Leander's Lies

a novel

by

Nancy Werking Poling

APRIL GLOAMING

Publisher's Cataloguing-in-Publication Data

Poling, Nancy Werking
Leander's lies / written by Nancy Werking Poling
ISBN: 978-1-953932-41-9

1. Fiction – General 2. Fiction – Historical: General 3. Fiction – Southern I. Title II. Author

"Quite a story! Leander's religion-fueled ambition takes the reader on an odyssey in postbellum America, from North Carolina to North Dakota. A cautionary tale for genealogists seeking to learn more about their revered forebears."

– Vicki Lane, author of *And the Crows Took Their Eyes*

"A compelling read that I predict will garner the attention it deserves. It presents a character study of a complex Southern man determined to follow his calling and willing to compromise personal integrity to do so."

– Julia Nunnally Duncan, author of *The Flood of Remembrance* and *All We Have Loved*

"Meticulously researched and richly detailed. Poling demonstrates how elusive ancestors, fractured records, racism, and deliberate deceptions confound family historians while honoring the complex and complicated human stories beyond what we find in records."

– Rev. Kate Penney Howard, pastor, genetic genealogist, and international speaker specializing in brick wall research

"[E]vocative historical fiction that plunges readers back into the decades after the Civil War and a lovable scoundrel's efforts to climb out of poverty and recreate himself."

– Marylee MacDonald, author of *Surrender*

Leander's Lies is a work of fiction. My imagination accounts for all personalities, motivations, and specific events.

However, there was a real Leander. A novice in genealogical research, I grew in my ability to expose his lies and uncover the truth. I learned how to maximize my use of Ancestry.com and Find a Grave. My husband and I made multiple trips to Burke and Cleveland counties, where we located churches, graves, and spoke with old timers. Meanwhile, I communicated with historians and read multiple books and articles about the historical climate of late nineteenth-century North Carolina.

I cannot write about our efforts without acknowledging the extensive genealogical research my mother-in-law and father-in-law, along with one of their sons and a niece, did in the 1980s. Though they worked under the assumption that Leander had told the truth, their findings were valuable in my quest to understand the man and his time.

I'm especially indebted to North Carolina historian Dr. Gordon McKinney for his counsel. I also turned to others with historical expertise: Dr. Thomas A. Kinney, author of *The Carriage Trade: Making Horse-Drawn Vehicles in America*; Bill Kostlevy, former Church of the Brethren archivist; Mattie Richardson, author of North Dakota historical fiction (Appaloosy Books); and Dr. Stephen Ray author of *Do No Harm: Social Sin and Christian Responsibility*. Despite their input, I am responsible for any errors in historical details.

Terms referring to persons of African ancestry are in keeping with the historical period.

Part I:
Elias

Chapter 1

Had Pinckney not been dazzled by the beauty of Mrs. Elliston, who eight years after the Yankees killed her husband at Petersburg, still wore widders weeds. Had black not become her, and had she not engaged in pleasant conversation with Pinckney, fifteen years her junior, Elias and his big brother would not have been walking along the dirt road as wood thrushes and chickadees broadcast their final notes of the evening. The boys would not have been in near darkness when the ground shook like the walls of Jericho falling.

"Horses!" Pinckney said. "A heap of 'em."

He grabbed Elias's braces, tugged him toward the nearby corn field, pulled him to the ground. The honey jar, Mrs. Elliston's payment for a repaired buggy wheel, slipped from Elias's hands, the puddle of golden sweetness oozing away.

"You made it break!" he hollered, crawling toward the shattered glass.

"Hush!" The urgency in Pinckney's voice made Elias forget the honey. "Follow me." Backs hunched, the brothers made their way deeper into the field.

The ground stopped shaking. They could hear horses snorting, hooves restlessly prancing not far away—men's shouts. Pinckney dropped to his hands and knees. A jerk on Elias's braces signaled he was to do the same.

Inching over a slight rise, they came within sight of Jeremiah Arnold's home just as the kerosene lamp inside went dark. Raised on rock piers, the unpainted frame cabin with a sloping shingled roof looked like a strong gust of wind could blow it away.

Men on horses, several carrying torches, formed a semicircle in the clay-packed yard. Faces were concealed by flour sacks with holes cut out for eyes, a beard painted on one, a few with bulls' horns sticking out. Two riders wore ragged Confederate army uniforms, another a long black robe.

Before the war Jeremiah Arnold had belonged to Silas McDowell, who, even though he owned four slaves, made it clear to anyone who would listen that he thought owning a human being was a sin. Folks around were still angry about old McDowell giving each of the freedmen plots of his land, then dying. Some thought he'd done it deliberately, the dying, so nobody could hold him accountable.

"You, boy, come out here!" a raspy voice commanded.

"Bitch, you and the pickaninnies come out too," another called.

Two riders got off their horses, stomped across the wide wooden porch, and put their shoulders to the door. Those astride their horses cheered when the door fell in. Seconds later two masked figures dragged Jeremiah, his wife, and two girls in nightgowns out on the front porch. The girls clung tightly to their mother.

Another man, short and skinny as a cornstalk, signaled by pointing a whip. "Bitch, take the 'lil ones over yonder. You," he said to Jeremiah, "stand over agin' that tree." He cracked his whip in the air. "And take off your shirt."

Jeremiah took halting steps toward the giant oak.

"Now hug that there tree."

Had the man with the whip been a dog or a pig, Elias thought, Papa would have drowned him in the trough. That's what he did to runts, so there'd be more milk for the healthy ones.

A crack of the whip! "Fast!" Runt-man hollered.

Jeremiah Arnold stretched his arms around the tree. The whip whistled as it sailed through the air. With a *phwup* it met flesh. Lash after lash snaked across his back. His wail—as loud as when Mama gave birth to the baby that died— penetrated the darkness.

Elias winced. Pinckney whimpered. "Do somethin'," Elias whispered.

"Can't. There's fourteen of 'em. Only one of me." He wiped tears from his face with his shirt sleeve.

Elias lost count of how many lashes landed on Jeremiah Arnold's back before he slumped to the ground. Runt-man kicked him.

"Now, boy, you been livin' on stolen property. This here's white man's land."

"Mr. . . . Mr. McDowell, he . . . deeded me this place."

"Well, Mr. McDowell ain't around to tell us no different, now is he? And we're saying it's stolen. This here's a warning. You ain't welcome in these parts. Time you skedaddle."

"No, no . . . it's mine." Jeremiah Arnold's head briefly lolled before dropping to the ground.

"I repeat, boy, you better git goin'," Runt-man yelled over his shoulder as he walked away. Back on his horse he kicked its sides and jerked the reins. The others fell in behind him, everyone whooping and laughing as they headed back in the direction they'd come from.

Once the riders were out of sight, Pinckney, with Elias trailing, ran toward the Arnolds. The woman knelt at her husband's side, sobbing. The girls huddled nearby.

By now darkness had set in. The moon revealed only half of itself, yet its brightness offered enough light to move about the dirt yard with sure feet. No one spoke as Pinckney helped Jeremiah's wife lift the barely conscious man from the ground and half-pull, half-carry him toward the house. They gently lowered him to the edge of the porch. She hurried inside, returning with a tin tub of water and strips of cotton. Jeremiah winced as she washed his wounds with a gentle touch then wrapped the strips of cotton around his torso.

Elias went to stand near the girls. He cleared his throat. "Terrible to watch your pa get beat like that." His instinct was to reach toward them, create a cluster of security. But they were colored. He could only say, "I'm sorry."

At Sunday afternoon gatherings he often played church with the other children. He'd call on someone to lead singing, saving for himself the sermon and the lifting of a prayer.

"I'll pray with you, if I might," he told the two girls. Without waiting for a response he bowed his head. "Our heavenly father, we have beared witness to a terrible thing. These girls, their pa's been treated real bad. For these are the days of tribulation. Thou knowest who those bad men are. Pour thy wrath down on 'em.

Oh, and thank you for sending your only begotten son who died for our sins. Upon that cross at Calvary. And bless us all. And our food to its intended use. In Jesus's name we pray, amen."

On the walk home, in darkness barely penetrated by the half-moon, the terror of the evening overcame Elias. Holding firmly to Pinckney's hand, he wept. Tears on behalf of Jeremiah Arnold and his family. Tears on behalf of himself, of the horror he had witnessed. After a while he stopped crying and started to hum "This world is not my home," sung at church on Sundays. If he were Jeremiah Arnold, he'd load the wagon and move on.

1866. Not the best year to be born. The War of Northern Aggression had ended only a year earlier, leaving North Carolina reeling from the loss of more than 33,000 men and a shattered economy. Over much of the state, homes and businesses had been destroyed, the region's workforce—emancipated or stolen, depending on which side of the conflict you supported.

During the war preachers had cited Holy Scripture in defense of the Peculiar Institution, though owning a great number of slaves was mostly impractical in the western piedmont. The land wasn't suitable for large crops of rice and cotton. The many tributaries of the Catawba River, like bones of a carp, created small sections of fertile alluvial plane lending themselves mainly to subsistence farming.

The four-year war brought Elias's father, Joseph, few material losses, as he owned little to begin with. The devaluation and eventual failure of Confederate script mattered little to him or to his farmer neighbors who produced a small surplus for bartering. No battles had been fought nearby.

The Muller family's possessions included a structure of river rock, where Joseph worked as a wainwright. Most of the time he repaired wagon parts and built wheelbarrows, but when he and Marshall Albright, the blacksmith, got an order for a new wagon, they could build it in eight days and earn one hundred and twenty-five dollars between them. On those rare occasions Joseph took the family over to Lincolnton to buy shoes.

An insubstantial, unpainted barn sheltered a cow, a mule, and an assortment of farm tools. The two-room log house, with a tin roof and porch across the front, stood close enough to the workshop that Elias's mother, Hattie, could holler out when it was time for dinner. At the sound of her voice, Hector the mule bellowed his *aw-ah-aw* from out in the barn.

Behind the house fifteen acres were partially cleared, planted in corn and wheat with space left for Hattie's vegetable garden and a decent-sized apple orchard. Apples not filched by bears and raccoons provided a dependable product for bartering with general store owner Mr. Gruen, who turned them into hard cider. Beyond the orchard the Mullers' hogs foraged for chestnuts and acorns in the wooded area and over onto land belonging to Silas Barber.

At the time of Elias's birth, in addition to his father's workshop and eight rustic homes, the settlement consisted of a grist mill, a blacksmith shop, a general store, and a one-room Methodist church. The Muller family, however, traveled half an hour by wagon to attend the Baptist meetinghouse down the road a piece. Joseph was convinced that God required baptism by total immersion, certainly not the sprinkling of a few dribbles of water on the head of an infant.

Except for the crumbled stone shell of the mill and gray boards of an abandoned building, its purpose long forgotten, no signs of the settlement remain today.

Elias's saucer eyes stared at the map Miss Pritchard had spread out. All thirty-seven of the United States, some of them pale blue, others pink, or green, North Carolina in yellow. Towns he had never heard of, all across the country.

"What are those?" he lisped through gaps where he'd recently lost two front teeth. He pointed to curved lines with cross dashes.

"Those are railroad tracks. One of these days you'll be able to get on a train and go all the way across the country."

Elias placed his index finger on the map. "And we're somewheres in through here, ain't we?"

"*Aren't we*," she corrected. "Right where the top of the R connects to the bottom."

"And up here, that's Dakota, ain't—isn't it?" Elias pointed to a yellow rectangle. "Where my big brother died."

Making Papa slow to forgive the Yankees, despite what Holy Scripture said about forgiveness. Not willing to forgive the South either. A foolish effort, all the young lives sacrificed. And for what? The O'Brian boy killed in action, one of the Warlick boys too, many others coming back without an arm, a leg.

During recess, Caleb, a nine-year-old of flabby frame and matching jowls, told Elias that Andrew had deserted, run off right after Gettysburg, him and another boy. "You know what you get for desertin'?" Caleb taunted. "You get kilt, that's what they done. They shot your brother cause he was a coward."

Elias stepped closer, looked up at Caleb defiantly. "They did not. The Yankees captured him and carried him off to some prison in Maryland, and he died up in Dakota. Of dysentery." He wasn't sure what dysentery was, but he'd heard his father use the word in regard to Andrew.

"You're lyin'. He was a coward and he got hisself kilt."

Elias swung a furious fist, but Caleb, at least a foot taller, caught his arm mid-aim and twisted it. Elias's hollering brought Dorothy Jane running, screaming like a banshee as she came up behind Caleb and jumped on his back. "You leave my little brother be!" Now the scuffle was between the two of them, Dorothy Jane the aggressor, Caleb the assailed, hands in front of his face to deflect her clawing, children yelling, "Git 'im, Dorothy Jane! Git 'im!" until Miss Pritchard appeared out of nowhere, a petite one herself, and pulled them apart. Back inside the schoolhouse she made Dorothy Jane and Caleb yield to the humiliation of the hickory stick.

All this furor left Elias incensed over Caleb's accusation and guilt-ridden over Dorothy Jane getting punished in his stead. Scowling, he returned to the map on the table, towns all across the country identified by fancy lettering. The space between the two parts of the R, tiny like the points of Mama's pins. The map didn't even show the world. There was Africa and India and China.

Fishing in the shallows of Jacob Fork with Pinckney, Elias already yearned for deeper waters, for unfamiliar land on the opposite bank and river bottoms that held buried secrets. He wanted to be swept downstream by strong currents, deposited like soil carried from the hilltops to rest on distant shores.

He welcomed being sent on an errand to the general store, where he'd get the mail and sometimes trade wheat or apples for salt, tea, or a paper of pins for Mama. The store owner, *Herr* Gruen customers called him, had been a peddler before settling in Burke County. From Prussia, he spoke with a heavy accent. *Frau* Gruen wore a dirndl revealing far more of her ample bosom than local custom condoned.

The couple lived above the store. The building had a weatherboard exterior with a stepped-parapet façade, a double-door entrance, and wide front windows in which the Gruens displayed an assortment of tonics and liniments to treat nearly every complaint, from catarrh to piles. The store's interior was dark and crowded, with barely enough space to walk between barrels of nails and tables stacked with ammunition and crockery. Harnesses and lanterns hung from the ceiling. Lining two walls, chestnut cabinets and shelves held dry goods and bins containing edible items such as coffee, salt, and sugar. A wide wooden counter ran the length of the room. Once a week mail was delivered to the community post office in back, with individual boxes for residents who had to travel as far as ten miles to collect letters from kin who had moved on to Tennessee, up to Illinois, all the way to California.

Sometimes Mama gave Elias a penny for candy. His gaze moved along the shelf just above eye level as he studied one jar, then the one beside it, then the one next to that, trying to make up his mind whether he wanted butterscotch or peppermint or horehound flavor.

If not busy, Herr Gruen would lean over the counter and share boyhood memories of life along the Rhine River. That he was a Jew fascinated Elias.

"You mean you don't eat no pork?" Elias asked. "How come?"

"You know Leviticus? God says animal what split hoof has and chews the cud, that animal can man eat. But if animal has only one or other—split hoof or chews cud—that animal man cannot eat. Pig does not chew cud."

Elias licked his lips. "Why'd God make it taste so good if we ain't supposed to eat it? A thick slice of ham, some biscuits, and a mess of collards, it don't get no better. You ought to come eat Mama's dinner sometime."

Herr Gruen smiled tolerantly and changed the subject. "*The Progress* arrived yesterday," he said, knowing the boy was curious about events beyond the settlement.

"Any news?"

"Good news, no. Ladies up in Ohio want women of America to unite against the making of alcohol drinks. The Women's Temperance Union, they call their nasty organization. Women take from man a great pleasure, the wine, the beer."

"Hmm. So God says you can't eat pork, and ladies in Ohio say you can't drink your beer. You're in a sad spot, seems to me."

Laughter. Herr Gruen's gravelly, Elias's in a boy's high pitch.

On winter evenings, when the ground lay fallow and winds roared, the Mullers would sit in the warmth of the woodstove. Hattie let out hems in Dorothy Jane's and Lizzie's dresses while Joseph told stories, most of them from the Bible. He added dramatic crescendos and diminuendos, flexing arm muscles to show Samson's strength, outlining with his hands the immensity of Nebuchadnezzar's golden idol.

Elias associated nearly everyone he knew with a Bible character. He could think of no better person than Papa—a forceful preacher when his turn came around at Sinai Baptist Church—to be the Apostle Peter, the rock Jesus built his church on. Mama was Mary, a holy woman wearing a gingham dress and sun bonnet. Dorothy Jane, who complained about having to help Mama in the kitchen, was the Bible Martha. Lizzie—he tried to picture her sitting on Jesus's lap and looking up into his kind face. No, she'd run off, giggling and daring Jesus to chase her.

Beyond family. Sister Davenport could only talk between sobs and hiccoughs about being in Lincolnton the day the defeated army marched into town, the lame ones and boys with one arm or one eye. And how her husband, God rest his soul, had gone into the war with strong feelings of victory. Sister Davenport was Lot's wife, who couldn't help but look back. A pillar of salt, her spindly frame with stooped shoulders masterfully chiseled.

Old Mr. Bisner, who'd stolen a horse back before there was a penitentiary and got branded with a hot iron as punishment, he bore the mark of Cain. Daniel Lewis lived down a long lane and greeted everyone who showed up on his land, peddlers and neighbors alike, shotgun in hand. He was King Herod, who drove Mary and Joseph away and wanted to kill Baby Jesus.

Elias gave careful thought as to who Herr Gruen might be. Paul had been a Jew, but he'd been mean until he saw the light, and Herr Gruen was real nice, and Elias didn't want to think about Herr Gruen being struck down and blinded for three days.

Miss Prichard acted as if conversation with Elias was one of her greatest pleasures. Pretty, too, except for wide pink gums that drew his attention when she smiled— which she did frequently. She had pumpkin-colored hair and freckles across the top of her nose. Queen Esther, Elias decided.

She had inherited twelve books from her father, volumes by Hawthorne, Dickens, and James Fennimore Cooper. Sitting on a hard bench near the warmth of the woodstove, Elias read with an avid craving.

On a morning when the threat of frost had nearly passed and fields were waiting for the spring planting, when the stove burned small sticks and a single log just to take the night chill off, Elias stood before Miss Prichard. He wore a pair of Papa's pants Mama had cut down and patched.

He handed her a book. "Thank you, ma'am, for letting me borrow this. I like Hawthorne plenty."

"What was your favorite story?"

He didn't hesitate. "'The Great Stone Face.'"

"What did you like about it?" The authority of her voice could halt a fight at recess, but at times like this, when Elias stood before her, she spoke with gentleness. And respect.

"I think of the boulders up yonder at South Mountain and the power nature has wrought. I see things there on the rocks, faces and such."

"And Ernest? What do you think of him?"

Dare he be honest? Express such a bold thought? He took a deep breath. "Ernest." He cleared his throat. "Ernest," he repeated. "I'm kinda like him. Only I ain't—"

"I am not," Miss Pritchard corrected.

"I am *not* expecting to discover 'the greatest and noblest personage' of my time. I 'spect to be that person, just as Ernest turns out to be the one."

Miss Pritchard leaned back in her chair. "Yes, Elias. Yes, I anticipate that you will be the greatest and noblest."

Anticipate. The word followed him through the rest of the day. She anticipated his success. Reading was about anticipation, he thought, the mind following the twists and turns, wondering what was going to happen to the hero. Anticipation. He was the main character of his own story, a boy for whom God had a plan. Not in Joseph's shop or in the fields, where there was nothing to anticipate but drudgery and hard physical work. No, Elias anticipated greatness.

And Queen Esther agreed.

It arrived in Silas Shuford's mailbox at the general store: a pamphlet published by the Atchison, Topeka & Santa Fe Railroad Company claiming the Cottonwood and Arkansas Valleys of Kansas were the Gardens of the West. The land was productive, the people happy. The latter assertion grabbed the attention of Silas's wife, Priscilla, who harbored multiple resentments toward the North Carolina piedmont: the heat, the cold, the dampness, the dryness, the harsh sunshine, the clouds, the rain, the lack of rain. The pamphlet listed land for sale. A month later the Shuford family was on a train bound for Kansas.

Silas's departure was a loss to men of the area, as he was the one who on winter afternoons read *The Lincoln Progress* aloud. Over Frau Gruen's protests—the men missing the spittoon and her having to clean up—Herr Gruen had placed six chairs with cane seats, along with a checkerboard, around the potbelly stove. But no one played checkers on newspaper-reading days.

With Silas Shuford gone, the men were at a loss over how to get the news. Herr Gruen could read, but Frau Gruen objected on grounds that he'd be sitting down on the job while she labored. At Joseph's suggestion, the group arrived at a solution: persuade Miss Pritchard to let Elias, now nine years old, leave school an hour early on Wednesdays. She didn't oppose the arrangement.

Seated on a nail keg, Elias read the newspaper out loud while five men, occasionally more, sat in a semi-circle around him. Arguments over the news were as heated as the top of the potbelly stove, half the group saying they planned to vote in favor of the amendments offered by the October convention, half—Joseph one of them—arguing it was a crime to turn over the control of county and township governments to the state legislature.

At other times conversations were about money: who had it (none of them), who didn't (all of them), and who was responsible for the disparities (President Grant, the goddamn bankers, the goddamn railroad owners).

Sept. 7, 1984

Dear Lydia,

Well, I finally got around to sorting through Mother's boxes. Yes, I'm embarrassed that it's taken me all these years. Guess I dreaded making decisions about what might be of value to posterity and what should be tossed. Last week, the weather being so dreary, I resolved to go down to the basement and get the job done.

First, the mundane results. Two boxes contain her clothes: the floral printed housedresses, nightgowns, and such. Moths have feasted on her wool sweaters. There are also those dreadful dark dresses, plus her black bonnet and the prayer coverings. I'm thinking we'll keep the bonnet. Shall I send it to you? Your Stephanie seems the most likely to someday be interested in family history.

Now the fascinating part, the mystery, if you will. One small box contains Papa's belongings, stuff I've never seen before. There's a really sweet picture of a baby girl, seven or eight months old, with straight dark hair parted in the middle. It's mounted and framed on heavy card, the kind that was popular in early photography. "Gastonia, NC" is stamped at the bottom of the frame. Who could she possibly be?

There's also a leather-covered loose-leaf binder containing outlines of Papa's sermons. Folded inside is a sheet of paper listing important dates in his life. His voyage around the world is there, as are his terms in Congress and his hunting trip with Teddy Roosevelt. I'll make a photocopy and mail it to you.

Another item seems significant. It's a worn book with ragged, yellowed pages, Christian Research in Asia with Notices of the Translation of the Scriptures into the Oriental Languages, *copyright 1812. Someone used blank pages to write names and birth dates in brown ink: Joseph Muller born March 20, 1820; Hattie Martin born Dec. 5, 1827; Elias L. Muller, born July 17, 1866. We know our grandparents were named Joseph and Hattie. Might Elias have been one of our uncles?*

I can't help wondering who that little girl was. How did her picture come into Papa's hands? You're the retired librarian. I leave the mystery for you to solve.

All is well here. Except for last week's rain, Vermont this time of year is lovely. I manage to walk two miles practically every day.

Love,
Dorcas

Chapter 2

"You're old enough to do a man's work," was all Papa said the spring before Elias turned twelve, leaving Mama to explain that circumstances had changed, what with Pinckney marrying and settling over in Rowan County.

Seemed to Elias he'd been doing a man's work for quite some time. Eased into it like every boy once he was tall enough to manage a hoe, strong enough to carry an armload from the woodpile. He helped Papa grub the fields, digging out stumps and roots. He'd chopped off branches of a downed tree before Papa and Pinckney dragged the trunk into the woodyard with a borrowed team of horses.

"Your daddy lives with a heap of sorrow," Hattie said in defense of Joseph. In case the boy didn't fully grasp her meaning: "Andrew dying up in Dakota, Franklin passin', Baby George going to heaven. Then Annie Elizabeth, too, back when you was a little tyke." Hattie reached in her apron pocket for the tatted-edged handkerchief and blew her nose. These were her losses too. Four of the twelve children she'd given birth to were now in their heavenly rest. "And there's all what we done lived through, the war and all."

Elias took rapid breaths, trying to hold back tears. What did Mama's explanation have to do with him having to quit his schooling? He hadn't even been born when his oldest brother died. His recollection of his oldest sister, who'd died in childbirth, was vague, like thinking you saw a panther up in the mountains but it was just a flash and afterward you didn't know for sure.

"Honor thy father and thy mother," Holy Scripture said, which he tried to do. Not begrudgingly, because his father was an honorable man. A wainwright and farmer most of the week; a preacher some Sundays, compensated mainly with salt and sorghum and hams. He wed the young and prayed over the dead; baptized those who confessed their sins, leading them down into the stream while witnesses on the bank sang, "Wash me and I shall be whiter than snow."

The night after Papa's decree, Elias followed his sisters up the pull-down stairs to the loft. At first he lay on his back, fingers clasped beneath his head, elbows extended. He rolled over, rammed his fist against the straw mattress.

"Stop it!" Dorothy Jane said in a loud whisper from the mattress she shared with Lizzie. "We're trying to sleep."

She had quit school at ten, but she was a girl. Folks expected girls to start learning women things so that when they married they'd be skilled at running a home. A hard-working man needed to be confident that food would be spread before him and his clothes would be clean.

"I want to go to school!" Elias said through gritted teeth.

"I know you do," she said, "but Papa needs you. Besides, Mama says we don't got the money. If I had a way to earn some, I'd give it to you." And she would, Elias knew. He could depend on Dorothy Jane more than anybody.

Long after his sisters were making the deep inhalations and exhalations of sleep, Elias, again lying on his back, peered up into the darkness. An idea came to him. On a shelf beside the Bible, there was a book passed down from Cousin Ephraim: *Christian Research in Asia with Notices of the Translation of the Scriptures into the Oriental Languages*. Elias committed himself to studying it and the Bible.

He would educate himself.

He was expected to sweep the dirt floor of the shop, sharpen Papa's tools with a mill bastard file. He returned chisels, mallets, straightedges, and steel framing squares to their rightful peg. Mistakenly toss out a piece of wood with a penciled design on it, or hang a tool on the wrong peg—Papa's usual gentle drawl morphed into a syllable-by-syllable reprimand. Not that he was a harsh taskmaster. A hand on Elias's shoulder or the occasional pat on the back acknowledged a job well done.

Elias understood the expectation behind his father's corrections. As had been true for generations, the son of a wainwright would become a wainwright, just as the son of a shoemaker learned to become a shoemaker, a merchant's son the eventual store owner. That's what being a father was about: a man shaping his son's future.

But what if the son wanted something different? What if the son didn't want to be poor? What if he wanted to employ his mind rather than muscle? Was there a way to say *This is not what I want to do with my life* without disrespecting a father's legacy?

Chapter 3

Corn stalks stood brittle not far from the long iron bar where mules, broodmares, and a few well-bred mounts were tethered. Some waited in resignation, eyes shut in drowsiness, while others, eager to stretch their limbs, pawed the straw scattered underfoot. Faded green wagons lined the east perimeter of the chestnut grove; tents were pitched in the meadow.

Folks came to camp meeting from neighboring counties, no fewer than a thousand believers—Methodists, Presbyterians, Baptists—living up in the hollows and along winding, rutted roads. Some hungered for inspired preaching, others for social engagement.

Freeing Elias of work responsibilities was Papa's way of moving along the call of the Lord. Baptists believe that turning from sin and choosing to be baptized is an adult choice. To Papa fifteen was adult enough.

Between preaching services, while children chased each other under the eyes of their mothers, older youth congregated. Boys gathered in clusters, girls gathered in clusters, members of each group stealing glances at the other, laughing over something said about those across the invisible chasm.

"Who is she?" Elias nodded toward a girl whose gingham dress did not conceal feminine curves pleasing to his male eye. He heard her laugh, not a girlish giggle but smooth in tone, welcoming others into her circle of humor. Welcoming Elias.

"Emma Broder," his friend Isaac said. "From down in Cleveland County."

A wisp of auburn hair escaped Emma Broder's braids coiled at the back of her head. An arch of freckles stretched across her nose. Her brown eyes, when their gazes met, were bold, inviting. When she left the group of girls to stand alone under a beech tree, Elias abruptly cut off conversation with Isaac and approached her.

He was not shy; neither, it seemed, was she.

Elias sat toward the front of the brush arbor shelter, body hunched over, head in hands. His whole life he'd heard sermons about victory. Victory over envy. Victory over lust. Victory over the sins of drinking, gambling. And victory of all victories: a moral victory over the enemy, the North. When those men preached about God's chosen, they meant sons and daughters of the Confederacy.

After meandering through all these topics, the afternoon's preacher settled into victory over lust. He paused in his sermon so that worshippers might sing a hymn:

Rock of Ages, cleft for me,

Let me hide myself in Thee;

Let the water and the blood,

From Thy wounded side which flowed,

Be of sin the double cure;

Save from wrath and make me pure.

Make me pure, make me pure, make me pure. Across the center aisle, on the women's side, Emma Broder sat between her sister and her mother. As she sang, her torso swelled, deflated, swelled, deflated.

Make me pure, make me pure. Elias had caught glimpses of Dorothy Jane naked and knew that beneath Emma's gingham dress her breasts were shapely mounds with brown nipples. He wanted to touch them.

Oh, Lord, take these thoughts from me and make me pure. Cleanse my heart. I am a sinner in need of your mercy.

It was there, the preacher proclaimed: God's grace. Available if Elias would proclaim his guilt in front of all. Confess that he resented having to quit school. That he wanted more than anything to read and study and learn—a lazy boy's diversion from work, many here would think.

Confess his sins of a carnal nature too: his curiosity when he went with Papa to get Flossy bred. Papa's brief explanation that men and women did the same had later been supplemented by older boys who passed on their knowledge. And there were the downstairs grunts and moans Elias heard some nights when he put his ear to the hole in the loft floor.

Now this desire for Emma. Only God could relieve him of the guilt, if only he'd confess and promise to give up his resentment and dreams and lust. Under conviction he began to sob into his hands. Joseph put a hand on Elias's shoulder. "Go, son."

The aisle up to the mourner's bench seemed endless. "Forgive my sins, oh, Lord, forgive my sins." Over the din of other repentants, Elias called out for deliverance. At the bench he knelt, repeating, "I am a sinner. Forgive me, dear Father in heaven."

Over the blessing of redemption he didn't shout as others did—their rebirth the agonizing sounds of a woman in the travails of childbirth—hollering that the Lord had saved them. Instead, a stillness came over him. Gratitude for victory over his sinful nature.

Two weeks later a fall drizzle saturated the frosty October air. Believers from all around— at least two hundred of them—stood on the bank of the creek running through the Abernathy farm. Brother Hoyl's extended hand guided Elias into the water, pressed his shoulder as a signal to kneel. "In the name of the Father, Son, and Holy Ghost," Brother Hoyl said, thrusting the boy's head backward into the frigid water.

"Halleluiah!" Elias shouted as he stepped out of the creek into his father's embrace.

Dorothy Jane was first to recognize the signs. How Papa's pace had slowed, the way he held on to a post, to the table, to any secure object he passed. His coloring was off, she pointed out, his skin the shade of oak bark in the winter. Elias began to pay attention. His father had coughing fits and spent fewer hours in the wainwright shop, more time in his rocking chair.

As Joseph declined in strength then took to his bed, he was haunted by images of the trestle collapse over Indian Creek, the train tumbling into the ravine, stoves in passenger cars catching fire, screams of people burning to death.

"Elias, tell me again, had James Henderson been baptized?"

"Don't know, Papa."

"John Bloom, did he know the Lord?"

"Don't know that either."

"I keep seeing the fire that consumed 'em. Can't bear to think that some on that train have been condemned to eternal fire."

Hattie reported that during the night Joseph sat up straight and shouted, "Halleluiah! I saw him plain as day, Andrew standing there before me calling 'Papa, come home.' I'm comin', son, I'm comin.'" He fell back on his pillow, mumbling, "I'm comin', I'm comin' home."

The following day Joseph clutched Elias's hand with surprising strength and whispered, "Son, promise me you'll see to your mama and sisters, ya' hear?"

"Yes, sir, I promise."

During Joseph's final hours, neighbors and family came to sit by his bedside, their chatter at times so loud that Hattie chased them outside. Gladys Conner later broadcast area-wide that she was by his bed the Thursday afternoon he departed this earthly life. She saw the glow of heavenly lights surrounding him. His labored breaths, his eyes opening for a brief moment, him smiling at Gladys—all of this she said she personally witnessed when Jesus called Joseph home. Making herself the center of attention, Dorothy Jane complained to Elias.

Neighbors and church members arrived for the sitting up, bringing with them pies and cakes, platters of fried chicken and ham, bowls of fresh peas and new potatoes. Seated in the main room, waiting for the spirit to leave the body, some sang hymns while others ate. Through it all, Hattie, in her black Sunday dress, pursed her lips. A widow was expected to keep her emotions in check.

Elias stood away from visitors, staring out the window. The gloaming cast yellowish hues on the garden: greens salad-ready, peas already producing, the plot of bushy sweet potato plants that would feed the family all next winter. His attention drifted to something out of sight, on the opposite side of the house: Papa's shop. A vise inside. Pressing, pressing, unrelenting expectations. He had promised Papa that he would care for Mama and his sisters. From now on their well-being depended on him.

A hand on his arm startled him. "I'm awful sorry about your daddy." It was Emma Broder. Her voice was velvety.

He continued to stare out the window. Tears moistened his cheeks. Emma's hand did not leave his arm.

"They say I'm man of the house now."

"Why yes, yes you are."

"But I don't want to be. I'm gonna end up spending my whole life here." He pounded his fist into the palm of his hand. "Why'd he have to go die, leave me with all this?"

"Why Elias Muller, that's no way to talk. Dyin' ain't something you just tell yourself not to do."

"Gonna run away. That's what I'm gonna do. Head out to Texas."

"Please don't. I want you to stay here."

He lifted his head. "Really?"

"Really."

A breeze wafted down from South Mountain, creating swirls of red dust, carrying it out of sight. The flutter of oak leaves forecast rain. Next to the smoothed field rock marking Baby George's final resting place, two church brothers opened the coffin to allow the family one final look at a body, hollow of spirit.

The church bell tolled. Muffled voices sang, "I greet Thee who my sure Redeemer art," as the pine coffin was lowered. The pit ran east and west, the better for Joseph to see Jesus when he returned on Judgment Day.

Hattie, who seemed to understand Elias's aversion to becoming a wainwright, wasted no time in selling Joseph's shop. With the money from the sale, she bought twenty acres of abandoned farmland. No matter the reasons for its having been forsaken, she claimed the ability to see beyond sight, not like an Old Testament prophet, but as things could be. *Someday. Someday* an orchard on that acreage would produce enough fall pippins to sell. Once Elias grubbed the acreage, she and the girls would plant apple trees.

His increased responsibilities exhausted him, so that in the light of the kerosene lamp, when he tried to read the Bible and *Christian Research in Asia*, he fell asleep at the table, head cradled in his arms.

Shotgun over his right shoulder, Elias tramped through the woods. Wandering among hardwood trees and scented pines offered the kind of quiet his spirit needed. And if he brought home a wild turkey, Mama wouldn't scold him for desecrating the Sabbath.

His legs stretched to climb an incline. A high-pitched cackle came from overhead. He strained his neck to gaze upward, hand over brow to shield his eyes from the intensity of the sun. An eagle circled. Gun to shoulder he followed the bird through the sight. Flapping its vast wings it climbed until it reached a thermal. With majestic smoothness it swept back and forth, searching for prey. Elias lowered the gun and continued to watch. A magnificent sight: the power of the bird, confidence in flights yet to come. The eagle turned westward, its disappearance like talons stabbing at Elias's heart.

Overcome by a profound feeling of reverence, he placed his gun next to the stump of a chestnut tree. Stooping there he traced its saw-jagged surface with his index finger. He considered what the tree had provided over its lifetime: chestnuts that nurtured animals and humans, shade for seedlings growing beneath it, shade for a Catawba boy pausing during a hunt. Finally, the tree gave its life. The eagle, the tree, they hinted at a message. He felt it, the tugging at his sleeve, at his heart, urging him to . . .

Later, up in the loft, a dream. Jesus hovering overhead, saying, "I have a plan for your future."

"Women's talk," Papa had called Mama's and the girls' chatter about dreams. Of being chased. Of biscuits burning. Of a storm coming through and ripping up trees. All imbued with hidden meaning they tried to uncover, their laughter over the possibilities.

He could ask Mama how to interpret his dream. But it felt like a private revelation with a meaning he himself must unravel, and more importantly, act on.

I have a plan for your future.

Nov. 2, 1984

Dear Lydia,

My, aren't you and Steven the adventuresome ones! I have about as much interest in camping as I do in collecting snake skins. I remember you as a fearful child, which makes me marvel all the more that you now set up camp among creatures that snarl and bite and sting.

I, too, am puzzled by what you found—rather, did NOT find—on your trip down to North Carolina. You located censuses with Joseph Muller as head of the family and his wife Hattie. There was a Dorothy, an Elizabeth, an Elias, but no Leander. Are you sure it's the right family?

You questioned why Papa never took us to North Carolina, especially since we frequently visited Mother's side in Missouri. I've always assumed he didn't go back because it was too painful. Whenever he spoke about losing his daughter to diphtheria, his eyes brimmed with tears. He never mentioned his wife's passing, but I think his periods of brooding might have been due to a lingering sadness over her death.

I hope all's well with your family. Bill and his kids are taking me out to dinner this evening. It's the first I've seen them in some time.

Love,
Dorcas

Chapter 4

It was a ploy, Emma telling her mother, "While you're delivering the butter, I'll just mosey over to Herr Gruen's and buy me some horehound drops."

Inside the general store she pretended to contemplate jars of candy. "Why hello there, Miss Broder," came from behind her. Not in the serious preacherlike voice she'd heard Elias Muller use before, more like the gentleness of "I Come to the Garden Alone." Without saying more, he exited the way he'd entered, then turned to make sure she was following.

Once she rounded the back corner of the store, Elias reached out, caught her by the hand, and pulled her into a lair of elderberry bushes. Briefly they stood facing each other, an arm's length apart, looking into the other's eyes. She smiled and stretched her arms around his neck. Emma had been kissed before. By the Jacobs boy, who lived over on the other side of Casar, and by James Warren. Elias's kisses were different, like he was empty inside and needed filling up.

"Emma," her mother called. "Time to go home. Where you at, girl?"

"When can I see you again?" Elias's eyes said he'd perish if it weren't soon.

"Tomorrow. In the woods behind the McCarthy place."

"Before suppertime. Four o'clock?"

She stepped away from the bushes and hurried in the direction of her mother's call.

"There you are," Frances Broder said, looking at Emma askance. "Where's your candy?"

Emma shrugged. "Decided to save my pennies."

Mother and daughter remained silent as the wagon bounced along the rutted road toward home, Emma thinking all the while about Elias's translucent blue eyes gazing into hers. About his hands. Callused and rough when her fingers traced the lines, gentle when he swept an escaped strand of hair from her brow.

Clandestine meetings in the thicket behind the wainwright shop progressed to stolen kisses behind the springhouse of the Broder farm, which progressed to Emma carrying a quilt up to the barn haymow, which progressed to . . .

Elias scrubbed off the day's grime in the trough, shed overalls reeking of sweat and manure, put on his other pair stiff from Mama's washing, and headed down the road toward the Broder place. Whistling "Blessed Assurance," he admired the bright yellow coreopsis blooms along the way and the winged tufts of clouds floating overhead.

He didn't find Emma in either of the usual places. Not waiting on the rickety porch steps, squinting for a glimpse of him rounding the bend in the lane. Not perched on the rope swing either. "Emma," he called. "Emma." Only clucking hens searching for worms in the dusty red soil answered. Walking around to the back of the Broder cabin, he finally spotted her seated on the ground, hugging her knees. The calico sunbonnet hid her face, but he could tell from the way her shoulders shook that she was crying.

Not a new revelation, this melancholy part of Emma's nature that left him disoriented. One day she'd welcome him with a smile that made him go weak in the knees. Come another day and nothing in God's creation brought her the tiniest bit of joy. Finally, he would resort to caresses and kisses, until the two of them were up in the haymow, his trousers undone and the hem of her dress gathered at her waist.

Studying her profile now, seeing the tremor of her shoulders, he felt an expectation to make right whatever disturbed her. Sometimes, though, her needs felt like a burden.

He approached, stood above her, his bare feet shoulders-width apart. He sighed deeply, reached down for her hand, and brought her to a standing position.

She flung her body against his. "Oh, Elias." More wail than affectionate welcome. Beneath the sunbonnet her eyes were puffy, her cheeks rash red. She took his hand and tried to pull him toward the copse of trees.

He kept his feet firmly planted.

She tugged harder. "I gotta tell you something."

"Tell me here."

"No. Mama or Eula's somewheres about."

"Tell me here."

She looked up at him with pleading eyes. His resolute stance did not change. She whispered, "The pip—it stopped."

"The what?"

"The pip." Her lower lip quivered. "My monthly. It stopped."

He looked at her, squinted, turned an ear toward her as if he hadn't heard.

She took a deep breath. "We—we're gonna have a baby."

"A what?"

"A baby."

He stepped back, shook his head in confusion.

"Elias Muller, don't you know how babies are made?"

"Course I do."

Her tone turned honey-sweet. "You're gonna be a papa."

He stood there, slack-jawed. "But we ain't married."

Hands on her hips, Emma scowled. "Now you don't expect me to have no briarpatch baby, do you?"

"No, no. But . . . but . . . I'm too . . . This ain't God's plan for my life."

"Not God's plan?" Emma scoffed.

He was confused by her change in demeanor. Crying, when he first saw her from a distance, then talking sweet as molasses, now this jarring anger.

"You think God don't want this baby born? Or does God think you're too good to marry me? The pious Elias Muller, the preacher's boy, shouldn't be tied down. That what you're saying?"

"You know that ain't what I mean. Our heavenly father wants me to get an education . . . and do something with my life."

"Well, I've got a thing or two to say about father and son. You are gonna be a father and the boy who comes out of my belly is gonna be your son." She stomped her foot. "Now are you or ain't you gonna marry me?"

Hands pressed together, fingertips to chin as if praying, Elias stammered, "Of . . . of course I want to do the, the right thing. But you gotta see—you, you got to understand—you know I want schoolin.'"

"It's time you got to thinking real clear. Even if you wuddn't gonna be a daddy, you're stuck here. You've got you a mama to take care of. And two sisters. I'd say God don't have such big plans for you after all."

"Just let me think about it. At least get used to the notion."

He turned abruptly and headed down the lane toward home. A Delilah. Emma Delilah Broder. She had led him up the ladder to the hay mow. Encouraged his curiosity about her body, undoing the buttons of her bodice herself. Under the quilt, their bodies side by side on the prickly hay, she had wanted him to reach beneath her dress, move his hand along her hips, bring it up between her legs. Until there was nothing a boy could do to stop the want, until he needed the release.

He couldn't be blamed for yielding to Emma's desire.

At recent conference meetings of Sinai Baptist Church, members had rebuked Melvin Bryson for drinking spirits, Athenia Louder for taking the Lord's name in vain, Winston Lail for gambling.

Now, on the women's side of the aisle, Hilda Tallant stood, posture straight, chin raised. "In sisterly love I must do as the Apostle Paul has instructed. 'If any man that is called a brother be a fornicator, or covetous, or an idolater, or a railer, or a drunkard, or an extortioner; with such a one eat not. Therefore, put away from among yourselves that wicked person.' It breaks my heart," she continued, unconvincingly to those who knew her well, "to bring to the attention of the body of Christ that Elias Muller and Emma Broder have fornicated."

A dramatic pause, a waggle of the index finger. "And that she is carrying his child!"

There were gasps—of disbelief or confirmation, it wasn't clear. Eyes turned to the back of the women's side, where Emma, her face flushed, began to cry. Elias, on the men's side, took a deep breath and closed his eyes.

"Stand, the two of you," Brother Hawkins commanded.

Emma stood, her body shaking as if overcome by a chill. Next to her, Frances, instead of looking in her daughter's direction, maintained a glazed stare out the nearby window.

Elias did not immediately stand but sat slumped over, hands clasped between spread legs. He mopped his forehead with his handkerchief. Like a caged animal he could only think of escape. Escape this building. Escape Emma. Escape the whole county. He had seen himself destined for—if not greatness, at least significance. He wanted to defy the brothers and sisters, stand tall and unrepentant, yet he knew what had happened when others refused to repent. They were excluded from the fellowship.

He stood.

"Are the sister's concerns true?" Brother Hawkins directed his question to the women's side of the aisle.

"Yes, sir," Emma mumbled.

Brother Hawkins turned to Elias. "And you, Elias Muller?"

"Yes, sir," Elias said, barely above a whisper.

"Please come before those gathered here."

Emma and Elias made their way to the front of the meetinghouse without acknowledging each other. They stood side by side, her shoulders dropped and shaking, his posture straight.

"You know, do you not, that your sin injures the glory of God and your eternal soul?"

"Yes, sir," both replied.

"We read in First John 1:9, 'If we confess our sins, he is faithful and just to forgive us our sins, and to cleanse us from all unrighteousness.' Do you, Elias Muller and Emma Broder, confess before God and this body that you have committed the sin of fornication and that you will turn from your sinful ways so that flesh will no longer master the spirit?"

"Yes, sir," both replied.

"And do you appeal to the Lord for mercy and pardon?"

"Yes, sir."

"Therefore, by the authority granted me by this body, because you have confessed your sin, I rebuke you and the sin you have committed. As our blessed savior said, 'Go and sin no more.'"

Many a young pregnant bride had stood before Merlin Hall. He never bothered asking a couple's ages, didn't want to lie, just wrote eighteen in the designated columns. Emma was twenty, Elias only seventeen.

Following the *I Do's*, Justice Hall made a perfunctory statement that marriage was the union between man and wife.

For a lifetime.

Dec. 21, 1984

Dear Lydia,

This memory may or may not be relevant to your family research. The event was confusing for a little girl, which could explain why I remember it so clearly. Papa was pastoring the Phoenix church. I was holding his hand while we waited to cross a downtown street. A man came up and said, "Don't I know you? You're from North Carolina, aren't you?" Papa suddenly lost his Southern accent. His pronunciation became very exact. He said, "No, I have never lived east of the Mississippi." His grip on my hand tightened and he practically dragged me across the street.

Might it have been the truth, though, and that's why you haven't found him in any census? On the other hand, he had that thick drawl, and the way he'd strike up a conversation with strangers (the encounter in Phoenix an exception) has always seemed quite Southern to me. But why tell us he was from North Carolina if he wasn't?

Well, Christmas is upon us. I always wanted to write to Santa, but Papa wouldn't permit it. He believed little girls should think about the birth of Jesus, not about material yearnings. Was it at the Myrtle Point church that he told Ladies Aid to take down ornaments they'd already hung?

Back to your search for the Joseph Muller family. My memory of the Phoenix episode aside, maybe you did find the right family. We know Papa had a sister named Dorothy. But why isn't his name on any census? It's too bad the one from 1890 was destroyed.

I don't think I need to encourage you to keep digging. You're a driven woman, you are.

I wish you and Stephen a Merry Christmas.

Love,

Dorcas

Chapter 5

Sally Wortman getting herself *that way* had set the church women to gossiping for a spell, but Sally's life was turning out just fine. Folks made a fuss over little Mary Sue, and Floyd was proving himself to be a good husband. Emma anticipated the day when she and Elias would have their own plot of land. He would farm while she carried out her womanly responsibilities, their transgression forgotten.

But for the time being she was an outsider in the Muller home, made to feel like the crowded cabin was her fault. Her fault that she and Elias got the only bedroom while Mother Muller slept in the main room, and Elias's sisters had to climb the ladder up to the loft each night.

Dorothy Jane was especially unfriendly. She wore her dark hair parted in the middle, tightly pulled back into braids coiled around her head like a rattler. Acted like a rattler, too, waiting to strike, as if Emma were to blame for entrapping the family's precious Elias. Only Emma knew he'd come after her body like ospreys diving for fish down on the Catawba.

Such disapproval might have been more tolerable had she felt confidence in Elias's affection. But if she lifted her face for a kiss, he turned his aside. If she brought his hand to her belly to feel the baby, he quickly pulled it away. There was no denying: He resented the baby; he resented her.

A mist hung over the piedmont, making Elias's floppy felt hat droopier, the distant mountains undiscernible. With audible grunts he thrust the pitchfork into the ground, jostled it back and forth to loosen the soil, dropped sweet potatoes into a bushel basket. Now and then he wondered what was happening inside the house. Mama said it would take a while, this being Emma's first.

He tried to focus his attention on the sad state of national affairs, the economy doing so poorly, wishing he were old enough to vote in next year's election. Papa had supported the Republican Party, as Elias planned to do once he had the opportunity.

His thoughts meandered to his disagreement with Jacob Abbott, who argued that parts of the Bible didn't hold water anymore: "Like some of them rules in Leviticus." Elias argued that Holy Scripture was the word of God and such notions were sacrilege. The next time they were together he planned to cite Second Timothy.

"Elias. Elias!" From out the back door Dorothy Jane's shout interrupted his thoughts.

"It's time to go fetch Granny Branson."

What had been a mist turned to a gentle rain as he raced to the shed. Hector refused to cooperate, avoiding the bit and shaking his head up and down, back and forth, with a loud *aw-ah-aw*. "Damn you, mule!" Elias shouted. Bit, bridle, and reins finally in place, he hitched Hector to the wagon. It was nearly five miles to the Branson place, and no amount of snapping the reins could coax the mule to move along any faster.

Elias found Granny Branson at the table with her husband, eating fatback sandwiches and fried potatoes. They were an ancient couple, their craggy faces resembling dried apple dolls. They had lost their only son, Willie, in the war and were pitied for having grieved ever since. Their last letter from him had come from Fredericksburg, asking his mother to make him some pants and socks. Nobody knew for sure how Willie died. Hiram Coulter, coming home with only one arm, refused to speak much about what he'd endured on the battlefield. Would only say he'd last seen Willie in Winder Hospital and that Willie had taken a bullet to the shoulder. The Bransons had written letter upon letter to the governor, to Presidents Grant, Hayes, and Arthur, pleading for information, never receiving any.

Upon Elias's arrival, Granny Branson rose from the table and fetched a basket covered with a piece of quilt. "Don't rightly know when I'll be back," she told her husband as she walked out the door.

She and Elias exchanged few words as they rode. Along the side of the road, dark red sumac berries still clung to stalks. Early rye and wheat planted in October were breaking through, no doubt thirsting for the drizzle of rain.

Entering the Muller home, Granny Branson straightened her bent spine as much as she seemed able and jutted her chin into the air. She was now in charge. Dorothy Jane led her into the bedroom where Emma lay sweating and moaning.

"I know, darlin', hurts something terrible, but it don't last forever," Elias heard Granny say. To him she said, "Bring in more wood. Tell your sisters to boil up some rags."

Then Mama ordered him to resume his outdoor work. Standing around wasn't going to hurry the process along. Back at his task digging up sweet potatoes, he fumed. A secret society, women were, like the Masons, not letting outsiders know what went on in there. Some kind of magic. He'd seen animals birthing. Couldn't be much different from that.

Elizabeth, a sister he'd barely known, had died in childbirth; Myrtle Tweed—not more than a year had passed since she and her newborn baby girl died. Briefly, Elias entertained the notion that Emma's death would free him of responsibility. He hastily repented of such thoughts. "Please, heavenly father, don't take my wife from me. But if it's your will . . ."

Dorothy Jane insisted he eat supper out on the front porch. My, women were bossy when birthing was going on. Nobody cared that it was cold out there. As he took bites of barely heated leftovers, he heard the heavy double doors of the nearby wainwright shop slam shut, a cow bellow in the distance.

"Elias," Dorothy Jane finally called from the doorway, "you got yourself a baby boy." He downed the last bite of apple cobbler and stepped into the house.

Robert Clarence was a puny infant, all the time crying, refusing breast milk. Refusing, too, the sugar tit Mother Muller made from a rag dipped in honey. His face purple with rage, little Robert screamed, *You are a bad mother!*

Mother Muller said it was Emma's state of mind, her nerves, that made her milk disagreeable. Elias admonished her for resisting his mother's advice and for having breasts so tender that nursing was painful. Blamed her, too, for the constant wailing when he tried to read of an evening.

On a Thursday afternoon she secretly put on her coat, bundled Robert in two quilts, and set off down the road. She was tired by the time she reached her parents' cabin, but Robert, tightly wrapped against her body, had fallen asleep.

Her mother and Eula were stooped over in the garden, pulling leaves off collard greens. Frances took the baby from Emma and led the way inside the house, with its welcoming scent of burning hickory. Seated by the hearth, Frances removed the layers of quilt, held Robert close, and hummed as she rocked him. He continued to sleep.

Home, Emma thought. Here she felt no condemnation. Eula took her by the hand and guided her to the bench at the table. Emma leaned into her sister and sobbed.

"I can't make him happy. Mother Muller says my milk ain't good, and he ain't growing like he ought to."

"Well," Frances said, still rocking the infant, "she's had—how many, ten young uns?—and I only had you two. But Eula here, she was a fussy one. I had to use a pap boat. Maybe milk from a cow mixed with a little soaked cornmeal, maybe that'll satisfy him."

"Elias done let Flossy go dry. He said give her a rest, like he done it on purpose, but I think he wasn't paying no heed. The calf was eating grass."

"Even with our butter making and what we give Granny Babcock, we've got plenty to share. A jug of milk will last you real good if it's chilled."

After that, against the wishes of Mother Muller, Emma kept the milk Eula delivered every other day in the springhouse.

Then, despite drinking a cup of pennyroyal tea every day, she was pregnant again. The women of the household seemed to take her pregnancy in stride, but Emma knew Elias held it against her. Another child meant more obligations. He let her name the second boy: John Amos.

Chapter 6

Folks turned to "Doc" Howard when the wadded inner bark of the devil's walking stick offered no relief for a toothache, and they'd just as soon be done with the darn tooth altogether. On a November afternoon Hattie returned from Doc Howard's farm minus a molar, hand pressed against her jaw, a strip of fabric wrapped around her head. Dorothy Jane applied cotton saturated with oil of cloves to the wound and put her to bed. But not before Hattie's muffled announcement that she and Doc had made a deal, a mighty good deal. The only way to get ahead, she said, was to farm more land, and that day she'd signed papers to rent ten acres from him. The first two years were free.

It went without saying that Elias was expected to farm this *mighty good deal*. Legs spread, hands on hips, he squinted into the morning sun as he examined the acreage. Not usually a cursing man, he spat out a stream of *goddamns*. Twenty years or so had passed since a plow had dug into the soil. There were young elm and poplar and maple trees, along with a few loblolly pines. Here and there two trees shared a base. Whoever originally cleared the land had failed to dig out the roots.

What were the chances that once Elias made this suitable for farming, Doc Howard would decide not to rent it out anymore?

"You all right?" Emma's hand rested on Elias's shoulder as she took his empty dinner plate.

He'd stayed seated at the table, head in hands, eyes closed. "I reckon," he said. He opened his eyes and looked up at her. His gaze rested on her breasts, filled with milk. He wanted to bury his head in her bosom and cry.

"The day's pertier than any we've had for a spell, and the boys are nappin'," she said. "Why don't I walk with you over to that new piece? You can tell me what you're planning to do."

Planning to do. That was the problem; he had no plan. Still, he saw a bit of gaiety in her brown eyes and recalled that just a moment ago he'd wanted to cling to her.

The autumn day glistened. They passed bare-leafed thickets and fields of corn stubble. Emma took hold of his hand. "You realize, 'cept for nighttime this is the first time in a coon's age that we've been alone?"

At the plot Elias pointed out the dimensions: the eastern boundary marked by the walnut tree over there, the western boundary by the ditch over there. Nearby a woodpecker hammered at a hollow tree. A sharp-shinned hawk flew high overhead.

Emma spoke: "I'm thinkin' you see this as one big job when it's really a lot of little ones. You ain't gonna get all ten acres cleared in one winter. How 'bout you start over yonder? Cut down all them pines and young maples over there. That'll give you a sunny section for planting in the spring. You could just leave them poplars out in the middle for a season or two. I'm sure Pa can help you. And what about your Cousin David, your Cousin Aaron? You've helped them plenty. They can come out here this winter with their big saws."

"Yes, yes, that might work." Impulsively he leaned down and kissed her on the cheek.

There was camaraderie in such an undertaking. Two men creating a rhythm in the back and forth of a crosscut saw; shouts of warning at the cracking sound of an about-to-fall tree; periods of rest when Emma, Dorothy Jane, and Lizzie brought dinner down the road—Lizzie carrying on a flirtation with Aaron, even though he was her cousin.

Some days Elias worked alone, offering ample opportunity to think. Lately he'd been contemplating three realms. First, the eternal realm, where God ruled supreme and Jesus sat at his right side and bodies were made whole.

Second, the domestic realm. The here and now, where Elias worked and slept and ate his meals. He was head of the household, but he relied on the women, whose feminine sensitivities made it function. Along with hard work of course, theirs and his, in a paradise turned topsy-turvy because of Adam and Eve's sins.

Seemed there was a third realm too: the world of ideas. Some men made a living from reading and writing then applying their knowledge to the law or politics, sometimes writing down their ideas for others to read, sometimes speaking to a crowd. Such men were respected.

St. Paul had enough education to engage with the scholars of Athens. "Let us honor human learning," the author of *Christian Research in Asia* had written. "It is indispensable in preaching to the heathens." *Human learning. Let us honor human learning.*

Buggies and wagons clattered into the churchyard. The steeple bell urged believers to hurry along. Elias tied Hector to the hitching post and dodged mounds of dung.

He was there to learn a thing or two about preaching. Three years earlier, Sinai Baptist Church had ordained him as one of its preachers. The other two men, when it came their turn, relied on the Holy Spirit's instant guidance. Elias, though, always prepared a mental outline.

Seated in a large chair resembling a throne, Reverend Gibson wore a black robe with a starched white collar. For Presbyterians, being a preacher was like being a doctor or lawyer. *Reverend,* how they addressed their ministers. A certain level of education was required. There were standards.

They lacked Baptists' fervor, Elias quickly noticed. No shouts of *Amen* or *Praise the Lord.* Standing or seated, their bodies were stiff, their faces emotionless. They sang sturdy hymns.

Today he leaned forward, eyes watching Reverend Gibson's every gesture, ears taking in each word coming from the learned man.

"Behold, a sower went forth to sow," Reverend Gibson said. "Now, we're country folk. We know you can't just scatter seeds any old place. You don't plant them along a path. Birds might get them. You don't plant them on stony surfaces. The roots are going to be shallow, and when the sun shines, your crop is gonna dry up. And you don't scatter the seeds among the thorns. The thorns, they're going to choke out your seeds. But this sower—maybe he was conducting an experiment, because he scattered seeds in four different kinds of places.

"The fourth place? you ask. He scattered seeds on good, healthy—it was like our soil, good old bottomland soil. We know what happened. Those plants grew and grew, and Jesus says they produced abundant fruit.

"Now, not even his disciples understood what the Master was getting at, so he had to explain."

Elias recognized what Miss Pritchard had tried to instill in her students. During recess schoolboys had imitated her, raising the pitch of their voices to make her sound as prissy as the queen of England. Instead of joining in their humor, Elias had paid close attention to how she spoke. Reverend Gibson used proper English too.

After the service, Elias lagged, waiting as the minister greeted worshippers at the door. He watched some in attendance walk over to the adjoining graveyard to pay their respects, others as they climbed into buggies.

Standing tall, wanting to make a good impression, he approached Reverend Gibson. "Sir, my name is Elias Muller. I am a conscientious student of Scripture."

The reverend gave the young man an evaluating once-over. From worn shoes to threadbare coat. Nodded his head. "Conscientious student of Scripture," he repeated. "Well, welcome to you, Mister Muller."

Elias cleared his throat and recited the speech he'd rehearsed. "With winter approaching I have extra time for study, and I'd be much obliged if you would tutor me in Greek and in the interpretation of the Holy Word. I'll repay such kindness with a good supply of wood to keep you over the winter."

Giving Hector a loose rein on the way home, Elias lifted his arms and shouted to the sapphire blue sky, "He accepted my offer! I am going to get to study! He accepted my offer!" Seeds needed rich soil to produce in abundance, and he, Elias—could Jesus's parable also be about the seed itself, its needs? What if the person—what if Elias was the seed? Living in this place, among people who had little interest in matters of the mind? He had been planted among thorns. Didn't he have a responsibility to find good soil?

Parlors were for people who had enough space to be divided according to use: for sitting, talking, drinking a cup of hot tea or sweet lemonade. This one had a piano. Elias, as he passed it, couldn't help but reach over and press a key, pleased by its low rumble.

Reverend Gibson was a robust man, his blond hair combed away from his face, carefully cropped around the ears and at the neck. He had a mustache the color of cornsilk. A well-fed man, judging from the taut buttons of his waistcoat. From his waistcoat pocket draped the gold fob of a pocket watch, which on subsequent meetings he would remove at the end of an hour and announce the session's end.

The two met regularly in what Reverend Gibson referred to as his study, a room with heavy draperies and book-lined walls. A colored woman named Betsy, wearing a crisp white apron over a gray dress, set cider and cookies on the table where they worked. Heads bent over a Greek lexicon, the older man and the younger one unraveled biblical mysteries.

Elias's questions often prompted Reverend Gibson to approach the bookshelves. Chin lifted to better see through his reading glasses, he ran an index finger along the titles. "Ah, here it is, something I suggest you read." Elias might return home carrying a commentary or a volume by John Calvin.

Or a book by Charles Spurgeon. Elias imagined himself as America's Charles Spurgeon, preaching before people who valued scholarship. His words would be published and read by millions all over the world.

On a January afternoon the drapes in Reverend Gibson's study were pulled to block cold winds blowing from the northwest. Warmth radiating from the fireplace cast a cozy spell. The two men had just finished translating one of Paul's letters from the Greek when, without explanation, Reverend Gibson left the room. Alone, Elias stood, moved along the rows of books, reverently touching several.

Reverend Gibson returned with a package wrapped in paper and twine. "May God's blessings be upon you," he said as he handed it to Elias. Elias looked at him questioningly, not knowing what to do. "Open it," Gibson had to instruct.

Cruden's Concordance. Elias's own biblical reference book. Not counting his Bible and *Christian Research in Asia*, it was the beginning of his library.

Elias and Cousin Aaron grunted as they positioned notched logs. Hands on hips, Emma squinted into the afternoon sun.

"Seems kinda small to hold a bed," she said.

"Ain't gonna be a bedroom."

"What you doing then?"

Elias wiped his forehead with a red handkerchief. "Building me a study."

"A what?"

"A place I can have me some peace and quiet."

"A study," she muttered, then turned without saying more.

The room had a single window facing east, a door to the outside, and a small corner fireplace of river rock. Elias built a sturdy table of chestnut, placed an inkwell on it, the pen passed down to him by his father, five sheets of paper, and his three books.

"Elias! Elias!"

Through the fog of slumber, he heard raspy blasts of coughing like the bay of a hound dog. Heard Emma say, "We need to get steam going, help him breathe."

Elias had given little credence to Emma's recent fretting over the boy's runny nose and lethargy. Women had a way of turning minor trials into tribulations.

Unlike Robert, who stuck to Emma like spruce resin, Johnny, practically from birth, had responded to Elias. Wrapping tiny pink fingers around dirt-stained, calloused ones. Focusing his eyes on his father's mouth when Elias spoke. Holding out his arms to be lifted and nuzzled with funny sounds. Outdoors, the baby was spellbound by words beyond his comprehension about corn breaking through the soil and bees buzzing. He would shift his gaze from Elias's face to the flower or leaf or clump of dirt as if intent upon understanding.

Groping in the darkness, Elias lit the oil lamp. Now he saw the terror in Emma's eyes matching the terror in her voice. In the main room he stirred the barely-alive embers of the evening fire. He added wood from the wood box and made sure the kettle contained water.

"We need to get him to Dr. Campbell," Emma said.

"You know we ain't got the money." It was a stab to the heart, hearing himself admit he was too poor to afford a doctor.

"The Ferris boy, he died of the croup."

"It's probably just a bad cold. Young-uns get colds and get over 'em." He wanted to believe it was so.

She spoke emphatically. "This is not a cold."

"I've already started praying."

"Now ain't the time for prayers. It's the time for doing somethin'. If you won't take him to Dr. Campbell, I will." She hastily wrapped the baby in a blanket, then headed toward the door with emphatic steps.

"Wife, you come back here." He took big strides to clutch her elbow. "How you gonna hold him and keep control of Hector at the same time? Besides, you ain't going nowheres without more blankets around—why you're not even dressed." He pried Johnny from her arms. "I say we pray some more. If he isn't doing better in the morning, we'll take him down to—I'll find some way to pay the doctor. Now then, fire's warmin'. We're gettin' a little steam."

Emma looked up at him with pleading eyes. "It can't wait," she whimpered.

"There's no moon and—two hours it takes even in daylight, when you can see the ruts and all. We can't risk the—"

"Give him to me." From the surrounding darkness Mother Muller reached for Johnny. Until now the couple hadn't noticed her and Lizzie and Dorothy Jane standing in their nightgowns. "You—" she pointed at Emma, "slice an onion real thin and sprinkle sugar on top. We'll give him the juice from it."

"Do as she says," Elias ordered.

Emma sliced the onion, tears of fear merging with tears from cutting the onion.

The night was long. Nestled between Emma and Elias, Johnny had fits of coughing and crying. Until he could only whimper and his breathing came in gasps.

Early morning, while it was still dark, Elias hooked Hector to the wagon, all the while praying, *Please God. Please place your healing hand upon my boy's brow.* On their way toward Polkville, Emma held Johnny tight, sharing the warmth of her body. The sun broke through a heavy layer of clouds. Like lanterns scattering their beams, its rays spread across the horizon.

"Elias, stop! Stop!" Emma screamed when they'd gone no more than a mile. "Something's wrong. He's gone—he's gone limp." She whimpered. "He ain't with us no more." Her prolonged moan penetrated the morning calm.

Elias took the child from her and slapped his cheeks as if to awaken him. "You, God, don't let it be this way. Heal him! Heal him!" He crushed Johnny's small body against his own.

Heads leaning over the inert body, Elias and Emma clung to each other. In the distance a rooster crowed. A dog barked. In the stubble of the corn field, a flock of crows searched for nourishment. Until the sobs of mother and father drowned out all else.

They buried Johnny next to his grandfather in the church cemetery. In a tiny pine coffin, a narrow slab for a headstone, JAM carved into the slab.

For months afterward Elias tried to assure everyone, himself included, that Johnny was with Papa and Jesus up in heaven. Sometimes, though, while clearing the rented parcel—swinging the axe and digging up roots that seemed to extend to Earth's core—when no one was around, he allowed his mind to go to that sorrowful place in his heart. He'd stand beside a tree stump, not even trying to compose himself, just stand there sobbing until the fountain of tears ran dry.

His fault, his son's death. The delay in taking Johnny to Dr. Campbell. Even more damning, his inability to afford a doctor.

Emma, he knew, also blamed him. It was as if her specter carried out her duties. She seldom spoke, and then only a simple response to a question. Clean clothes were put in the drawer, food appeared on the table. Nights, like a rag doll, she let him use her body for release.

Fifty cents! A frivolous gift, but perhaps it would lift Emma from the sorrow she hadn't been able to let go of. She hung the mirror beside the door of their bedroom, but to Elias's knowledge she'd not once peered into it, not witnessed her own sallow complexion, the dark circles under her eyes. Surely, she'd want to do something about her appearance once he shared his news.

Yes, he'd have to do something about himself too. He'd ask her to give him a haircut. First, though, he needed to tell her why.

In the bedroom he lowered the wick of the kerosene lamp, then took familiar steps in the darkness. The cornhusk mattress rustled as he lay down.

"What do you say we go to camp meeting this year?" he asked. She rolled over, turning her back to him. He repeated, "What'ya say we go to camp meeting?"

She mumbled, "You're all the time saying farming keeps us from getting away."

"Not much of the corn's tasseled, it being so dry. Mama and the girls'll look after things."

"If you want to," she said in resignation.

He turned her to face him, pulled her close so that her breath brushed his chin.

"A lot of your friends'll be there. Lucy Tallant, she'll probably go. There's all the inspiring singing and preaching. You like to sing. And they only ask the best preachers to speak, you know."

"It's a lot of work," she mumbled unenthusiastically, "getting the bedding ready and gathering enough vittles for one week."

"They asked me to preach," he finally admitted. "Thursday evening service."

He wanted her to share in his excitement. This was an honor, especially his being only a month beyond twenty years. It would be the most people he'd ever preached to, and a chance to win souls to Jesus.

"Then I reckon we'll be going." She removed his hand from her hip and again turned to face the wall.

Six chickens cackled frantically, protesting imprisonment in a crate tied to the back of the Muller wagon. Near the crate, a week's worth of provisions: flour, dried apples, and vegetables from the garden. Elias lightly held the reins as Hector leisurely clopped along the clay-packed road. Emma, now warmed to the notion, sat next to him on the wagon bench, Robert on her lap. While she hummed "Onward, Christian Soldiers," she pointed out the turkey vultures circling in the distance, a bluebird perched on a cornstalk.

By the time they arrived at the campground, other families had already pitched tents or parked wagons. Sites were organized in two concentric circles; between the circles, a cleared strip of land for cooking fires and walking paths. In the center of everything, at the heart of all the activity, stood the brush arbor tabernacle, an immense open-air structure of poles supporting a roof of tree branches.

Before settling in, Elias drove the wagon around both circles, greeting people he did not know, as well as acquaintances. "Howdy, Brother." "Hello there, Brother

McCoy." Finally, he chose a site next to Cousin Lemual and his wife Sally, with child and rotund as a cracker barrel. Their little boy immediately began to chase three-year-old Robert, who squealed with delight.

Men who had organized a livery stable were getting horses and mules settled in for the coming days. There were three wagons of straw for bedding, six wagons of hay.

Women prepared communal suppers over open fires, taking a moment to holler out greetings to friends just arriving, inviting others to combine resources. Already the aroma of sizzling pork permeated the campground. By nightfall, women had divided responsibilities so they could take turns attending the week's inspirational events.

Worship that evening was brief, allowing families to settle in. While Emma tried to calm Robert for the night—his being so overstimulated by the day's activities—Elias felt the need to go off and meditate. He stepped beyond the outer circle of sites. Away from the muted sounds of conversation, away from the campfires, from the neighs and stomping of horses and mules. Into the surrounding forest.

There was no path, only a thick carpet of pine needles. Had Elias been looking down, he would have seen the tree root the size of a giant snake, but he was gazing upward, trying to catch a glimpse of the moon between trees. He tripped. Sprawled on the pine needles, he was stunned more by surprise than by the fall itself. Leaning against a tree, he brought his hand to his mouth and tasted blood.

He continued to sit there, running his tongue over the injured lip, worried it would swell. He wanted his sermon to be perfect, for people to marvel over his eloquence. What would they do when they greeted him afterward? Would they see the lip and, instead of extending words of praise, express sympathy and offer advice for the lip's care?

No voice of condemnation came from above, no prophet stood there and admonished him. Yet he recognized that like a swiftly flowing stream, the current of his own sin was pulling him under. He was not the attraction; he was a tool.

Thursday evening arrived. An elevated platform accessed by a flight of stairs stood at the front of the open-air tabernacle. As if there to lend credibility to the young preacher, five bearded men of wide repute sat alongside him on the platform. From up high he watched worshippers enter and take seats on planks supported by tree stumps, the men to his right, women and children to his left.

Abner Jenkins lined a hymn, the congregation's response a mournful chant:

"My mother has gone to bright glory

My father is still wandering in sin."

When it was his turn to preach he stood and looked out over the gathering. Mothers nursed babies, children wriggled restlessly. Uninterested men turned their gazes to the ground. Worshippers seated in the back rows seemed miles away. His voice had to carry that far. He stood as tall as he could, reached deep into the lower range of his voice, declared The Word loudly and with gravitas.

His choice of scripture was short: only the beginning of two sentences, both from Genesis. "Here we see it clearly, already at the very beginning of creation, 'And God said . . . And the serpent said . . .' The Lord speaks, the serpent speaks. From the very first page, the Bible warns us about the goals of the evil one. His fangs thrust through all the rose petals and the summer beauty of life and time.

"If I look abroad upon the earth, I cannot but find proof enough that there is an enemy today. Call him by what name you please—Satan, the Devil, the Evil One—account for him as you like; deny him if you will. Only be mindful that God has an unslumbering enemy." As Elias preached, more heads turned upward toward the high platform.

After an hour he concluded the sermon with "'Behold the lamb of God, that taketh away the sin of the world.' Amen."

It was time to call repentants to come forward and confess their sins. Worshippers sang "Just as I am Without One Plea," women's and men's voices raised full throttle.

A pause in the song, Elias's right hand raised. "Will you join Jesus at the throne of God or will you face unending agony in the throes—"

The ground began to tremble. Babies ceased crying. The squeals of horses and mules pierced the night air. Panicked faces looked up at the swaying of the overarching arbor. A branch fell on the head of Wilber Weinsap, known for his perfidy and frequent drunkenness. He fell to his knees. Anna Whitmore shouted, "Lord, Jesus, save me," and sobbed into her hands.

Elias stood confused. Was the kingdom at hand? Because of his sermon? He fixed his gaze upward, half expecting to see God floating above it all. Telling him what was going on. And what to do. *At his wrath the earth shall tremble.* Why would God be angry?

Earth's shuddering stopped.

From both sides of the aisle, women and men ran to the altar, crying women carrying crying babies, men pleading in agonized voices for God's mercy. Elias could only stand there dumbfounded as the other ministers on the platform descended the steps and welcomed the sinners.

More than three hundred souls were saved that night.

Later, as Robert slept soundly between Emma and Elias in the wagon, Elias tried to make sense of what had happened. Out in the forest he had prayed that God would work through him, and he believed God answered prayer, but . . . but . . . He rejoiced that many sinners had repented and wanted to be baptized, but . . . but . . . he couldn't help but feel sad. All the joy and laughter of the past three days as children chased each other, as women prepared meals together, and men played horseshoes—strange how salvation had scared cheerfulness away.

Waves of people had crammed the aisle. Surely, not all of those men gambled or took the Lord's name in vain. And the women—what did they feel so guilty about? He could not fathom the amount of remorse people had laid at the feet of Jesus.

Two days later, word spread through the campground that there had been an earthquake centered down in Charleston. Emma's words to Elias: "Just remember,

Elijah was up on that there mountain, and it come an earthquake, but God, he wudden't in the earthquake." *

Dorothy Jane got married. At age twenty-six she wed Peter P. Collins, a widower thirty years her senior. Instead of settling Dorothy Jane into a house of sadness—his first wife and three children having died of diphtheria a year earlier—he moved Dorothy Jane and his two youngest sons, ages fifteen and seventeen, to a farm up in the far northwestern corner of Burke County.

Compared to neighbors, the Collins family was a family of means. During the war Peter served as a 2nd Lieutenant in the 55th Infantry. His father had big holdings of arable land, and before the war owned a dozen slaves.

As he witnessed the marriage, Elias figured everyone present had reason to be relieved. Peter, because he'd found a woman to run his household. Dorothy Jane, because she wouldn't be an old maid. Mama, because Dorothy Jane and Peter invited her to live with them in a sizable house; Emma, because she no longer had to work under Mama's and Dorothy Jane's supervision; Lizzie, at age eighteen, because she was a romantic at heart. Elias was grateful for two fewer mouths to feed.

Following the wedding Peter tied Hattie's and Dorothy Jane's trunks to the back of his phaeton and carried the two women off. Elias watched the buggy make the turn in the road and disappear from sight. Since his birth Mama and Dorothy Jane had praised him, scolded him, told him what to do, how to behave. Now they were gone. Emma took his hand, seeming to remind him that he was not on his own. Five-year-old Robert continued to wave goodbye.

Alone in his study Elias considered the chapter of his life that had just closed. The memories were many: carrying wood for Mama's cookstove and the fire under

---

*On August 31, 1886, 9:00 p.m., an earthquake centered in Charleston, SC, was felt in Lincolnton, NC and surrounding areas.

the laundry tub; plowing her garden, he a mere boy holding firmly to Hector's reins; and helping Papa build the bedroom she wanted. Papa had been man of the house but Mama was the one they all wanted to please.

Two weeks after Dorothy Jane's wedding, a letter came from Pinckney's wife over in Rowan County. A falling tree had killed him while he cleared land. He left behind a widow and seven children. Pinckney was the big brother Elias looked up to. Along with Papa he had taught Elias how to fish and hunt. How to be a man.

Each of life's chapters seemed marked by loss: the death of Papa, Johnny, and now Pinckney. One day he'd greet each loved one up in heaven. But his despair over recent losses was far more intense than hope.

March 16, 1985

Dear Lydia,

You've been in my thoughts all day. Last night I dreamed Papa was making you stand behind the door (his discipline of choice, when it came to making you tow the line), and you were screaming for me to rescue you. I wanted to but he held me back. I woke up frantic.

It seems you were always being punished for something. Even though I was younger, I wanted to protect you. I recently read about the "Mothers of the Disappeared" of Argentina. I'm prone to defending Papa, but it seems to me that punishing a child by making her stand behind a door was "disappearing" her. Not on nearly as harsh a scale as murder, obviously, but my, how you hated it.

Because of your investigative efforts (and probably because I'm at "that age"), I've been thinking about memories. Some will die with me. They're little ones of no interest to anyone but me, and maybe you. One recently came to mind. I was seventeen. You were living at home but spent most of your time at college, so I don't think you were there. Papa got the telegram saying his sister, Dorothy, had died. I still see him holding the telegram in his hand, leaning against the icebox and crying. I wrapped my arms around him, trying to comfort him. He often said I reminded him of her.

As for the here and now, I have no news. The kids lead busy lives but manage to stay in touch. Sharon drives over once a month. She so reminds me of our gentle and sweet mother, with her deep-set green eyes and full cheeks.

I hope you and your family are doing well.

Love,

Dorcas

Chapter 7

By the time Frances Broder prayed on the women's side of the meetinghouse, she had already that morning killed and cut up two chickens, peeled potatoes and set them aside in cold water, and doubled the recipe for breakfast biscuits so that when dinnertime came she only needed to reheat them. As they did most Sundays, Emma, Elias, and the boys—which now included Spurgeon, named after Charles Spurgeon—came for dinner. Elias said grace: gratitude for dinner and the hands that prepared it; the confession of sins—gossiping on behalf of Emma and Frances, profaning God's name on behalf of Amos, mentioning no sin of his own. He thanked God for the recent rain and asked that God would "get us through the trials and tribulations of these times." Immediately following Amen, he reprimanded Robert for wiggling during the prayer.

Later, while Emma and her mother cleaned the kitchen, Spurgeon napped and Robert ran in large concentric circles outside.

Elias and Amos played checkers on the porch. "I've got Papa's original fifteen acres," Elias said. He kept two fingers on the red checker, hesitant to finalize the move. "Plus the apple orchard I doubt'll ever produce, plus the ten Mama's been renting from Doc Howard."

"You're lucky he ain't decided to farm it hisself, you having cleared every damn inch of it."

"Isn't that the truth. But what I'm getting at is this. Every year I borrow against crops I haven't planted yet. Even in a good year I barely make enough to support the family. I'm never going to get ahead." He lifted his hand, letting the checker rest on the black square. "Lately this paper, *The Progressive Farmer*, it's called, it's been coming to the general store. Takes the position that the time has come for the government to step in and help the farmer."

Amos Broder's right hand rested on his knee. He never talked about the war. Didn't need to, the amputation of three fingers a testament to what he'd endured. A gunshot at Gaines' Mill had left him signing documents with an X, though truth be told he'd not known how to write his name prior to the war. Now, with his left hand he picked up a black checker and jumped two of Elias's red ones. "Last thing we need is for the goddamn government to interfere. If you need cash, make likker." He spat a glob of tobacco juice out on the ground.

"You know how I feel about that. I've seen what whiskey can do to a man."

"I ain't suggesting you drink it. A business, that's what it is, a business. Only way a man can make hisself some cash."

"I've been here on a Saturday night. Not a sober fella on this here porch. Even if you didn't drink much—not saying that's the case—you're tempting others. Take Oscar Fisher. You hear how our womenfolk have organized to protect Nellie? Every time somebody spies him drinking, one of the ladies fetches Nellie and the girls and hides 'em somewheres safe."

"I ain't never sold to that son of a bitch."

"Makes no never mind. I'm saying I don't want it on my conscience, selling to a man who beats his wife and children."

"How'd we get from talking about how you're gonna get yourself out 'a debt to talking about hooch? You're just stallin' cause you ain't got nowhere to move that sucker."

In 1887 Helmut Gruen died of a heart attack. Kneeling by the bed at night, hands folded in prayer, Elias begged God's forgiveness for not making an effort to convert the kind-hearted Jew.

Frau Gruen now managed the store, which she did quite capably, though with less tolerance for tobacco juice on the floor than when her husband had been present to moderate. Nowadays, the men who congregated around the stove during the winter—usually five or six of them— were a younger lot. Three had been raised fatherless, required to do a man's work at an early age. All, including Elias, were tenant farmers, every year borrowing money for spring supplies against crop success, often owing more after harvest than they'd taken in. Their language was coarse, their hair ragged and greasy, beards straggly.

Conversations usually began with observations about the weather. The rain or lack of it. How cold it had been lately. Warmer than usual for these parts. Prospects for an early spring. Prospects for a late spring. The talk moved from the weather to politics, voices growing in amplification and, on occasion, resorting to a shout of *bullshit*, causing Frau Gruen to order everyone to leave the premises. Not with English words the men understood, but the intent of her tone and her index finger pointing toward the door was unmistakable.

As the 1888 election approached, Elias, now twenty-two, took his recently acquired franchise seriously. For the most part the current Republican Party stood for values he shared. He, too, opposed the federal government giving railroads and corporations land in the public domain, but Harrison's support of tariffs ate at farmers' earnings.

"Why would anyone want to bring Republicans back in power?" one of the men said. "They don't respect the South none."

"Harrison, now he's with the small farmer. He's for silver and gold both backing our money, and for railroads giving us a fair shake. His plan to repeal the tobacco tax, that's good for North Carolina."

"You vote Democrat and you're working 'ginst yourself. We ain't seen no evidence that

Cleveland gives a damn about the South."

"But Republicans are all about makin' Blacks equal to whites. By his very nature he ain't got the intelligence to vote."

"Now, hold your horses. The colored farmer, he's struggling too. All of us, colored and white, gotta work together. Stands to reason he'll vote his interests, just like us."

And so on, and so on.

The nearby town of Dallas had been trying to build a reputation as a virtuous place. A year earlier, vigilantes had demolished six houses of ill-repute run by white women. Now newspapers reported that the court had ordered the hanging of a colored woman accused of killing her baby.

"We got to go see it for ourselves," Allston Paine insisted, a wad of tobacco making his jaw bulge.

Elias was no stranger to death. He liked to hunt and had shot One-Eye when the dog was in agony. He'd helped Pinckney prepare their father's body for burial. Lynchings, he'd hear about after the fact, white thugs taking it upon themselves to settle manufactured grievances. Any excuse to execute a colored man.

As for a court-ordered hanging: "I have no interest in seeing justice served," he told Paine.

"But ain't you even a little bit curious? A man ought to see these things for hisself so he can decide if they're right or wrong."

Yes, Elias reckoned he was a bit curious.

The atmosphere on the day of the hanging had the festive atmosphere of the Fourth of July. They came from miles around, more than a thousand people.

"This n——'s gonna get her comeuppance, ain't she?"

"Them Yankees judgin' us for selling heathen babies. Better than lettin' them poison their own, that's what done come with freedom."

Suddenly, the crowd hushed. Caroline Shipp, no more than twenty years old, rode past in a wagon pulled by a single horse. She was perched on her own pine coffin, singing for all to hear, "O Beulah land, sweet Beulah land! As on thy highest mount I stand"; shouting, "I am innocent. I loved my baby"; praying, "Father, forgive them, for they know not what they do."

Then she was climbing up the steps to the gallows. Overcome with nausea, Elias turned away as the hangman placed the noose around her neck.

"She just dropped the handkerchief," Paine whispered breathlessly. "That means she's ready."

Elias returned his gaze to the gallows. The box she stood on was pushed away. Yet she did not die. The hangman tugged on her legs. Her neck snapped, the muscles of her body twitched, her face swelled. "Look, she shat herself!" someone hollered. The crowd's cheer drowned out Elias's moan.

He saw the glee in everyone's eyes. What kind of people were these, that they found entertainment in a human life being taken? What kind of man was he, that he'd agreed to come?

Nights afterward he had vivid dreams, some with the hangman's noose dangling as if waiting for him. Other dreams with Caroline Shipp herself pleading her cause, telling him she had not killed her baby.*

"You ask her about it yet?" Emma whispered.

"You ask her. You're the one who noticed."

"She's your sister. And you're head of the house."

Men mainly entered women's realm for meals, and Lizzie was the kind to go quietly about her work, not asking to be noticed. But once Elias bothered to move his eyes up and down her body, pausing in the middle, he saw what a loose-fitting dress and an apron partially hid.

Head of the house. His responsibility to . . . Long into the night he lay awake wondering what to do. He couldn't think of any man who might be responsible. And Lizzie's condition definitely required a man.

"Lizzie! Lizzie! You come down here," he shouted up to the loft the next morning.

She cautiously descended the drop-down stairs in her nightgown. Her unbraided walnut-colored hair hung in crinkled waves down to her waist. At the bottom of the steps, she smiled at Robert, who reached for her hand. More than anyone else she was sensitive to the fretting he had not outgrown, holding him

---

*Though out of sequence, this was inspired by an actual historical event.
On December 18, 1891, Carolina Shipp was executed in Gaston County, NC.

through his spells, humming a gentle tune while rubbing his back. Now her smile signaled that he need not fret over the adult conversation and anger about to erupt. She would be safe.

She faced her brother with lifted chin.

Whore of Babylon. Harlot. Jezebel. Who's the father? Who's the father?

"Let him who is without sin cast the first stone!" Lizzie finally yelled. Which had the intended effect. Elias turned on his heels and stormed out of the house, into the overcast morning.

Not many days after the confrontation, a warrant was delivered to the post office in the back of the general store. Lizzie was ordered to appear before the Justice of the Peace.

"Who reported it?" Elias wanted to know.

"Lot of folks to choose from," Emma mused. "I reckon someone at church. That's the only place anybody ever sees her. Had to be a woman. Only women notice such things."

Peter, Dorothy Jane, and Hattie made the day-long journey from northwestern Burke County to accompany Lizzie. Peter, a man of means and a former lieutenant in the Confederate Army, still carried influence in the county. He, not Elias, could provide a more imposing male-in-charge presence.

Later, Dorothy Jane provided details of the meeting.

Mr. Collins—she always called him Mr. Collins—had known William Cobb from their war days, when Cobb presented every man up the ranks with chickens, whiskey, and other goods acquired in raids. Toadying up to leaders had become a lifelong practice, for no sooner did Democrats retake the state in '77 than Cobb was appointed Justice of the Peace.

In the front room of his two-story house, William Cobb administered justice from behind a large oak desk. He came out from behind the desk to shake hands with Mr. Collins, Cobb's swagger suggesting he wanted his importance noted. He acknowledged that they had fought side by side, and it was unfortunate how things had turned out, honorable men losing to the damn Yankees.

Three women had been ordered to be present. One, obviously pregnant, was accompanied by an older man who turned out to be her father. The second, a middle-aged woman, carried an infant. The third, Lizzie and her entourage.

The father of the other pregnant woman said he would assume financial responsibility for raising his grandchild. He would pay the bond. The woman carrying a baby, when pressed, surrendered the name of its father. Mr. Cobb ordered that he report to court.

"Miss Muller," Justice Cobb said when Lizzie stood before him, hands clasped beneath her rounded belly, "you have been ordered to appear before me because you carry a child and are not married to its father. Therefore, the county requires that you answer these questions: One, are you a lifelong resident of this county?"

"Yes, sir."

"Are you single?"

"Yes, sir."

"Have you ever been married?"

"No, sir."

"When was the child conceived?"

"I don't rightly know, sir."

"Can you estimate?"

"Late August, sir."

"Who's the daddy of your child?"

Lizzie gazed directly at Mr. Cobb and pressed her lips together.

"I asked, Miss Muller, who is the father?"

Lizzie's voice shook. "I cannot say, Justice Cobb."

William Cobb shuffled papers before him. "You know the law, Miss Muller. The county is unwilling to bear financial responsibility for bastards. Is there someone who will bear responsibility and pay the bond?"

"Yes, sir. My sister's husband will."

Mr. Collins stood.

"I assume you are not the father, Lieutenant Collins."

"Correct, sir. As the husband of Miss Muller's sister, I am paying the bond."

The next monthly conference of Sinai Baptist Church requested Lizzie's presence. She refused to attend. She was "excluded on her own regress," that is, expelled from the fellowship.

Peter Collins came and took Lizzie to his and Dorothy Jane's home. Andrew Muller was born in May. Named after Hattie's and Joseph's oldest son—who'd died in Yankee captivity—who'd been named after Joseph's oldest brother, who'd been named after that brother's uncle.

For more than a week Elias had practiced the statement. *This is the man we need!* someone would shout, and he'd be propelled to . . . He'd again been considering politics. Not as a topic of interest one reads about in newspapers, but as a vocation, a calling. Mayor of a city, perhaps, or member of the General Assembly, then on to the House of Representatives. Why not aim for the U.S. Senate?

The schoolhouse was already crowded when he arrived, adult men stuffed into student seats, others standing and leaning against the wall. Open windows did little to lessen the pungent stench of sweat and tobacco breath.

Elias stood in front, beside the schoolmaster's desk. He rocked heel to toe, toe to heel, a rhythmic motion. Now and then he swept a hand through his slicked-back hair.

"This is not our fathers' South, where the labor of every man was respected. The New South, they're calling it, business folks wanting us to leave the land and work in their factories and mills. The New South, where bankers and railroad owners are kings, us farmers are the peasants. Men who are driven by profit decide our fate. They're financial manipulators who care nothing for the ordinary man.

"But farmers across the country have been joining together. Out in Texas they started what they're calling the Farmers' Alliance, and it's been working its way across the country. Farmers need to organize, they tell us, and some places in North Carolina they've been doing just that. I'm proposing that we organize too."

"A body can't never get ahead," John Nesbitt shouted from the back. He nervously chomped on the tobacco wad in his bulging cheek. "Not by hisself."

"Old Cecil Bidwell done lost everthing." This from a man called Raccoon, whose wife had created a dozen recipes for coon, him being such a sure-shot. "Them sons of bitches up in Morganton leavin' us all suckin' on the hind tit."

Elias had spent hours on this speech and sought the group's undivided attention, but chaos was taking over.

"We don't want nothing like the Grange," D.W. Payne hollered. "Landowners done took that over. Gone all secretive, like the Masons. The Grange ain't worth chicken shit to us."

Elias held up both hands to silence the men. "All over the South, farmers are uniting. They're demanding that the government step in to regulate the banks and take over the railroads. Cotton farmers are building warehouses where they can keep their cotton until the price goes up. Some places farmers are forming cooperatives, where they can pay discounted prices for supplies."

"That's what's killin' us!" Thomas Downs shouted, "Morganton, Lincolnton, Shelby— wherever you go, they scalp you. Me, I ain't sure I can make it through another season."

Elias wanted to shout over the din that he was in charge. Then it came to him: The purpose of joining with the Alliance was to give farmers a voice. To give those here in the schoolhouse a voice. He took a seat behind the schoolmaster's desk— hands clasped behind his head, elbows extended—and listened as men vented their anger over conditions beyond their control.

"I got a question." This from Chester Burns, who was leaning against the back wall. "Are Blacks included in your organization? I ain't joining if they're part of this."

"The alliance," Elias said, "it doesn't include them. They have their own. Now, I myself, I don't have much admiration for them. But regarding this matter, it seems to me it'd make sense for all of us, colored and white, to work together."

Again, Chester Burns spoke out: "The powers that be in Raleigh, you think they'll pay any heed if we're acting all friendly with the n——s? Let 'em keep their own body."

"They're hurting too." That from Jacob Kirby, a hefty man squeezed into a student desk.

"You heard him," Raccoon yelled, "they ain't allowed!"

Elias wanted to end the meeting. Quickly, while goodwill existed. He lifted both hands as he did when offering the benediction at church.

"I say, brothers, it's our sweat that puts food on the nation's tables. But the cost of moving our goods by railroad eats up what little profit we make, and we stay indebted to the store that sells us seed and tools on credit. Only in unity can we survive."

A week after Frau Gruen announced the impending sale of the general store and her plans to go live with her daughter out in California, Thomas Downs loaded her two trunks onto his wagon, extended a hand to help her climb to the bench beside him, hollered "giddy-up," and flicked the reins to urge the horses onward. They were headed to the train station up in Morganton.

That same week the new owner, Edward Hubert of Lancaster, Pennsylvania, arrived with two wagons loaded with farm supplies. He was accompanied by his wife and three sons—between ten and fifteen years of age, local folks guessed. Within a month he and the boys had built an addition for his increased inventory and cleared a large area outside the store, leaving everyone to wonder what he planned to do. Word spread that he'd taken four wagons over to Lincolnton for a big shipment coming in by train.

A crowd gathered to watch Hubert and his sons unload the returning wagons. Shiny new grain drills, cultivators, a manure spreader, a three-blade plow, a spring-toothed harrow, and a reaper-binder now occupied the cleared outdoor space.

With a hairless pate, a walrus mustache, and a crooked front tooth, Hubert was foremost a businessman, who could do a string of sums in his head. He had little time or interest in conversation, and when he did speak, his mustache concealed his moving lips. When he removed the chairs from around the pot-belly stove, Elias tried to explain the importance of this meeting place, how it kept local men abreast of current events. But Hubert, who'd already overheard two such discussions, said he was there to help farmers, and voices of dissent were not welcome in his store.

For more than a year after Hubert's arrival, Elias averted his gaze when he passed the display outside the store. Once a man bought a piece of equipment, he'd want another, he told himself, and there'd be no end to accumulating worldly goods. No end to debt.

1891. The harvest was bountiful. It allowed him to reimburse Edward Hubert for seeds and hand tools purchased on credit, and pay rent on Doc Howard's land, with nearly a hundred dollars left over. But his success had required working in the fields from sunup to sunset, March through November, leaving him bone-weary at the end of each day. His study had gone unused.

1892, the first Monday of the new year. Elias granted himself permission to veer off the path leading into the general store and step closer to Hubert's display. He ran a hand over the blades of the plow and considered the benefit of three blades over the single one he steered behind Hector. He climbed up on the seat of the manure spreader, imagined himself holding Hector's reins, letting the spreader do the work of dispersing the wagon's contents over a wide swath of ground. Modern farming equaled smarter farming. If he had just these two pieces of equipment, he could bring in a bigger profit. He went inside and negotiated with Edward Hubert to purchase the manure spreader and a three-blade Sulky plow, the amount to be repaid in full after fall harvest.

"I know for a fact," D.W. Gosner said, spitting into the dirt, "that fertilizer salesmen come by here and offer Hubert a commission on every bag he sells of their kind of fertilizer. What we buy ain't necessarily the best. He gets the commission *and* charges us interest from spring till November."

"I been thinking," John Nesbett said, moving a stalk of grass from one side of his mouth to the other, "why can't we order a ton of fertilizer and divide the cost amongst us?"

"Who's got the cash to pay for it in the first place?" D.W. asked.

"Why can't we find a salesman ourselves, buy it directly from the company on credit but at a discount?"

"It comes to Lincolnton by train," Elias said. "We can't just divvy it up there, and none of us has a good enough wagon to tote it back here."

"Lucy May's brother, he's got a couple heavy wagons and a barn. I 'spect he'd give us a hand."

Not long after that discussion—at whose invitation, nobody would say—a stranger came to the settlement. A city man, tall and thin, with a skinny mustache and blond hair cut short, wearing a suit and waistcoat. He introduced himself as Jacob Holsinger and asked what chance there was that he might speak to a group of farmers. He wanted to present an offer that would assist them in the season to come. Herman Self, having the biggest front room and being of such a nature to trust a stranger, agreed to host the event.

Elias wasn't so trusting. Were Edward Hubert to wrongly measure a product or miscalculate a cost, all the farmers knew how to find him. Not so with the salesman. He could take off for California, and nobody would get their money back. Nevertheless, he—Elias—decided to listen with an open mind.

Mr. Holsinger stood next to the hearth and cleared his throat. "I represent S.W. Travers and Company of Richmond, Virginia." He put a boot of fine leather on the ladder-back chair he'd vacated and, resting his forearm on his thigh, leaned forward. "You gentlemen have been buying fertilizer individually through Mr. Hubert, but I can make y'all an offer that will save you money and increase your production beyond belief."

He removed his foot from the chair. Standing erect, he placed his thumbs in his waistcoat pockets. "Let me say a little about our product. Here in the South we are the sole importers of Ochilla Guano. Down in South America, as y'all know, sea birds leave their droppings on rocks, and because they eat fish, the guano is rich in phosphorus."

Elias was familiar with guano, knew its potential to increase productivity. If several men went together . . .

"A while back we introduced this product, this Ochilla Guano, to farmers up in York County, Pennsylvania, and those farmers have had great success. It's been used in the poor soil of eastern Virginia, which now grows clover, the quantity and quality second to none.

"Now, what I'm offering y'all is this: a chance to purchase Ochilla Guano as a group. That is, you would buy it in a large quantity and get it at a fraction of what y'all are now payin.'"

A February snow weighted down evergreen trees in the nearby woods. The ground crunched beneath Hector's hooves. Reins hanging loosely in his hands, Elias kept turning to look at the field behind him, brown on white, pleased by how clumps of manure made their way to the back of his new spreader, were broken up by a beater, then scattered on the ground. Manure in the winter, guano later.

He'd done the calculations and figured that with the new equipment he could farm more acreage. So, he'd made a deal with Floyd Hoke to rent more land, fifty acres in all.

That spring he planted wheat and corn and produced enough sweet potatoes to sell to wholesalers in Shelby, who then sold them in Charlotte. Had the season not been so successful, Elias probably wouldn't have bought a five-tine cultivator and a double disk grain drill on credit. Had Hector not died—at age forty—and had the following year not looked as promising as '92, Elias probably wouldn't have bought a spry, young gelding named Whirlwind.

1892 also marked the year Elias and Emma's fourth son was born. Named Leonidas, after Leonidas Lafayette Polk, leader of the Farmers' Alliance.

He remembered reading it could be predicted. Or maybe he'd heard one of the old timers say how it happened about every twenty years or so. He remembered the last one, the recovery taking so long. He'd been but a boy then, reading the news to men gathered at the Gruens' store, trying to make sense of how confidence—or lack of it—influenced markets. Despair was like a disease, contagious, and once one segment of the population caught it, it spread quickly.

Now, indeed, twenty years had passed, and newspapers confirmed it. Reporting first that the stock exchange had crashed. Then investors were demanding their money. In businesses and industries, workers were idle. It was the worst economic crisis the country had ever experienced: the 1893 Panic. Ordinary Americans, many unemployed, had no income to purchase farm products. By harvest time no markets were buying.

And Elias was in debt up to his ears.

He was in mental anguish. When he had a chance to read, he couldn't concentrate. When his turn to preach at Sinai Baptist Church came along, he had nothing to say. Of an evening, he reminded himself that a man should not allow fear and emotion to overtake him. *I will look rationally at the matter at hand. God is with me. God will guide me.*

But self-recrimination won the battle of the moment. He had a duty to provide for his family, and he was failing. He was failing as a farmer. He had applied scientific practices recommended in *The Progressive Farmer* but made the mistake of overextending himself.

No, Grover Cleveland was at fault. With Democrats in power, the government could not be trusted to look out for the little man.

He wanted to believe that God was in charge of his life. If that were so, why did God keep placing so many obstacles in his path? No, God wasn't to blame.

Other men in debt simply took off without telling anyone where they were going. They left their wives with no choice but to move to a mill town. For forty cents a day, boys swept lint from the floor and climbed machines to put on new spools, girls worked as spinners. No, Elias would never have his boys working in a mill.

He could go west. Twenty years ago, after Papa's Cousin Leland encountered a Mormon missionary in Charlotte, he sold his patch of land, packed up his wife and three children, and headed to Utah. Up in the loft at night, Dorothy Jane and Elias had whispered about him just wanting to have a bunch of wives, and giggled about which one he'd be reunited with in heaven. Now Elias admired Cousin Leland for his ability to imagine a future in a different place. Indeed, opportunity had come his way. Out in Utah he'd opened a store that sold supplies to men going out in search of gold. The last anyone heard, he'd built a big house and his children attended that Mormon college out there.

There was talk of cheap land in the western part of the state. Not that he had money to buy land. Timber companies were paying good wages out that way. One winter afternoon, when four men had sat around the fire at John Nesbit's place, Nesbit said he'd heard that sin ruled the lumber camps. Which made the men's eyes light up, sin being mentioned, offering them an excuse for reciting the many ways a man might sin: drinking, or fornicating, or blaspheming the Lord's name, among them. Elias was thinking the camps might provide a mission opportunity, a chance to lead souls to Jesus. Besides, logging being such dangerous work, somebody needed to be on hand to pray over the dead.

Baptists, if they had an organized mission out that way, might pay a trifling salary, but not nearly enough to solve Elias's problems. His limited schooling did not qualify him to teach children. To start a business, a man needed capital. Even so, Elias lacked knowledge about any suitable venture. All he knew was farming and preaching. Neither would ever get him out of debt.

May 2, 1985

Dear Lydia,

I understand your disappointment that another trip down to North Carolina produced so few results. How fortuitous, though, that you were able to locate and meet Dorothy's grandson and his wife. It's mystifying that he'd never even heard of Papa. Dorothy had to have been proud of her brother serving in Congress and hobnobbing with important people in Washington. It was a big deal and something you'd think she'd have bragged about to her children and grandchildren.

Thanks for sending pictures of the three of you at the graves of our grandparents—that is, people we assume were our grandparents. I find it fascinating that Joseph and some other Mullers are buried in the same cemetery, but Hattie is buried on the opposite end of Burke County. Do you have any clues how that might have come about? I imagine a feud of some kind, maybe with the "good people" of the church.

Our cousins—are they first cousins once removed?—did burst one bubble, two if we count their not knowing about Papa. All these years I've pictured his homeplace the way he described it: a lane lined with moss-laden oak trees and a big house with pillars. So they were positive Dorothy came from a poor family but married into affluence.

Also, I'm scratching my head, as you are, about the Mullers being in North Carolina before the Revolutionary War. Papa always said both his parents were born in Germany and that they spoke German at home. He even peppered his language with a few German words now and then—those and his quirky Southernisms. Is it possible that you found the wrong Dorothy Collins?

You've got to contact that relative in New Jersey they told you about, the one who has a family Bible. I hope you'll be able to get a photocopy of relevant pages. That might tell us a lot. I should say, tell YOU a lot, as I will deserve none of the credit. But then I AM cheering you on.

Love,
Dorcas

Chapter 8

He saddled Whirlwind and set out at sunrise for Linville Township. Emma had packed enough food for five men, it seemed, the apple cake a present for Mama and Dorothy Jane.

It had become a routine announcement, Dorothy Jane writing Mama's in a bad way. Since spring Elias had twice made the all-day trip northward, expecting Hattie to be on her deathbed, only to find her sitting by the fire, delighting in the antics of Lizzie's little Andrew and Dorothy Jane's little Jennie and asking how the apple orchard was doing. Knowing she would offer a mouthful of advice were he to tell the truth, that in recent years the trees had not been particularly productive, he'd said—as he planned to repeat this time— "They'll do well this year,

Mama. We'll have us a good crop."

Dorothy Jane also wrote that Lizzie had married. She and her new husband had taken off for Texas, leaving Andrew with Dorothy Jane and Peter. When Lizzie and her new husband got settled, they'd send for her son.

Elias rode along at a gentle trot, taking in the day's wakening: the sun's friendly countenance as it rose in the east, the scent of last night's rain still clinging to meadows and woodland, the chips of cardinals and robins. The land was preparing for winter's dormancy, shades of yellow starting to appear. In fields farmers had picked only enough corn to feed their animals, leaving the rest to stand dry and bend over. With no markets buying, why go to the trouble of harvesting?

His observations came to an abrupt halt. Recent rains had washed out the bridge over McCoy Fork. Whirlwind shied away from entering the rushing stream, pacing backward, prancing around while Elias urged him forward. Finally, an insistent kick against the ribs motivated him to enter the torrent, slowly make his way across unseen rocks until the waters nearly reached his underbelly. Several times he slipped and would have tossed Elias into the churning current had Elias not clung tightly to his mount's withers.

The section of road up to Morganton was familiar, as Morganton markets had in the past sometimes offered better prices than markets in Lincolnton or Shelby. He rode by cabins close to the road, one woman sweeping the patch of ground surrounding her home with a broom, another hanging laundry on a clothesline. Protective dogs chased after him, nipping at the horse's legs. "Git," he'd yell at them. In other places large houses were hidden back tree-lined lanes.

He passed the Morganton asylum for the insane. On its pastoral grounds some patients sat on benches, others paced and talked to themselves. Mama's cousin Adeline—he remembered her as a woman who took up a lot of space, not physically, but having a big nature. She entered a room like she was the Queen of Sheba, stirring everyone around to stop whatever they were doing and pay attention. As a boy, he'd relished being in her presence—before he learned that some nights she'd sneak from the house and go play the piano at a Lincolnton saloon. Her husband said she was crazy and had her committed. If a man couldn't control his wife what choice did he have?

After Morganton, Elias came upon a group of colored men in prisoner garb repairing a railroad bridge. As if to impress Elias with his authority, the guard hollered, "Unless you get to totin' more of them rocks, you gonna wish your sorry black asses was back on the plantation."

"Yes, sir," several said in unison.

Elias had not stopped since leaving home, and though this was neither the best time nor the best place to stretch his legs, he nonetheless dismounted. He offered Whirlwind oats from a canvas bag.

The guard nodded at Elias. "Judge only give me thirty n——s, and they lazy as a rattler sunnin' itself on a rock."

"Looks to me, sir, like they're working mighty hard."

The man's countenance changed. He scowled at Elias, gripped his rifle tighter. "Better keep travelin' through, young man. Just keep on travelin' through."

Elias passed a plantation house, shutters askew, paint flaking from its massive pillars. On an earlier trip he'd ridden up the short lane for a closer look and seen that it was abandoned. Beyond the house stood shanties for slaves, now occupied by colored families, children chasing each other around.

At the edge of a settlement—one not much different from where he lived, with no more than ten houses spaced far apart—he stopped at a church to water the horse and let it rest. Like a starched apron, the church had a prim and proper appearance, with a fresh coat of white paint on its board-and-batten siding and a box-shaped steeple. A picket fence surrounded a cemetery with more graves than he would have expected, given the small building.

He'd stopped here on previous trips and come across no one. This time, though, a colored man was inside the picket fence, pulling weeds around slabs inscribed with "Gone to be with Jesus"; "Suffer the little children"; "Gone but not forgotten."

"All right if I take a drink from the well?" Elias pointed toward the pump as he called to the man. "I'm thirsty as a dry road."

"Yes, sir. Help yourself."

Elias grasped the pump handle. Pushed it down, let it rise, pushed it down, let it rise, repeated until water gushed out of the spout into a low, narrow cement trough. He filled the gourd dipper hanging from the pump and gulped the cool water, welcoming its trickles down his chin onto the collar of his shirt. Then he led Whirlwind to drink from the low trough.

He took four ham biscuits from the saddlebag and walked back to where the man was working. "Here you are, friend," he said, holding out two biscuits. "Can you sit a spell?"

"Much obliged, sir," the man said, putting down his sickle.

It was difficult to tell how old he was, probably between forty and fifty, Elias guessed. A man who knew hard work, judging from callouses equal to his own, as the ham biscuits passed from hand to hand. Legs spread, knees bent, they sat in the shade of a large oak tree.

"This a colored church or a white church?" Elias asked.

"Well, we got us six colored members and fourteen white ones. This is a gentle community where we all get along. Fonta Flora, it's called."

Elias sensed a gentle quality in the man, the way he chewed slowly as if to savor the ham's saltiness, the biscuit's crust. Not like those who swallowed without tasting.

"Fonta Flora. Fitting name, especially this time of year. You been around long?"

"Since war's end, sir. Me and the wife and some other folks, we come from two plantations in South Carolina, made our way up here. We helped each other buy some land until—well, several years back it come about that we all finally had a plot to farm. Our labor, it be for us. We been blessed. Yes, sir, we been blessed."

"You've got a family, I assume."

"Yes, sir, a wife and five young-uns. Born free, all of 'em." As if in disbelief, he shook his head and smiled. "Grandbabies too. All of 'em gettin' schooling."

Elias took the last bite of a ham biscuit and stood. "A gentle community, you say. A real pleasure to know such a place exists. Now I must be on my way."

Northwest of the settlement the road curved over and around rolling foothills. The sun was dropping lower in the sky. A blessing just to be free and have some land, the man had said. Winter evenings, when Elias used to read in his study—that's when he'd felt blessed. Farming? It was like a thick leather belt strapping him to dirt. And now the debts.

Three years short of being thirty, he already felt dead inside. Reverend Gibson had often prayed, "Heavenly father, we ask that thou wilt direct this young man in the way thou wouldst have him go."

Once Elias asked, "Will God speak directly to me, or will I be gently steered?"

"You'll know when the time is ripe," his mentor had said.

Elias was still waiting.

Dusk had settled, mountains to the west had turned dark blue against a fuchsia sky. While not ostentatious, the Collins's home exhibited the owner's prosperity, with two stories, a gable in front, a large side addition, and a wide wrap-around porch. The exterior was painted white, trimmed in green.

"Evening, Mr. Muller." The colored boy, John, took Whirlwind by the reins.

"Evening, Nimrod. I brought you something." Elias withdrew two books from his saddlebag: *Treasure Island* and *Gulliver's Travels*. Though he grieved over parting with any book, he'd decided that these two were not among the ones he held most dear. They should be shared. "Next time I come, we can talk about them."

Dorothy Jane and two-year-old Jennie greeted him at the top of the wide steps. Since he'd last seen his sister, her little boy had died. Sadness still marked the lines of her face, reminding him of his own sorrow over losing Johnny.

She immediately led Elias upstairs to see their mother, stretched out on a feather mattress. This time Dorothy Jane's description of her state had been accurate. Hattie's face was the color of the sheets she lay between, the strength he'd always seen in her eyes replaced with feebleness. He pulled a tapestry-covered chair to her bedside and held her cold hand. His visit seemed to renew her energy, for she immediately began speaking, though in a raspy voice unfamiliar to him. She spoke of Lizzie marrying a good man, and little Jennie being so sweet, and how was her apple orchard doing? He started to answer, then saw she had fallen asleep.

A supper plate had been saved for him. A cold slab of beef with slaw and biscuits, a large square of gingerbread. He ate alone at the dining room table while Dorothy Jane put little Jennie to bed. After a short visit with Dorothy Jane and Peter, he climbed the wide stairway to the guest bedroom.

Larger than the main room of his own home, it had polished walls and a ceiling of yellow poplar. After hanging coat and pants and shirt on the row of hooks beside the chest of drawers, he quickly fell asleep in the canopy bed, with its factory-made mattress and feather pillows.

The next morning the aroma of frying sausage awakened him. A young colored woman brought a bowl and pitcher to his room for washing. He dressed and descended the stairs to the dining room, where Dorothy Jane and Peter already sat at the table.

Despite all the death Peter had witnessed—the war and the loss of his first family—he'd maintained friendly eyes and a mischievous smile behind a full white beard and mustache.

And he liked to talk. This morning he harkened back to the days before the war. How kind his father had been to the slaves, who were all like family. "Old Habakkuk is with me to this day. He's not able to do a heap of work—he slops the hogs—but I let him live in a cabin down by the creek, and Dorothy Jane takes him a bag of cornmeal whenever we send someone to the mill."

He wiped his mouth on the napkin, took a plug of tobacco from his pocket, bit off a piece. He leaned back in his chair, got that glimmer in his eyes signaling he was about to throw a hook into the waters of discourse. "And now we've come to this. At least we've got Grover Cleveland back in the White House. After that dastardly Harrison."

Peter relished debate, all the better if he could get his opponent riled up. On earlier visits Elias had hesitated to disagree with a man forty years his senior. *Yes, sir; no, sir,* Elias had repeated until Peter Collins shouted, "Dad-burn-it, boy, don't you have a single thought of your own?"

Now Elias knew he was expected to say what he thought and state it with conviction.

"Please, Mr. Collins," Dorothy Jane said, "not over breakfast."

Her husband waved away her concern with a flick of the wrist. "One billion dollars," he lamented. "Harrison squandered all the work Cleveland did to build up our treasury during his first administration."

Elias leaned forward in his chair. "What good is all that money in the treasury if nothin's going for helping folks during these times? Democrats were loath to regulate the railroads, and see where that got us. Loath to regulate anything. It's their fault the whole country's going to hell in a handbasket. They don't care a fig about the ordinary farmer."

Peter spoke full throttle. "You forget I'm a farmer too. It's not government's responsibility to take care of us. We gotta look out for ourselves. Regulations are a gross overreach. Mark my word, the economy will work itself out."

Elias's laugh was without mirth. He refrained from reminding Peter that he had inherited a vast acreage of tillable land and that his father's slaves had cleared the land and created a profitable venture. He said instead, "Yours is more than a farm. It's a business. Tobacco business. My survival depends on the price I get for every ounce of grain. And nowadays, thanks to the Democrats, I'm not getting a red cent."

"Son, I know you think government spending's a good thing, but even you've got to admit the Republicans done gone too far. Not just using the federal government—why, they're wanting to make the Blacks equal to white men. Can you believe that? They can't read, can't—"

"A lot of white men can't either. For years I read the weekly to men at the general store."

"That's different. Their kind know how things are supposed to be run. Republicans, they've done all they can to destroy our Southern way of life."

"Well, this Southern way of life was good for folks like—"

Dorothy Jane cut him off. "Just the other day, Elias, we got a letter from Richard out in California. Did I write to you that Mr. Collins's brother invited him out there?"

Elias recognized and accepted her effort to avoid conflict. "Oh, is he on vacation or—"

"No, he's planning on staying. Mr. Collins's brother has a goodly amount of land in some valley, but him being an invalid and all, he needs help. He likes it plenty out there, Richard does."

"Things going well for your boy Adam?" Elias asked Peter. "He's in business, isn't he?"

Peter Collins also seemed to accept Dorothy Jane's leading the discussion away from an argument she feared would destroy goodwill between the two men. "Yes, yes, he is. He has a general store down near my other farm."

"Mr. Collins set him up," Dorothy Jane said.

"Splendid," Elias said, trying to sound more enthusiastic than envious.

The heavy parlor draperies had been pulled back to allow light in. Elias and Dorothy Jane sat in upholstered chairs on either side of the fireplace. Above the mantle a mirror hung, its walnut frame carved into curlicues with gilded ridges.

Elias saw himself in his older sister's oval-shaped face: the wide forehead, prominent nose, the dark brown hair parted in the middle, hers pulled back in a bun. Since childhood, when the two of them and little Lizzie slept in the loft, she'd been the one he could open his heart to. Her dark eyes had always communicated her affection for him. As they did now.

Now and then he caught sight through the doorway of little Jennie trailed by a colored girl no more than fifteen years of age. A dark-skinned woman—the girl's mother, he was guessing—placed a tray on the table and poured two cups of coffee from a silver pot. Elias stirred a spoonful of sugar into his, emptied some coffee from the cup into the saucer, blew on it. Saucer to his lips, he savored each swallow. He and Emma could only afford chicory sweetened with sorghum.

"I'm glad you came up here," Dorothy Jane said, "as I've been considering your state for many days now."

"My state?" Elias waited while she took several sips. How would she know the extent of his indebtedness?

She spoke as if she'd rehearsed a script. "As you can see, in spite of the times, Mr. Collins's sons are doing good for themselves." A smile of satisfaction on the verge of haughtiness spread across her face. "We didn't even talk about Jacob. He'll be heading to law school come fall. The University of North Carolina."

Dorothy Jane's lifted chin, her straight-as-a-board posture, and her store-bought dress bore testimony to her having adjusted to being a woman of means.

"I've been thinking how you're every bit as smart as they are." She let those words register a moment, as if waiting for Elias to say something. Somewhere in the house little Jennie squealed in delight. The clock on the mantle ticked away the seconds.

Reverend Gibson, though a generous man, lacked any understanding of what it was like to be poor. Dorothy Jane was the only person Elias could confide in. He set his cup and saucer down, lowered his head, stared at the faded knees of his pants, down at his scruffy brogans.

"What you're—I think you're hinting at thoughts that have been on my mind. I wanted to see Mama, but even more I wanted to talk with you about—I'm not sure what I wanted to talk about."

Though he did know. Her words just now had expressed what had long been on his mind, thoughts he nurtured while he plowed or cultivated fields. "Seems like a real man—no, that's not the direction I want to go. What I want to say is there's more to life than—I'm meant for more. That's what I want to say."

"Yes, that's what I'm talking about. What I know you can become."

"I come across—I *came* across some verses in Jeremiah. They're God's words to the captives, and I—I feel like a captive. The words, they're about hope, that God has a plan for his people. He's saying I'm gonna give you a future. But—but—I'm nearly past believing it applies to me."

Elias put his head in his hands. For weeks, months even, he'd felt this muddle of despair, this feeling of being rudderless. For the first time he allowed himself to cry. Not teardrops but sobs originating deep within, punctuated with gasps for breath.

Dorothy Jane came to kneel beside him, her hand on his knee. "You're meant for more, I know it. You're meant—you're meant to have you a future. That's what I'm saying, little brother." The two stayed that way while the clock continued to tick, brother and sister bonded by blood and history, until she said, "You know I'll help any way I can. Is there something you need? Before you figure out what you're gonna do?"

Over breakfast he'd nearly asked Peter for a loan so that he might reimburse Mr. Hubert sooner rather than later. Now with Dorothy Jane, he took a deep swallow. He could only bring himself to say, "Yes, I need spectacles."

Chapter 9

Just yesterday Emma had accomplished more in half a day than she often did in all her waking hours. Spurgeon had been on his best behavior, helping her dig up beets and pick greasy beans. She'd laughed at Robert galloping around the blanket Baby Leo lay on. Her cheerful outlook had remained as she returned indoors where the bread was rising.

Spurgeon had wanted to help her string leather britches. "No, Sugar, I don't want you accidently pricking your fingers with a needle."

"I'm a big help, ain't I, Ma?" he'd asked more than once.

"You surely are, sweet one."

That was yesterday. This morning an unease of mind kept her in bed. Elias had risen and brought the baby to her breast then gone out to the kitchen to prepare his own breakfast of ham slices and cold cornbread. Robert and Spurgeon fed themselves.

Finally, she forced herself to get up. Elias would be coming in at noon, expecting dinner. The stove had not yet been lit for the day, an insurmountable task it now felt like. Reading her intention, Spurgeon gathered yesterday's ashes from the grate and dumped them into the pan below. He made a small pile of shavings and twigs to start the fire but knew better than to strike the match himself. Emma struck the match and as soon as the kindling started to flame, placed a log on it.

What if she moved closer and allowed sparks to climb up her bodice sleeve? As had happened to Aunt Mirabel. People wondered whether it had been deliberate, for every woman knew the dangers. Every woman knew that if her clothes caught fire she should drop to the floor and roll over and over, better yet wrap herself with a rug if one was nearby. But Aunt Mirabel hadn't even yelled out as flames moved up her arm and across her bodice. Emma understood the blurry boundary between wanting to die and wanting to live. The weariness, the loneliness.

The day continued in the same manner. She trudged through basic tasks: cleaning the lamp chimneys, applying black wax to the stove. Time and again she hollered at Robert and Spurgeon, whose never-ending energy annoyed her. Why couldn't she have had daughters instead? Daughters were companions, like she and Eula and Mama were to each other, working side by side, singing in three-part harmony.

Without purpose she entered the bedroom. As she walked past the mirror on the wall, she stopped to study her face. In the faint light she saw that her eyes were dull, her face dry like onion skin. She tried to smile, some confirmation to herself that life was not so miserable. Impossible, the smile.

When barely out of girlhood she'd seen herself through Elias's eyes. His lust for her body had told her she was beautiful. Sometimes she still felt a desire for bodily pleasure equal to his; at other times she cringed at the thought of his hands, rough as a corncob, running up and down her body.

Evening came, dishes were put away. While Leo slept in the cradle, Robert's and Spurgeon's whispers up in the loft drifted downward. Elias was out in his study, where she and the boys were not welcome.

Hands folded across her belly, Emma rocked in the main room. All summer long Elias hadn't been himself. He still got up early in the morning, but when she washed clothes she saw they weren't very dirty.

"Next time you go down to Shelby—" she'd started to say the other day.

He'd cut her off. "Nothing's happening down there."

"Well, when you go to Morganton . . ."

"They're not even opening up the markets," he said. "Nobody's buying."

She wanted him to talk to her, tell her what was wrong. He'd only say, "The whole blasted economy, that's what's the matter."

Forward and back in the rocking chair, its motion a rhythmic squeak. She reached down to the floor and removed the thimble and needle from her sewing box, lifted the fabric beside it. *Skilled fingers bring a calmer mind.* The pieces were on her lap, cut from a worn skirt with a frayed hem, a patch where a spark had burned a hole, another patch where she'd caught her skirt on a nail. The material had faded but there was enough to make shirts for the two older boys.

The door opened behind her. Emma was still growing accustomed to Elias's spectacles. They made him appear older, though not like Mr. Hubert at the general store, who was at least sixty and had to lift his chin in the air to better read a list. Elias's spectacles set him apart, like he wanted everyone around to notice his intellect.

"I don't understand why you can't sometimes sit in here and visit with me," she said.

"A woman innocent of book learning wouldn't understand." The words came out harsh, and she winced at their sting. He took big strides toward her, planted his legs apart, and looked down at her. "Soon as you've put the garden food up, you need to go live with your folks a spell."

The needle slipped, pricked her finger. She brought it to her mouth to suck the trace of blood. "With Mama and Pa, you mean? Whatever for?"

He put his hands behind his back. "Economy being what it is—every man around here—I ain't alone. All of us got fooled by last year's markets. We did good, so we borrowed to buy machinery and fertilizer. Now the panic. I'm not even harvesting what I can't use to feed the animals. Come November, I'm supposed to pay Hoke his third, and Hubert, he's got a lien on everything. He'll take it all, and what he can't get, he'll send the sheriff for. That's why I've got to leave."

"I don't understand. Where you going?"

"Can't tell you. That way you won't have to lie."

Her head started to throb. She closed her eyes and took a deep breath. "I, I—" she groped for words but none came.

"I sit in my study praying, and God—God does speak. He's telling me to move on. Once I get established, I'll come back, get you and the boys."

She stood. Her sewing fell to the floor. "You're going over to the mountains, ain't you? Winter'll be settling in before long. They say some places a body'll git froze like a fence post."

"If I go now, I can find a place and be working on it over winter, so's by spring I can plant then come back for you and the boys."

"You ain't never even been out there. You got no idea what it's like. Folks say a body gets lost back in them hollers, and once winter comes you get snowed in and don't see nobody for months on end. How you gonna preach the Gospel if'n you can't even get out of your cabin?"

With the back of her hand she wiped away the tears. Brought her apron up to blow her nose. Her jaw quivered. "You know, it makes no sense a-tall. Why haven't you talked this over with me, just sprung it on me instead? Like oh, Emma, I forgot to tell ya, I'm moving you and the boys to your ma and pa's?"

"I'm talking it over right now."

"You ain't!" she shouted. "You done decided."

"Shush, you're gonna wake the boys."

"So, you don't want them to know their daddy's a selfish, a selfish, a . . ." The only word she could think of was a nasty one her father used. She yelled out, "Wake up, children! I want y'all to hear what a bad man your daddy is. Wake up!"

Elias grabbed her, pulled her against him, and clamped his hand over her mouth. "You've done gone crazy, woman!"

She leaned into him, sobbing. He continued to hold her firmly against him until her breathing evened out.

"Who's gonna keep house for you?" Emma whimpered. "Cook your meals? Wash your clothes? At least . . . at least . . . Spurgeon's big enough and he's a good worker. Let him come along and help you." She stood back and smiled like she'd just solved their problem. "No, we'll all come with you."

"I've made up my mind." He walked out of the house.

On the rare occasion she wanted to enter his set-apart room, she would rap gently on the door and wait for him to grant permission. This time she didn't give him a chance to close the door in her face, but pushed her way in at his heels. "Elias, I do not want to live with Mama and Pa. I want to go with you."

"It's a hard life where I'm goin'. You're not up to it. And the boys—they would—I don't even have a place to go to yet."

"I'm a stronger woman than you think."

Elias sat down and placed his elbows on the table cluttered with books and papers. He buried his face in his hands. Accustomed to household spills, Emma stepped to his side and moved the glass inkwell. He scowled disapprovingly.

"Emma—" He sounded as if he were speaking to a young child, soft yet firm: "The Apostle Paul says, 'Wives, submit yourselves unto your own husbands, as unto the Lord. For the husband is the head of the wife.' I've been in prayer over this. It is God's will."

Who could argue with God's will?

June 4, 1985

Dear Lydia,

Thanks for sending me photocopies of the photocopies. Do we have any idea who the Bible originally belonged to? Obviously one of Joseph's descendants, as his name is at the top of the left page. And we can assume, can't we, that it once was Dorothy's, as one of her descendants now has it. Is it possible that Elias L. was Papa, and the L. stood for Leander? It's strange, isn't it, that the month and date of birth are the same, but the birth year is different.

So, if Elias L. was Papa, this tells us when he was baptized, when he was ordained a deacon, and when he was "liberated to preach." What an interesting way of putting it: "liberated to preach." But Papa wasn't a Baptist. He was Brethren.

I noticed something on two adjoining pages that may have escaped your attention. The feminine-looking handwriting on the left page (Dorothy's maybe?), under the heading "Joseph," records births AND deaths of him and five of his children. On the right page, printed crudely, are the names of four people who seem not to be dead. Otherwise, their death date would be included. Elias L. (Papa?) is the first name, below that is Emma. I think your assumption that she was another girl in the family is wrong. She doesn't show up with the family anywhere else. The other two people listed there, Robert and John, were born in '83 and '86. Joseph, our grandfather, died in 1882, so they couldn't have been his children. Also, our grandmother would have been past the childbearing age. So, who were Robert and John? Who was Emma?

Dear sister, you're uncovering more questions than answers.

Have a great trip across the country. Hasn't anyone told you it's hot in the summer?

Love,

Dorcas

Chapter 10

Elias lied.

To take advantage of half-fare train tickets available to preachers, he told the agent that he was on his way to a church conference in Topton. His appearance bore witness to the claim: his only suit—readymade, a close-fitting jacket accentuating a muscular build—and a black tie. He was clean-shaven, his straight dark hair parted in the middle.

It was his custom to converse with fellow travelers. Ask a stranger a simple question, he'd learned, and you'd get a story.

"Where you headin'?" he asked the man seated next to him.

"To Asheville. I hear a fellow's got his pick of jobs there. They've got a big buggy company, wallpaper, timber too. And a man named Vanderbilt, he's building hisself a castle. More than one thousand workers he's takin' on."

"Bringing your family to join you, I 'spect."

Tears filled the stranger's eyes. "My wife, Annie, Lord how I—she died nigh unto three months ago." He pulled a handkerchief from his jacket pocket and blew his nose. "Our baby girl too. I'm only twenty-six and done buried two wives."

Elias shook his head in sympathy. "A man shouldn't have to live with so much sorrow."

After a while the train began its ascent through the Swannanoa Gap. Two engines strained to pull their load up torturous switchbacks, every turn offering a new vista. Ridge beyond ridge beyond ridge, those in the distance a hazy blue, nearer ones a disfigured landscape of jagged tree stumps left behind by timber companies. Passengers gasped each time the train suddenly thrust them into the total darkness of a tunnel. When they finally reached the summit, everyone's breath came out in one loud exhalation, as if the engines' exhaustion had been their own.

At Topton Elias disembarked and purchased a stagecoach ticket to Aquone. A treacherous journey into the highlands, the four passengers forced to hold tightly to overhead leather straps. The coach following an unpaved, pockmarked road along cliff edges, with steep climbs and downgrades. Whenever the carriage rounded an S-curve, it swayed from side to side.

One man was a timber speculator from Massachusetts. When he allowed his eyes to follow the first steep drop to the bottom of a deep gorge, he turned the shade of a green apple. A second man, returning from Raleigh after meeting with "gentlemen of influence," passed around a flask. The speculator took desperate swigs; Elias declined the offer. The fourth passenger, an older gentleman returning from a visit to his dying daughter in Asheville, also accepted. Elias, not having given any thought to an account of his own situation, quickly concocted a story: he came from Wilkes County and planned to set up sheep farming in the western part of the state. The explanation crossed his mind when the coach had to wait while a drover coaxed a flock of sheep across the road.

Rather than gaze down precipitous inclines just feet from the coach's wheels, Elias kept his eyes on the distant horizon. Mountains reached majestic heights; colossal granite boulders seemed on the verge of tumbling down near-vertical slopes. Whenever the horses sped down a steep descent, he stiffened, certain they would miss the sharp turn, sending the stagecoach plummeting over a cliff. *Yea, though I walk through the valley—over the precipice—of the shadow of death*. His bones rattled every time a wheel sank into a hole and the coach lurched. Twice it toppled onto its side, and the men had to get out and push it aright. The only harm was to their dignity and to their dust-covered suits.

Finally, the coach arrived at the Aquone station, a sturdy two-story frame building. While the driver hitched a fresh team of horses, the four passengers disembarked. The timber speculator, to vomit behind the station; the man who'd been in conversation with "men of influence," to the privy; the elderly gentleman returning from Asheville, inside for a mug of hard cider. The driver climbed onto the roof of the coach, and along with a small mailbag tossed down Elias's carpetbag of clothes and his leather satchel heavy with books.

"Who's getting off here?" the station mistress asked as she picked up the mailbag. The driver nodded in Elias's direction. She squinted at him, her chin lifting then lowering. Lifting again.

Laura Jacobs was a sturdy woman with breasts like pillows. Her teeth were yellowed, her hair askew with strands poking out from braids coiled like snakes. When walking, she leaned on a stout rhododendron branch. She thumped it against the porch floor to get Elias's attention.

"What're your plans, mister? You be needin' a room here?"

"I'll be making my way to the home of my cousin, Ephraim Langford," Elias said. "I plan to stay there a spell."

"Well, son, you're plumb out of luck, I'd say. That family done moved to Asheville last spring so's their young-uns can get some schooling. New folks living down there now, Hopkins their name."

"Moved to . . ." Elias stammered, shaking his head in confusion, ". . . moved to Asheville?"

"I can put you up for the night with another feller. He's plannin' on a timber company taking him on soon as they get to these parts. Any day now, folks been sayin'. Something you might do."

Elias was all too familiar with the dangers of logging, and clearly, Aquone wasn't big enough to offer many other opportunities for employment. The man on the train had said there were jobs in Asheville. Should Elias head back east? *God will provide*, he assured himself. *God will provide.*

The upstairs room Mrs. Jacobs rented out smelled like socks before washday. The bed Elias was to share with another man had a mattress stuffed with corn husks, a single quilt. He set his carpetbag and leather satchel down on the grimy floor.

Enough daylight remained for him to explore Aquone. *Moved to Asheville. Moved to Asheville. God will provide. God will provide.* The only road, narrow and rutted, followed bends in the Nantahala River, its waters roaring as they crashed against boulders then skirted around them. A water-powered grain mill stood where a rushing creek emptied into the Nantahala. A row of enterprises—a post office, blacksmith shop, three stores, and Mrs. Jacob's establishment—lined the elevated riverbank. Evening's sunrays highlighted gold and red leaves on the opposite steep slope.

At the edge of the settlement, he came to a white frame structure with a belfry, narrow windows, and double front doors. He took the liberty of entering what appeared to be a vacant public building. The air was musty, the temperature the same late-October chill as outdoors. A home to spiders and assorted insects, judging from the web he walked into and gauzy threads along the ceiling. Two slate boards looked nearly white, so much dust had accumulated on them. In a cupboard he found *McGuffey's Readers* and spelling books, their covers splotched with mildew, along with two small rolled-up American flags and a picture of George Washington. With his handkerchief he wiped dust from the chair behind the teacher's desk. He sat and looked out over the room. A schoolhouse without a schoolmaster, it seemed.

"Mrs. Jacobs," he said back at the waystation, "I'm curious. You say my cousin moved his family to Asheville so the young-uns could get schooling, yet an excellent schoolhouse stands right down the road. It appears not to have been used for a spell."

Mrs. Jacobs placed both hands on the tabletop to keep her balance as she dropped her ample frame onto a chair. She motioned for Elias to sit as well. "Mr. Burnside—three years ago, I think it's been, maybe four. You know how time gets away from a body. Well, he just up and went to Dakota, though it beats me why a soul would head for such a place. Cold as a witch's tit, I hear tell.

"Well, not long after his departure, Estella Meachum—now she was one of his students. A lovely girl, fourteen years old she was, with the pertiest blond hair, almost white it was. Well, she took to missing. Her pa and ma worried in the worst sort of way, thinking she'd done got herself lost in the forest or carried off by a bear. Whole town searched and searched for her until we just gave up. Had a funeral for her, though of course there wasn't no body, and we all sobbed like we was pleading with St. Peter to let her enter the pearly gates. Wouldn't you know, a year or so later they get a letter from her saying she's with Mr. Burnside up in Dakota and has a baby girl." She slapped the table. "Don't that beat all?" Mrs. Jacobs heaved a sigh. "So, we've been without—say, you talk like a man of learning. Ever give thought to being a schoolmaster?"

Elias hesitated. Employment in service of one's mind certainly held more appeal than working at a lumber camp. "Why yes'um. It's a heap of responsibility, though a blessed one, taking on the teaching of youth. With whom might I speak concerning the matter?"

"That'd be Mr. Cunningham who's heading up a committee, such as it is. I'm sure they ain't paying much, else we would 'a had us a schoolmaster by now. Folks in these parts, they think education's a waste of tax money. But he's got three boys and a girl, and Mrs. Cunningham, well she wants in the worst way for them to get some schooling. I'll let him know you're interested."

As Elias climbed the steps to his room, he overheard Mrs. Jacobs say to Mr. Jacobs, "With whom—that's what he said—with *whom* might I speak concerning the matter?"

That night, Samuel Byrne, the other lodger, cursed Elias's restlessness. Elias tugged on the quilt as he tossed and turned, Samuel tugged it back. Finally, Elias rose and gazed out the window into the darkness.

Some places wouldn't hire a schoolmaster with only six years of schooling. Yet the citizens of Aquone couldn't be particular. And had Dorothy Jane not said that his intellect was greater than that of her stepsons, who attended Rutherford College and became widely respected lawyers and businessmen?

The next evening Elias came downstairs for the interview shortly ahead of schedule. He wanted to assess committee members as they arrived, check on any mannerisms that might offer clues about how to relate to them.

The main room of Mrs. Jacobs's waystation had a low ceiling, two outside walls lined with wooden benches for those waiting to board the stagecoach—not that they were ever of a sufficient number to occupy all that space. For passengers partaking of drinks or repast, there were ordinarily three rectangular tables in the center of the room. Somebody, most likely Mr. Jacobs, had rearranged the tables. One now stood alone, a single chair facing three opposite it.

Mr. Cunningham may have been chairman of the committee, but obviously it was Mrs. Cunningham, a mite of a lady wearing a freshly ironed dress of blue cotton and a gray shawl, who entered with swaying shoulders and lifted chin, her every step asserting efficiency. Mr. Cunningham, in soiled overalls, taller than his wife by at least two feet, shuffled in after her. Sawdust covered the overalls of Mr. Parker, the other man, who had a wide forehead and timid eyes.

Elias pulled out a chair for Mrs. Cunningham and pushed the one on the opposite side of the table slightly to the left so that he might look into her face more directly.

"I'll tell you right offhand," Mrs. Cunningham said, "we can't pay no more than twenty dollars a month. School goes from October through April, though we're partway through October. And we give the schoolmaster a place to live."

Elias masked his disappointment over the meager salary. He peered into her eyes with his intense blue ones, nodded, and forced the corner of his mouth into a half-smile.

Mrs. Cunningham leaned back in the straight chair and folded her arms beneath her breasts. "So, tell us a mite about yourself."

Elias hesitated. It was unlikely but not impossible that someone would know someone who would know someone from Burke or Cleveland County. "Well, I came over here from Wilkes County." It was already clear that Mrs. Cunningham needed to be impressed. "I was a schoolmaster there, of a school about the size of yours. I came out this way thinking—well, you know, a lot of young men head out for a bit of adventure. That's part of my reason for coming here."

"So, how much schooling you had?" Again, it was Mrs. Cunningham who wanted more information.

God sometimes willed an untruth. Jacob, with intellect and drive, knew—he knew he was God's chosen. That's why he held out an arm covered with lamb skin and said to his blind father, "It is I, Esau. Bless me." Of what value was the birthright to Esau, who lacked the capacity to use it to its full advantage?

"I attended up through ninth grade. I wanted to go more, but my father needed me on the farm." Elias lowered his head. "He and my mother both passed last spring. Of typhoid." He wished upon himself a single tear, brought on by a recollection of lowering his father into the grave on that overcast autumn day. "That's why I needed to move on. To forget the memories. If you've lost someone dear to you, Mrs. Cunningham, you'll understand the sorrow I live with. Why I'm trying to escape."

She brought a handkerchief to her eyes. "I understand, Mr. Muller."

The interview took no more than ten minutes, with Mrs. Cunningham offering him the job. As for Mr. Parker and Mr. Cunningham, they remained silent, except for "Pleased meetin' you," with a nod of the head as they walked out the door.

A job! A real job! But it wasn't just the relief of gaining employment that elated him. He had forged a past and been believed. Believed!

A sense of civic duty seemed to have inspired community women to clean the schoolhouse and sew curtains for the four windows. They'd hung the two small American flags above the picture of George Washington and removed ashes from the stove in the middle of the room. The slate boards were now free of the dusty coating.

Apparently, civic duty had *not* inspired anyone to prepare the two-room—cabin, shack, hovel?—for occupancy. *Cabin,* Elias finally decided. A frail structure atop stone pillars, it had windows that didn't open and gaps between logs. It had a rough-hewn floor and, like his old homeplace, now in the hands of Horace Landis, a ladder to a low-ceilinged loft. Mice or other creatures had left a thin mattress in tatters, and the few kitchen utensils hanging from hooks were rusted. A heavy layer of dust had settled over a small table. The rush seat of the single chair had a hole in the middle. Worst of all was the stench of a dead opossum's decaying remains.

Outdoors he walked along the creek, water gurgling around boulders, carrying along leaves of russet, crimson, and pale yellow. On the other side of the creek, a steep slope was covered in a forest of chestnut, sycamore, oak, and yellow-poplar trees, many over a hundred feet tall, the closer ones adorned in autumn's rich shades.

Behind the cabin stood a second structure—*stood*, perhaps a misnomer—a shed in no better condition than the cabin but large enough to shelter equipment and a few animals. He trod through weeds that had overtaken an orchard, persistent wormy apples still clinging to twelve long-neglected trees. Though Cherokees had named the area the Nantahala, "land of the noonday sun," this small section of the hollow had a meadow with a broad southern exposure, and mountains to the west were far enough away not to block the afternoon sun. Elias added and subtracted in his head. Twenty dollars a month might get him by, but it wasn't enough to support a family, much less pay his debts. He needed to make the land here profitable.

The next day Laura Jacobs told of a family soon to set out for Texas. Elias paid three dollars for all the belongings their wagon couldn't accommodate: furniture, bedding, cooking utensils, and tools. He loaded it all onto a borrowed wagon pulled by a borrowed horse.

"Smidgeon," children in the family called out as he left, "come back. Come back, Smidgeon." But their floppy-eared Plott Hound seemed convinced he was part of the business transaction and ran behind the wagon all the way to the cabin. He immediately established himself as companion and watchdog, though Elias questioned his loyalty, given how easily he'd abandoned his previous owners.

In his efforts to make the cabin livable, Elias was assisted by Samuel, the man with whom he had shared a bed at Laura Jacobs's waystation. They built an outhouse downstream from where Elias fetched his water; filled gaps around windowpanes with mortar of mud and straw. Elias compensated Samuel's labor by feeding him and providing a cornhusk mattress in the loft.

Aspirations to be a writer had brought Samuel to Aquone. The *Cincinnati Times* had reported that the Westmeier Timber Company had purchased land in the Nantahala region and would be hiring loggers. Samuel sought *a new experience with my masculinity,* an asset in becoming an author, he claimed. A naïve notion, it seemed to Elias, whose body bore the scars of repeated blunders with axes and saws. Samuel's bushy beard and fuzz on his arms were the same shade of red as the hair on his head. His fair Irish complexion testified to a life spent working indoors.

Mrs. Jacobs dropped her hefty frame onto a chair, tapped the rhododendron stick, and signaled with her head that Elias was to sit down too. He had asked about the cabin's history.

It had been built by a young family from Pennsylvania, she said, who had come down in 1845 and homesteaded the 160-acre tract. "Now the wife, it turned out, she had this—I don't know what you'd call it—this extra sense. At night she'd hear the voices of the Cherokees. She claimed their wailing and moaning kept her from sleeping, and it got to where she was accusing everybody in these parts of stealing Indian land, which of course the good folk didn't take kindly to. Especially her being an outsider with no right to say what was stealing and what was legally settlin' on untilled land. Finally, the family just up and left. Went back North, some said."

Mrs. Jacobs placed the tip of her rhododendron stick on the floor as if she intended to stand and get about her work. Then decided she wouldn't.

"Jacob Misner—he's long passed. Had in mind the cabin would be our schoolhouse. But folks, they wanted the schoolhouse closer to the village. That's how the cabin come to be the schoolmaster's place to live. Misner's boy owns the land around it. Has him a farm down near the Georgia line."

Acting with the confidence of one familiar with pedagogical methods, Elias directed the eight younger children to sit in the front desks, the four older students to sit in back.

"We will begin our day and our time together by considering Holy Scripture's teachings regarding learning. In the sixteenth chapter of Proverbs, we read, 'How much better it is to get wisdom than gold! And to get understanding rather to be chosen than silver!'" Standing before the class, thumbs in the pockets of his waistcoat, Elias pontificated on the importance of education and his hopes that in the months ahead all would work to achieve a greater understanding of God's world.

Through literature: He listed great works of Hawthorne and Melville and men of the

American Revolution, offering a more-than-adequate summation of their contents.

Through geography: He named and described in more-than-adequate detail the many places in the world he would like to visit, starting with the Far East and ending with Canada.

Through the study of scientific temperance: In more-than-adequate detail, he made a case as to why students should never partake of even a single sip of liquor.

After nearly an hour of speaking, he paused. Only then did he notice the rustling sounds of the young children wiggling, and see the older ones yawn and exchange smirks. His face reddened in embarrassment. "My apologies, boys and girls. I speak as one who loves knowledge and hope that I have not immediately frightened you away from the delights of learning. Let us now stand and pray the Lord's Prayer together, then begin the task before us."

Eager to escape the confines of their desks, students stood. Heads bowed, eyes closed, they recited, "Our father, who art in heaven . . ."

So began Elias's first day of teaching.

He followed Miss Pritchard's example. Worked with the eight younger pupils first, then brought the four older ones to the front. He signaled authority by tapping the ruler against his leg, reminding pupils during recitations to stand straight and

enunciate clearly. He prompted when lines were forgotten and urged the soft-spoken to speak louder. He recalled his eagerness as a boy to learn. He wanted to nurture that same commitment in these girls and boys.

On his three-mile walk to and from school he had plenty of time to think. Of Emma and the boys, of the quandary that had led to his hiding in the mountains of Macon County. Not an easy decision, selling Mama's parcel of land to Horace Landis before creditors could collect on their lien. Not an easy decision either, sending Emma and the boys off to her parents, penniless. Elias had confidence, though, that neither Mr. Hubert nor S. W. Travers & Company would beleaguer a poor mother for money she didn't have.

He felt justified not asking Mama's permission to sell her land, not telling Emma either that he'd brought the revenue along with him. Better that she not know of its existence. None of these decisions had been for his own benefit. No, all that he had done was for the family.

He considered the future. He'd earn extra income by farming the acreage south of the cabin, raising hogs, and growing apples, though the apple trees had been neglected and might take a year or two to recover. Added to the cash from the sale of his mother's land, he would save enough to return to the piedmont and pay his debts. By then he would have established himself as a schoolmaster, which would enable him to apply for a teaching position back home. After regaining his stellar reputation, he might run for public office. Under the banner of the Populist Party. Even if it took a few years, once Emma witnessed his success she'd appreciate his decisions.

Direct rays of sunshine warmed the cabin porch on a November Sabbath afternoon. The two men carried chairs and cups of steaming chicory outside. Briefly they returned indoors, Samuel to fetch the pencil and notebook he often carried with him, Elias to get his Bible.

"I hope you have no objection," Elias said, "if I read aloud from Holy Scripture."

Samuel leaned forward, sharpening his pencil with a penknife. "No, no objection at all. Goddamn—" He sucked the blood from where the knife nicked his finger.

Elias let it pass every time Samuel took the Lord's name in vain. Better a man release anger through his mouth than with his fist.

"He leadeth me beside the still waters," Elias read. "He restoreth my soul." He closed the Bible.

"That all?" Though not a firm Believer, Samuel was, in his own words, *disposed toward learning from the Good Book.*

"Yes, that pretty much inspires me at this moment." Elias reverently placed the Bible on the floor next to the chair, stretched out his legs with a sigh of contentment. "I am confident that God has led me to this place, and already my soul is well on the way to being restored."

Samuel took a cigarette and match from his shirt pocket, struck the match against the sole of his brogan, cupped his hands to light the cigarette, sucked like he was drawing venom from a snakebite.

They were silent, each in his own thoughts. Elias reflected on his present state. Restored? *Exhilaration* seemed a more appropriate word. The exhilaration of outfoxing his creditors. Of finding employment that used his mind.

He spoke without looking at Samuel. "I know you're hankerin' to write, but I'm thinking you might be escaping something too."

Minutes passed, Samuel inhaling, exhaling puffs of smoke in unhurried fashion. "Too, you said. You don't seem the type of fellow to be escaping the law."

Elias dodged the implied question.

"Guess you could say I'm escaping," Samuel said after a long pause. "She's been pressuring me to tie the knot. A lovely girl, kind and all, but I just couldn't bring myself—I have work to do, places to go, and I'll be damned if I'm going to let a woman tie me down."

"I understand." Elias tried to imagine that kind of freedom.

When Samuel's cigarette was depleted, he picked up his pencil. He pointed to the east. "Would you say that tree over there—would you say the leaves are the color of apple cider or a persimmon?"

"Persimmon, definitely."

Samuel wrote in his notebook. "And the forest. Every time I explore it I notice—how would you describe the smell? Not pleasurable, that's for sure."

"Oh, but it is. Pleasurable. The woods remind us that everything dies. We tread upon years and years of rotten leaves, yet it is that rotting that feeds the seeds that fall to the ground."

"Seems to me, you're the one who has a way with words. Sometimes I worry—no matter how much I want to be a writer, I'll never be much good at it."

"Course you will. You may not always have the words, but you're learning to pay attention. That'll serve you well, I'd venture."

"What's your ambition? I've seen the satchel of books you brought with you. You don't seem the type to be a schoolmaster in a backwoods place like this forever."

"Maybe I am, maybe I'm not. Don't know for sure." He took two swallows of chicory, which by now had cooled, its pleasure diminished. "I used to believe God was calling me to preach. Now, I'm ashamed to say, I expect more, though what more of an honor is there than to serve the Lord? I worry my aspirations are too lofty."

"Meaning?"

"Can a man feel called to preach yet hanker for—if I allow myself lofty dreams, I want to become an elected official. Not president of these United States, mind you. I'd start out with a local office, then maybe, God willing, a senator eventually." It was the first time he'd ever spoken so candidly to anyone, except maybe to Dorothy Jane. But she'd never asked about his aspirations, only spoken of her confidence in him.

"They're not unrelated, preaching and politicking. To get himself elected a man's got to be able to speak well and with conviction. Persuasion. The goal of both, is it not? Persuade listeners to follow Jesus, persuade listeners to follow you. In both cases, to take up a cause."

"Now that's a rather crass way of looking at preaching. I'd say it's about caring for your neighbor, wanting to save him from spending eternity in hell."

Samuel chuckled. "You think that's what's in store for me? You think I'm gonna burn in hell?"

Elias leaned back, his chair balanced on two legs. "I'd say you've got a good mind and you're seeking. 'Seek and ye shall find,' scripture says. I ain't—I'm not—worried about you."

That night the cornhusk mattress rustled like a critter in the brush every time Elias changed position. If the meek were going to inherit the earth, he was destined to forever come away empty-handed, for prior to meeting Samuel he had known few men he considered his equal. Not that those who'd congregated at the general store were ignorant. They argued cogently why President Cleveland was responsible for the Panic and whether or not North Carolina should be a dry state. Nobody, though, spoke of ambitions beyond getting better prices for their crops.

David and Jonathan loved each other as they loved their own soul, the Bible said. Was such a friendship between other men possible? A man needed a wife to provide a home, but a woman could never understand a man's thoughts, certainly not the lofty musings of the intellect.

Three weeks after his arrival in Aquone, Samuel got a job setting up the pole railroad at the soon-to-arrive logging camp. Once the muzzle loaders were up, offering him a place to sleep, he moved out.

The cabin and its contents were functional. A bed, a square table, two ladderback chairs, a rocking chair, a tin wash pan on a dry sink of pine, a woodstove that provided both heat and a cooking surface. The room's only touch of color was a crazy quilt with red gingham squares that might have once been the sewer's skirt, blue denim triangles most likely from a man's shirt, and geometric shapes of faded yellow.

When Elias gave thought to the single item he hankered for, he saw it in its finished state, not as expansive as Reverend Gibson's but of fine quality. At a sawmill he purchased two long walnut boards. With pencil and paper he calculated dimensions. Evenings, he planed the boards with great care, polished the wood with pumice. He lacked the skill his father would have brought to the project, so its craftsmanship might lack the marks of a master, but when it was finished, he stood back and admired his handiwork. A bookcase. He placed it away from the east window lest rain leak through, then with the tenderness of a doe for its fawn, placed his collection of books, eleven in all, on the smooth shelves.

The nearest Baptist meetinghouse was toward Briartown, along a twisting road often either too muddy for travel or blocked by fallen rocks. Road conditions and the fact that the congregation met once a month had prevented Elias from worshipping there before mid-November.

After services on his first Sunday, the Coleman family invited him home for dinner. Brother and Sister Coleman had three daughters, somewhere between the ages of sixteen and twenty, not beautiful but not homely either. Of the same height and wearing matching gingham dresses, the daughters were so similar in appearance that Elias kept confusing their names, calling Marjorie *Miss Caroline*, Caroline *Miss Agatha*, and Agatha *Miss Marjorie*.

The Coleman women set a fine spread. Elias didn't mind that they made a fuss over him, offering more fried chicken, more cabbage slaw, more of the squash and turnip dish.

"Brother Muller, how is it that a handsome man such as yourself ain't married?" Sister Coleman asked, obviously on behalf of her daughters, who all looked at him with moony eyes.

Instead of answering the question, he flashed a beguiling smile, smacked his lips, and removed the napkin from his shirt collar. "Sister Coleman, that was the best apple pie I ever tasted. Do you have some magic ingredient?"

"It's the apples. They're winter jons. Cook up real good, they do."

"I'm planning soon as winter sets in for real to prune the orchard next to the cabin. Reckon it's been a coon's age since anybody tended it, but I figure a little care and it'll bring in a fair to middlin' harvest. Tell me, Miss Marjorie—uh, I mean Miss Caroline—what are the town's future plans regarding a doctor?"

His question gave one of the Coleman girls a chance to flutter her brown eyes and address him. "We've done posted in the Franklin paper that all the logging coming in'll mean greater opportunity for a doctor willing to—"

"Brother Muller," Sister Coleman interrupted, "our Agatha plays the piano. Would you like to hear her when we rise from the table?"

"I'd be delighted." And he meant it. At Baptist gatherings he'd sung along with many a fine pianist, adding his enthusiastic baritone to the refrain.

Sister Coleman shooed the men into the parlor to sit on the settee while she and the girls, with the exception of Agatha, cleaned up the kitchen. Elias bobbed his head in time to the rhythms of Agatha Coleman pounding out "Stand up, stand up for Jesus, ye soldiers of the cross," closed his eyes in contentment when she played the soft strains of "Abide With Me."

He quickly saw an advantage of being unfettered. At twenty-seven he had mastered the art of charm and possessed a manner of speech that combined the language of the folk with that of the educated. Being the center of attention, as he was today, suited him fine.

Back in his cabin he gave thought to Sister Coleman's question about marriage. It had been on impulse, his changing the subject. He hadn't intended to mislead anyone. Did his denial not put him in the company of Peter, who denied any association with the accused Jesus? Elias had betrayed Emma and the boys.

A steady rain clattered a numbing rhythm against the cabin's tin roof. In his rocking chair Elias sat slumped over, chin against his chest, eyes shut, *Paradise Lost* on his lap. A knock at the door startled him. On the porch stood one of the Coleman daughters, a rain slicker covering the burden she carried in both hands, protruding far enough in front to give the impression she was with child. Inviting her in, he took the slicker, draped it over the back of a chair. The soaked dress clung to her body, her drenched bodice revealing the shape of her ample breasts.

"That's quite a load you have there, Miss Caroline," he finally managed to say of the heavy basket in her arms.

"I'm Agatha," she said without blame. "Mama, she thought maybe you—you arriving in these parts so late in the season—she thought you might could do with some root vegetables. So me and her collected these from some of the ladies in the church." The basket contained an abundance of white potatoes, carrots, turnips, yams, and squash. "And here's a jar of persimmon butter Mama and us girls made."

"Why, that's right neighborly of y'all. I've been getting by with cornmeal and a few supplies from the general store." He motioned for her to stand closer to the warmth of the woodstove. "You—you ought to dry out a mite before you return home. I have some hot chicory left over from breakfast. Would you like a cup?"

He was the one extending an invitation, yet the slight curve of her lips upward seemed to be inviting him to—he shook his head to clear it.

"That would please me," she said, pulling her wet bodice away from her breasts.

From the pot he kept on the stove, he poured the beverage into a cracked cup. "Apologies," he said, "for having no sugar or honey for sweetening. There's milk in it though." He scooted a chair closer to the fire. "Here, take a seat."

"Ain't no problem. I like it this way." Which he doubted but interpreted to mean she wanted to please him. And she did, please him. He took in her slender ankles extended toward the fire's warmth, his gaze moving upward, lingering again on her shapely breasts before rising to notice her dark brown hair coming loose from its knot in back.

"I've been mighty appreciative of everybody's hospitality ever since I arrived. It's a warm fellowship y'all have."

"Well, we don't often see new folks of your—of your importance. I mean your education and all."

The lilt of her voice had him wanting to hear her speak more. "So, how long you and your folks been in these parts?" he asked.

"Pert near five years. We come down from Illinois."

"Ah, I thought I detected an accent not usually heard in these parts."

"Papa said it was either here or out west. Maybe to Colorado, he was thinking. He wanted to live in the mountains. Mama, she said she wanted to go somewheres warm. Course us girls didn't get no say."

"Well, I'm awfully glad you came south instead of west. Otherwise—" He didn't need to finish the sentence. She blushed, seeming to deduce his meaning.

Yet he didn't know what he'd meant. The words had come out of their own accord.

"You've fixed up this place real nice like." Her eyes came to rest on his bookcase. "Course, I ain't surprised to see you got some books."

He walked across the narrow room to take a book from a shelf. Caressed its cover. "These, they're about theology. That means they're about the Bible and what it means and how to preach."

She rose and came to stand beside him. She placed her hand on his arm that held the book and left it there. "They mean much to you, don't they?" she asked softly. As if she understood his passion for learning.

He inhaled her scent, the wet wool of her shawl combined with femaleness. In his groin he felt a man's needs. He reached down to return the book to the bookcase, his movement compelling her to remove her hand.

"Thank you for delivering the vegetables," he said, his voice taking on a formal tone. "And the persimmon butter."

A signal she seemed to understand. She set her half-drunk cup of chicory on the table, smiled at him, and went to the door.

She threw the rain slicker over her shoulders. "Goodbye, Brother Muller." She stepped into the rain, beating down stronger now.

Closing the door behind her, Elias took a deep breath.

He tried to remember Emma's hand running up and down his body in bed. Removing a trace of food on his face. Her hands held his sons, they prepared his meals. They were no longer the soft hands of the girl he'd once been drawn to, but strong hands, a helpmeet's hands signaling he did not have to face life alone.

Winter set in. Not that of the piedmont, where nighttime lows might go down to freezing and a rare snowfall offered children the exciting opportunity to throw snowballs and build snowmen. Some days, mountaintops to the west glistened with hoarfrost; other days, snow blanketed the village and surrounding slopes. Mrs. Jacobs gave Elias winter clothes she'd acquired from a local widow: a man's wool coat, hat, and gloves.

Some sabbaths, when members of the Baptist Church didn't meet for worship, Samuel came to visit. By now he had acquired the appearance one might expect of a man who spent ten hours a day felling trees: the bulge of arm muscles discernible even under a heavy wool shirt, tangled red hair down to his shoulders, bushy red beard. His ruddy Irish complexion had darkened.

The two conversed over a dinner of ham, fried potatoes, boiled cabbage, and biscuits—always the same menu. Their conversations—energetic, argumentative, exhilarating—lasted so long that Samuel sometimes left in a rush to avoid walking back to the lumber camp in darkness. On political issues they agreed: Grover Cleveland and the Democrats were to blame for the financial mess the country was in; the government should take over the railroads; and senators should be elected by the people, not voted in by their cronies. On religious matters they disagreed. Samuel argued that every culture created myths to explain events and the world around them, while Elias insisted that the Bible was the authoritative word of God.

"That's bullshit. Blasphemy!" Elias shouted.

"It's science!" Samuel shouted in reply.

He had walked through knee-deep snow to get to Elias's cabin, bringing with him ground coffee beans and enough sugar to sweeten two cups. Now the two sat in the warmth of the woodstove. Though it was only slightly past noon, the sky outside was the dark gray of dusk.

"You sure?" Samuel asked, as he poured brown liquid from a flask he carried in his pocket into his cup of coffee. "Such a dreary day calls for this."

"Thank you, all the same."

Samuel took a swallow of his drink, signaled his pleasure with an aaaah and smacking lips. "He spent years observing. That's how science works. You observe, you collect specimens and keep records, and after a while you see patterns. You do believe in science, do you not?"

"I believe in God. Of course I value sound scientific research that informs farming. But not when it contradicts God's word."

"He started out studying birds. He took detailed notes about his observations and brought back specimens. Over time a species takes on the idiosyncrasies—it adapts so it can survive in its particular environment. Say the main food source for finches is some kind of seed that has to be pried open. That's what he observed. To flourish, finches there have to have beaks that can pry seeds open. If males with such a beak mate with females with such a beak, then their offspring are more likely going to have the same. That way the species can survive in an environment where those beaks are needed. That's what's called natural selection and ultimately survival of the fittest."

"Hogwash. 'And God made the beast of the earth after his kind, and cattle after their kind, and everything that creepeth upon the earth after his kind: and God saw that it was good.' God created the finch as it is."

"It's like breeding animals. You want the best milk, you breed Guernseys. You want a good hunting dog, you mate the best hunters, male and female."

"What about his notion that man descended from monkeys? Surely, you don't believe that rubbish."

"Think how similar we are. If birds change their physical characteristics to survive in a particular environment, why couldn't man have done the same? Started out looking more apelike but—well, they migrated, and survival—say only those with more developed brains survived, so they mated with each other. Over thousands of years they changed—or evolved, as scientists say."

"If that's true, it makes God's word a lie. And if Genesis is a lie, then what can we believe about the rest of the Bible? I tell you, fifty years from now people will laugh at this preposterous notion that man descended from the ape. It's an idea that we certainly don't want our children learning."

Throughout the long winter the sun dropped early behind mountains, tall evergreens cast their silhouettes against the skies. Mornings, frost caked the inside of cabin windows; outside, the rime crunched as Elias walked across it on his way to the schoolhouse.

Teaching was not going as he had hoped. While the young ones showed eagerness for learning, they squirmed and giggled much of the time, then cringed in fear when he reprimanded them. The two older girls seemed more intent on the attention of the two boys their age than on their studies and whispered with each other while Elias worked with the younger children. The two oldest boys were erratic in their attendance, claiming to be needed on the farm. This time of year? Then he overheard a younger brother of one say the two were panning for rubies that day. He assigned extra arithmetic problems to anyone displaying signs of disinterest. Practically every day he lectured on the importance of an education.

Sometimes in a pique of anger he applied the hickory stick. At other times he made offenders stand behind an open cupboard door. His ire increased when catching them peeking from around the door and making classmates giggle. Yet, he told himself, as he gained experience he'd likely become more comfortable with the children and fond of teaching. Maybe the following year one with an unquenchable thirst for knowledge would attend, grateful that someone understood him. And that boy—for surely it would be a boy—would later attend college, at least find an environment that fed his curiosity and encouraged his drive. He would acknowledge the important role Elias Muller had played in his education.

Winter winds whistled through the hollow, making the cabin shake. Somewhere out there a screech owl broadcast chilling territorial screams. Folks said they warned of death, at least misfortune.

Elias recalled piedmont winter evenings, coming in from his study to find Emma doing needlework while the boys slept soundly in the loft. He should write to her so she'd know he was all right. But any letter would be delivered to the post office in Hubert's store, and the postmark would expose Elias's whereabouts. Mingled with his fear of discovery was—he tried to push it from his mind—a wish *never* to be found. To be permanently unfettered and owe no man money.

Sometimes, returning from school on a cold, overcast evening, a fraction of the moon visible before darkness spread across the valley, his thoughts entered dark, angry corners. Anger at banks and corporations that blocked the ordinary man's success and bound him in debt. Anger at Emma and the boys for placing so much responsibility on him. Anger at her mood swings, which he could never anticipate, forcing him on those days when she could not rise from bed to take on her responsibilities in addition to his own. And if he allowed, anger at himself for desiring costly machinery.

In his more generous moments, thoughts of Emma's temperament reminded him of his current despair. Was this how she sometimes felt? Had her spells most often occurred during the dreary days of winter?

Grief, though, most often haunted him. "By the rivers of Babylon, there we sat down and wept, when we remembered Zion." Beautiful as the mountains were, they were not his Zion. He was in exile.

"Maybe you're thinking of this all wrong," Samuel said, tugging at his red beard. "Could be this is a time—as the Good Book says, for everything there is a season. You're young yet. Maybe these are the days to gather wisdom for someday taking up whatever battles you'll engage in."

In a cleared area, rough-cut boards formed a square platform, a hemp rope stretched around four corner posts. By the time Samuel and Elias arrived at the logging camp, everyone was already congregating, anger between factions spilling over, faces gnarled, teeth clenched, spit hurling. Appeals to God Almighty that souls be damned to hell. Insults implicating mothers. Cheers interrupted the diatribes as two burly, bare-chested men oiled with grease approached the platform.

"Which one you want to bet on?" Samuel asked.

"You know I'm not a betting man."

"Sure you are. You coming to these parts. You still don't know how it'll turn out. That, my friend, is gambling."

"Money's a precious resource. I'll pass."

Samuel wagered fifty cents on the man in black shorts.

Bare-knuckled, the two in the ring pummeled each other. Blood ran down faces, eyes swelled shut. Spectators shouted encouragement to their favored party. "Knock that motherfucker four ways from Sunday." The frigid mountain air was infused with the odor of sweat mixed with the sickly, sour-sweet stench of liquor. Fists swung outside the ring as well. Elias cringed each time he heard fist meeting flesh.

After half an hour the man in black shorts was carried off half-conscious. His opponent had a cut over his right eye, and his jaw was green and blue. Then another fight, followed by a third, after which the crowd gradually dispersed, shouts continuing the afternoon's grudges as more jugs were uncorked and passed around, long-drawn-out swigs taken.

"Haven't you ever been angry enough to fight?" Samuel asked, exhaling a cloud of cigarette smoke. The two stood at the camp's boundary, on the road Elias would follow back to the cabin. A mist began to swirl, caught up in the winds of early March, cold against hands and face.

"Sure. What boy doesn't get in a scrape now and then? But what we witnessed was of an animal nature."

"Are we not animals?"

"You trying to trick me into our same old argument? So I say, 'God created man in his own image.'" He slapped Samuel on the back. "And you'll answer, 'Elias, belief in your God has separated you from the true nature of man.' Which, according to you, is violence."

"You saw it right here. The beast in one man attacking the beast in another. And others taking pleasure in watching."

"I'll concede that the potential for violence is in the heart of every man."

"Logging draws such men—violent men who have nothing to lose."

"Or one who wants to write a novel. You brought me here to prove your point, that masculinity and violence are interwoven. I kept my eye on you. When a punch landed, a pained look came over your face. Your whole body cringed. You are a gentle man, a gentle poet at heart. That's what I admire about you."

Samuel put an arm around Elias's shoulders. "You're right, my friend. You're right. Now get back to your cabin before the sun sets."

Over the winter Elias had removed dead and broken branches of the apple trees. After honing the scythe blade to a sharp edge, he spent a spring Saturday attacking orchard weeds, employing the comfortable circular rhythm he'd learned as a boy. He hoed around the apple tree trunks, careful not to disturb shallow roots. He knew better than to hope for much of a crop this first year.

He bought a mule. Sassafras was neither an energetic nor cooperative beast, but she had love in her eyes. In gratitude, Elias was convinced, because he had recognized her worth. The amount of land he planned to put into wheat wasn't large enough to warrant a more expensive work animal anyway.

He bought a dozen piglets. As soon as they reached a suitable size, he'd turn them loose in the woodland across the creek, where they would fatten up on acorns and chestnuts.

Seeing that he had no seeds or sets for starting a garden, church members and students' families shared from their supply. Elmira Arnold, a single woman past her prime, with protruding upper teeth and weathered skin, brought him sweet potato starts. She lingered to ask how he was faring, saying how much she admired him, him being a schoolmaster and his knowledge of the Bible and all.

Wheat was in by late March and apple trees sprinkled their white blossoms on the ground. April brought a balance of sunshine and rain. Evenings, in the gloaming, the wood thrush sang its uplifting song. On the porch Elias nursed an optimistic outlook. His expenses were minimal, allowing him to have already saved sixty-five dollars of his salary. In a few weeks school would be out. Over the summer he'd work hard, get a bountiful harvest, and set aside more money. Another year, two at the most, and he'd return home and pay his debts. Only then would he feel free to get on with his life, whether the ensuing years be spent as a politician, a preacher, or a schoolmaster.

Verdina had vexed him from the first day. Her flirting with the boys and whispering remarks that Elias couldn't hear made the older students around her snicker. Here she was, again engaging in her antics, scrambling back to her desk when he looked up from listening to third graders recite their times-six multiplication tables.

The scowl on his face as he abruptly stood caused everyone to sit up straight, faces lowered as if intent on their studies. He grabbed his hickory stick and took large strides to the back of the room, coming to a halt next to Verdina. She looked up at him.

And smirked.

Whap! went the stick across her back. Large for her fifteen years, she stood and lunged toward him. "Don't you hit me! Don't you ever hit me!" She grabbed the hickory stick from his hand and threw it on the floor.

Elias gripped her shoulders in an effort to restrain her. She kicked him in the shin. He let go and slapped her face. She brought back her fist and swung it full force at his face, knocking off his spectacles. Suddenly, William Downey's muscular frame stood between the adversaries. Verdina turned, grabbed her jacket from a hook in the back of the room, and stomped out the door, yelling "Goddammit!"

Elias was panting; the children sat with mouths agape. William Downey stooped to pick up Elias's glasses.

"That'll be all for today, children," he said between shallow breaths. "You can go home."

Wordlessly, students got their lunch containers from the shelf, removed their jackets from the hooks, and left.

Elias sat in the empty schoolhouse, elbows on the desk, head in hands. He brought his fingers to his cheek and hoped there would be no bruise. Such an incident should not have happened. Yes, Verdina frequently presented disciplinary problems, but it was his job to maintain order, and he had allowed his anger to get out of control. Word would certainly get around the community, and people, Mrs. Cunningham in particular, would disapprove. With the school year near its end, parents might say he shouldn't be hired for another year.

How to manage the situation. After a while he smacked the desk with both hands, got up, and closed the windows, deeply inhaling a whiff of fresh air as he did so. With his books still open on the desk, empty leather satchel slumped on the floor, he exited the building.

He didn't even have a chance to knock on the door. Verdina's father sat on the porch, his torso erect, statue-still, a shotgun across his legs.

"Mr. Flynn!" Elias called out, not approaching the porch but standing at the edge of the road.

Mr. Flynn stared straight ahead. Elias didn't know what to do.

"Mr. Flynn!" he called out again. "I'm thinking you're as concerned as I am about what happened at school today. We're both honorable men who can talk this business through. For the benefit of the girl, I'm thinking."

Mr. Flynn stood, and with the gun over his shoulder, walked toward Elias. He was a big man with a bushy black beard and a thick neck partially covered by greasy black hair. The kind of man to run from, as Elias, with half Mr. Flynn's girth, was tempted to do.

Remaining on the road, Elias removed his hat and nodded respectfully.

Mr. Flynn stood before him, feet apart, his mouth a straight line. He heaved a sigh. "I'm 'bout ready to fix that girl's wagon," he mumbled. "Any whuppin' she got was surely comin' to her."

Elias said nothing.

"Been a problem since the day she was born." He motioned toward the porch. "Come sit awhile. She ain't here. Her ma sent her on some chore."

For nearly half an hour the two men sat, alternating between silence and Mr. Flynn pouring out a story of parental frustration.

When he was taking his leave, Elias stood at the foot of the steps and looked up at Mr. Flynn. "So, may I ask, sir, why you met me with a gun?"

"So's the wife'll keep inside. She'd a teared you to pieces, the way she favors that girl."

Elias noticed that his new piglets looked peaked, their tails limp, heads hanging down. Instead of wandering toward food, they huddled together and shivered. Hog cholera. No use trying to save them. He put them in gunny sacks and drowned them in the deepest section of the creek.

July 17, 1985

Dear Lydia,

I know you won't read this until you return from your trip, but I'm feeling a little melancholy. Maybe that's because you'll visit places that are part of my history too. I hope you're keeping a journal and will send me a detailed report.

Today would have been Papa's birthday. The year of his birth doesn't seem all that important. 1866 or 1870. In either case, he'd be over a hundred. He never made much of birthdays. He said it was because he'd grown up having every need supplied, so gifts didn't mean much. That's weird logic, if you ask me. Thanks to Mother, you and I always had a birthday cake. When we were little, we could depend on her making us doll clothes.

In your last letter you mentioned how strict he was with us. I must have been fifteen or sixteen when he discovered I'd snuck out to a party. He lectured me on the evils of dancing and made a big deal over the lust that went through a young man's mind when he held me close. But I detected—or thought I did—the hint of a twinkle in his eye signaling that he admired my rebelliousness.

When I went to college and he knew I'd quit going to church, he adjusted. Even when I started smoking, he lectured me once or twice then said no more. In one instance, though, I knew better than to go against his wishes—not that I wanted to. When I turned 21, he insisted that it was my civic duty to register to vote. As a Republican, of course. Not until the 1960s did I switch to the Democratic Party. I'm guessing that if Papa had lived that long, he would have too.

You, though, if I may put it bluntly, took him too seriously. You obeyed his every admonition. You never drank or smoked. You've gone to church your whole life. Yet in spite of your abject obedience, you were the brunt of an anger I never could understand. I still feel bad that he treated us so differently.

Those are my thoughts for today. I hope your trip is going well. Arizona in the summer!

Love,

Dorcas

Chapter 11

Elias was gone. He'd packed two satchels, one with clothes, the other with books. Hadn't even kissed her in parting or said goodbye to the boys. Trying to conceal his own sorrow over leaving, Emma wanted to believe. He just walked out of the Broder house, face toward the buggy where Billy Marshall waited to take him to the train in Lincolnton.

A husband—off to the mountains, she assumed, where he had no one to prepare his meals or wash his clothes. Leaving her with three boys and no money, forcing her parents to make room in their four-room log house.

"Why couldn't we go with Papa?" Robert and Spurgeon kept asking, all weepy-eyed. "Why ain't we at home?" "When's Papa gonna come get us?"

Emma wished for enough arms to enfold the two of them and, at the same time, hold Baby Leo. Jaw clenched, shoulders stiff, she tried to appear strong for all their sakes, at the same time repeating to herself, *He'll come back, Elias will come back to get us.*

For a spell Mr. Hubert had appeared at the Broder door nearly every day, at first demanding to know where Elias went, later ordering her to pay the debt, which had she had any money at all she would have spent on shoes for the boys, certainly not to relieve Elias of his responsibility for the fix they were in.

The home of her girlhood bore little resemblance to the one she'd returned to. Now, after supper, Amos shuffled to his rocking chair, where he immediately took to snoring and remained until all in the house went to bed. Frances still had the energy of five women, but her tongue had sharpened and she'd grown impatient. Emma saw the strain of adding four people, the youngest a fussy baby. Her parents had turned over the only bedroom to her and the boys, taking for themselves the tiny addition off the kitchen with barely enough space for a bed.

The boys' questions turned into defiance when they discovered they could ignore Emma's threats of the switch, unenforceable when their father wasn't there. "I ain't gonna mind you." "You can't make me." Her anger drove her to tears, making her appear all the more ineffectual. Finally, Amos took over, not in the way she wished but with a harshness foreign to her, though she'd long known it was there. The razon strop brought out, the boys spread across his knees. Or thrown to the floor and kicked. In the gut, in the head. The howling, Lord, the howling, which only seemed to increase the boys' belligerence.

Three times she'd cried out for her father to stop. He'd turned those eyes on her, bulging with fury, hand drawn back as if about to strike her. Instead of hitting her, he'd stomped out the door, his footsteps landing heavily on the porch floor.

Sometimes, while she mixed cornbread or washed dishes, Emma sang softly:

Dark and stormy weather

It still inclines to rain/The clouds hang over center

My love's gone away on a train.

The calendar on the wall turned from October to November, which turned to December. Harvest was over, but every day Amos took off in his winter army coat, often not even coming in for noontime dinner. Given his temperament, Emma was grateful for his absence.

Yet she was curious. "What keeps you busy all the time?" she once asked over supper, trying to sound pleasant.

"Oh, me and the men, we've got us some work up toward Morganton." He rose from the table, signaling the end of the conversation.

Sundays, Emma and the boys climbed into the wagon bed covered with fresh straw. Seated behind Amos and Frances, they bounced along the rutted road to Sunday meeting. Even when temperatures neared freezing and they could see their breath when they talked, church members were eager to socialize. Before and after services, children chased each other while men stood around arguing that the federal government had no right telling states how to run their elections, and women discussed the benefits of laxatives for mumps.

As long as Emma stayed outdoors, her body swaying gently as she and the sisters visited, Baby Leo was contented, but once she took a seat on the women's side of the meetinghouse, he would start to holler. On many a Lord's Day, instead of singing the hymns she loved and hearing the Word, she spent worship time in the chill of the outdoors, pacing with the baby, him crying in her ears. Her wool shawl wrapped around both of them, she held him close as he howled into the neighboring fields, over to South Mountain. Yelling into the world beyond her shoulders, demanding—what was he demanding? It seemed folks were all the time demanding something of her. Elias's mother and sisters had demanded her compliance. Elias too. If she only knew what little Leo wanted, she'd do what she could to make him happy.

Come Monday, there was again women's work to be done. Pails of water she carried from the spring to the washtubs spilled over, soaking her skirt. The heat of the fire caused sweat to roll down her face, while her feet were numb with cold. Her fingers were stiff and sore as she hung clothes on the line. Tuesdays, she and Frances took turns at the ironing board. Wednesdays, they baked bread.

Weeks stretched into months, with still no word from Elias. Because she couldn't read anyhow, she told herself at first, he'd see no need to write. If he wanted to, though, he could find a way to send a letter to someone else, so she'd at least know he was all right.

"You know how he is," she told her parents, her sister, the women at church. "He's a hard worker. He's probably so busy setting up a place for us that he don't have time to write." "Maybe there ain't a post office anywhere nearby." "He said he'll come and git us. That means he will."

Nights when she couldn't sleep, she created a future. Elias, after making enough money to pay off his debts, would come to get her and the children and take them to a small farm in a fertile valley. The house would have an upstairs and a kitchen off the back, cows and chickens and pigs, and she'd have a big garden that grew giant sweet potatoes. And there'd be a school for the boys just down the road. *Be patient*, she told herself.

She suspected her father's harshness with the boys partly came from working hard, never complaining as he eked out enough money to provide for the needs of three adults and three children. Once in a while, though, he teased the boys, who were fascinated by his missing fingers and the gray wool army jacket hanging on the peg just inside the door. They fought over getting to wear his kepi with the crossed rifles and begged for war stories. Amos would tell of Johnny Reb's bravery and Yankee cowardice, the glory of the South and the just cause of waging war against those whose armies invaded the homeland and stole food from their families.

"Take your daddy's oldest brother," he told the boys one evening over supper, "a galvanized Yankee, he was." And of Elias: "An idgit, he is, thinking book learning's—where's it got him so far? Can't look after his own."

"Papa, don't say such things," Emma would remind him. "I don't want them thinking bad of him."

In truth she *did* want them to think bad. Your daddy, he's a dreadful man, she wished she could say, taking off like he did to heaven-knows-where. Selling your grannie's piece of land before anyone knew. Leaving me to suffer for what he owes Mr. Hubert and leaving me not even a penny. It's his fault we're placing a hardship on my mama and papa. She held her tongue, the Bible teaching, as it did, that they should honor their father.

Spring brought Eula's frequent visits. With a Black woman to do her wash and ironing, Eula was free to go gallivanting around. She seemed to think it a wonderful surprise to show up in her fancy surrey, four children in tow, all jumping out, squealing and laughing. She had married into the Martin family, which owned enterprises in nearby Casar. Her husband and his brother ran the mill many in the area relied on for grinding their grains.

As if she'd forgotten the labors of ordinary folks, Eula would appeal to Emma and Frances to chat with her on the front porch while the children chased each other around the yard. Emma sensed the stress on her mother, who before long would excuse herself to perform some unnamed chore. Emma never knew whether to offer assistance, thinking she might just as soon want to be by herself for a while.

Some days were sunny and cheer-making, other days overcast, their gloom becoming hers, so that Emma would have stayed in bed had that not placed an undue burden on her mother. Her spirit cried out for release from feelings of abandonment, from the sadness that regularly enveloped her for—how long had it been since she'd been the animated girl Elias loved?

Marriage was supposed to be about two becoming one. But a man could divide his loyalties—in Elias's case, between family, God, and the esteem of other men. A woman, though, lived for the love of husband and children, and life without a husband's love felt empty.

She began to consider the possibility that he was dead. Wished it were so, then prayed it wasn't. Maybe he was killed by a bear. Killed by a Cherokee. Or he was chopping down a tree and it fell on him. Elias had locked her out of his heart; could she lock him out of hers? Nights, she cried herself to sleep.

Chapter 12

Cyrus Barktol brought his reaper. He and the fathers of two other students cut the wheat Elias had planted the previous fall, helped him tie it into sheaves, stacked the sheaves into stooks. The small amount of wheat brought a decent price, and the apple orchard Elias had nurtured back to health promised at least a few apples for turning into cider. The loss of the pigs in the spring had set him back some, but he looked to the future with optimism.

Long summer evenings, when physical labor left him exhausted, he sometimes sat on the rickety porch listening to the harmonies of crickets, frogs, and wood thrushes. Other evenings, in the light of the oil lamp on the table, he studied Augustus H. Strong's book on systematic theology. A trifle guilt-producing, its purchase, one of only a few indulgences since coming to Aquone. Sometimes he set the book aside, stared with unfocussed gaze toward the unlit woodstove, and allowed himself the honest shroud of loneliness.

The boys would be reading by now, eager to discuss with their father thoughts that literacy inspired. An opportunity they surely craved, given the ignorance of Emma and her parents. As for missing Emma, Elias wished he'd married a woman more his equal, one who could read and bring interesting topics to the conversation.

Only rarely did anybody stop by the cabin, usually some lady from the church bringing him a pie or a poke of blackberries. Otherwise, he only had Sassafras to talk with, she with her big eyes that looked upon him with affection.

"I've been studying the book of Ezekiel," he once told her. "How God defends sending the Israelites into captivity, and I'm thinking surely God has a purpose in exiling me to this place." Sassafras nodded her head in understanding then nuzzled at his pockets for an apple or carrot.

Fall brought the resumption of school. Fourteen pupils in all: four new ones, two of them young and wiggly, a twelve-year-old girl whose family had moved up from South Carolina, and a seventeen-year-old boy who'd had no schooling and couldn't even write his name. Two Cunningham boys had progressed to the upper level. Verdina Flynn, rumored to be pregnant, had dropped out.

There was a tedium to the weekday schedule, starting at the crack of dawn and lasting until five in the evening. He'd set off on the three-mile trek, light a fire in the potbelly stove to ward off the chill, ring the bell in the belfry, and lead the two lines of children into the building.

The day was filled with reading, orthography, and math instruction for the young ones and Matthew, the seventeen-year-old; physiology, United States history, English grammar, geography, and scientific temperance for two of the older students. Surely, they all were as bored as he was.

More than in the previous year, he found himself short-tempered, questioning why most of the students were even there, as reluctant as they were to learn. Not all that different from adults in these environs, who considered education an intrusion by outsiders and resented paying taxes to support it.

Autumn passed without Elias noticing the leaves turn gold and crimson and russet.

Smidgeon quit sniffing the ground and stood statue-like, ears lifted. Elias brought his gun to his shoulder. He anticipated dragging a buck down the mountain, the savory fragrance of venison roasting on an open fire, dried meat for later in the winter.

Men's voices. A conversational tone. Two—maybe three—men, it sounded like, on the other side of a boulder as big as Aquone's waystation. Smidgeon broke his stance and darted ahead, barking. So as not to appear threatening, Elias lowered his gun and walked around the giant rock. Beneath the overhang stood two strangers, not wearing the canvas pants of local men but bowler hats and wool capes over suits.

"Salutations," Elias said. He awaited an explanation for why two well-dressed men stood in the shelter of a boulder's overhang in the middle of the forest, but all he got were nods. "Elias Muller's my name."

The men exchanged amused glances, as if they considered this man wearing jean pants a yokel undeserving of their respect.

To correct that notion, Elias said, "I'm schoolmaster at our local school. Might I ask what leads two gentlemen to be standing here in our forest?"

The taller of the men stepped forward and extended a hand. "Our forest, heh? Pleased to meet you, Mr. Muller. I'm Walter Slaughter and this is Joseph Welty. We're from Massachusetts. In timber." With his thumb he indicated the elevation behind them. "Our company purchased this mountain from Mr. Misner. We'll start cutting next week."

Elias considered the tree he stood beside. He swept his foot along its outstretched roots. His gaze moved upward, taking in the blue sky between brown leaves stubbornly clinging to branches. He ran his fingers over the bark's twisted furrows, stooped to pick up a partially open chestnut burr.

He didn't intend to say it out loud: "That's a pity."

"Progress, Mr. Muller, progress. To build America's cities we must have wood."

Smidgeon was on edge, his bark raspy at day's end, body sagging with exhaustion. His eyes begged Elias to do something. Not until Elias was at home on a Saturday did he understand the source of Smidgeon's agitation: the grinding of crosscut saws, the clanging of axes, the thundering crash as chestnut trees as wide as men were tall crashed to the ground.

During nearly two years of living outside the village of Aquone, he'd found solace among the giant trees, sometimes hunting squirrel or deer or bear, sometimes simply taking in the beauty of giant chestnuts, oaks, beeches, sycamores, and yellow poplars, their canopies protecting verdant carpets of moss and ferns. He'd come to feel a kinship with the forested mountains, sensing their moods. The sun's scattered glitter on the narrow stream. Animal tracks in snow. Carpets of slippery red, yellow, and brown leaves. Early morning clouds nesting in the valley.

Now, on the mountain slope a few hundred yards from his cabin, jagged tree stumps rose from barren earth. Cougars and wolves had been driven to the next ridge; hawks forced to abandon nests reserved for next spring's young; food sources—acorns and chestnuts, insects and worms—destroyed. Elias's eyes spanned the marred landscape. He felt sorrow on behalf of the creatures.

And he missed Samuel, whose return to Cincinnati had been hastened by his mother's illness. Satisfied that he'd garnered enough material for his novel and bone-weary from grueling labor—for he was, like Elias, a man more inclined toward matters of the mind than of physique—he anticipated sitting at a desk, journals of his experience spread before him, writing his novel.

During their last Sunday together, he'd joked that Elias was the inspiration for the protagonist he would create: a man of intellect and ambition, forced by debt to escape his previous life. Except Samuel's protagonist would become a lumberjack who tragically never achieved his dreams. He gave in to the immorality surrounding him, drinking and gambling, negating his ambitions.

"That's not me," Elias insisted, offended by Samuel's assumption that his dreams wouldn't be fulfilled. "Besides, a novel's gotta have a happy ending."

"I'll give him a beautiful woman—like Rose McGee." Which brought a mutual chuckle. They'd often discussed the attributes of a certain young cook at the lumber camp: her ample bosom, black hair and high cheekbones, likely of Cherokee blood. Rose had not been subtle in her attraction to Samuel. "I think I'll have my character give in to her wiles and bed her."

Elias crossed his arms and winked. "What you gonna do about his wife back where he came from?"

"Many a man has wed two women. The fellows in your Bible—Solomon, he had seven hundred wives, concubines as well. Jacob had Rachael and Leah. Abraham—"

"Right, right. Anyway, it's against the law."

"Not if the law doesn't find out. It's a big country, my friend. Anyway, my hero—and he is a hero—he wins the woman's heart—rather, she wins his, they marry and have children."

"You said hero. How can he be a hero if he doesn't achieve his goals?"

"Ah, sometimes a man chooses the wrong goals. Our man is a hero because he overcomes his weaknesses. When the lumber companies move on, he stays behind with his new family and quits his drinking and carousing. His oldest boy, he's the one who achieves his father's ambitions."

January winds swirled through mountain gaps, whooshing in circles around the cabin. Tightly curled rhododendron leaves drooped. Gunmetal gray skies signaled soon-to-arrive snow.

One evening, in the warmth of the woodstove, he reread the *begets* of the Bible and remembered Papa's stories of the family's past. How Elias's great-grandparents—Opa and Oma, Joseph called them—made their way from Pennsylvania down the Great Wagon Road through the Virginia valley to North Carolina. With all of Elias's brothers now gone to heaven, the burden of taking Papa's place on the ladder rung of family history had fallen on him.

Samuel's ideas about evolution hovered over such thoughts. Not that Elias accepted Darwin's notion, but if . . . His own experience told him that the best stock came from breeding the meatiest hogs, the best producing cows, the swiftest horses. What about humans? Emma was not his equal in intellect. What if he had married a woman with a better mind?

Chapter 13

Another spring, another summer, another autumn.

Metal bowls on their laps, Frances and Emma sat on the porch stringing greasy beans soon to be threaded into leather britches. Amos, usually gone in the middle of the day, sat on a nearby step, hunched over, chewing a wad of tobacco.

"What you hangin' around this time of day for, Papa?" Emma asked.

Amos rubbed his beard stubble with his intact left hand. "Your mama's fixin' to tell you."

Frances cleared her throat. "Girl, uh, your pa and me, we're thinking . . . winter coming on and all. We're seeing how the boys, how they've been eatin'. They're growing, it's only natural. They're growing, and it takes a heap of food to satisfy 'em. We had a dry summer, and these are the last of the beans. The yams, the cabbage, everything did poorly this year."

"The times, the times—we're barely scraping by." Amos sounded apologetic.

Emma ran a needle through two beans and pushed them to the end of the long string. "What you getting at, Mama? Papa?"

"Well, uh, we've been thinking," Amos said. "Considering the possibilities."

Panic seized Emma. "You wanting us to leave?"

"Oh, no, no," Frances said. "Not that at all. But me and your pa, like he said, we've been thinking. And well, we come up with a plan."

Emma looked from her mother, beside her, to her father seated on the step, back to her mother. "Well?"

"At church Sunday," Frances began, "Sister Lattimore come up, she come up to me and says—she says something about her and Brother Lattimore getting older, and now that their boy David got hisself married, they could sure use some help."

"That Spurgeon," Amos said, "he's a workhorse. That boy, he could be a big help to 'em, chopping wood and grubbing the fields. If he goes live at their place before winter sets in and does some work, it would relieve us of some of the—"

"He's only nine years old! Relieve you of what? The burden of having us here?" Bitterness stuck to her tongue.

"Didn't mean to put it that way," Amos said, "but darlin', you know the times they're hard. The Lattimores' place, it ain't far. You'd see him now and again. At church. Think of this, besides. They'd have to keep him clothed, and they might be able to git him some schooling."

Spurgeon could be a difficult boy, his obstinacy infuriating. That didn't mean she'd ever give him up. What would Elias say when he came back and found their boy living somewhere else? No, she would not send Spurgeon away.

She said it out loud: "No, I ain't farming him out to nobody. He stays with me."

"Give it some thought before you decide for sure." Amos cleared his throat. "There's, uh, there's somethin' more. Now, I know you ain't gonna like this." He took a deep breath. "I need help at the still."

Emma jumped up. The pan in her lap fell to the floor, making a clanging sound. Beans scattered.

"You still got that? I thought Elias got you to quit makin' likker."

Amos rose from the step to stand in front of her, head thrust forward, his dark eyes challenging hers. "What the hell you think we been drinking when the boys come over of a Saturday night? Lemonade? And what do you think pays for the goddamn fertilizer and goddamn gingham you and your mama make clothes with? What do you think comes of those fields of corn over yonder?"

Emma leaned over to pick up the pan and scoop up beans, trying hard to hold back tears, knowing they were going to pour out anyway.

"His daddy," Amos continued, "that son-of-a-bitch don't understand it's the only thing between us and starvation. One of my men's taking off for Arkansas, and I'm finding myself short a worker. Better to keep it in the family so's to make it less likely somebody'll squeal to the goddamn revenuers. Robert, he's a husky boy, big enough to carry them heavy sacks of malt and cornmeal up and down the side of a steep mountain. The lad also—I been watching him, and he's got steady nerves. A lawman comes, and you've gotta keep calm. I need someone to pour out the slops and clean the still too. So the boy'll need to be doing that."

"Papa, what about . . .? What about the church? The covenant? We promise not to sell or drink—"

"—If you think I'm the only one doing this, you're a damn fool. How else do you think we all pay the tithe? It's a basic human right, providing for the family best way we know how. And I'm telling you, I gotta have the boy helping me."

"What'll Elias say when he comes back and finds out I farmed out one boy and let the other get into likker making?"

"Girl, it's time you got truthful with yourself. That man ain't coming back."

"How can you say that? Course he's coming back."

"Then why you got no word from him?"

"I'm sure he's wrote to me and the letter got lost somewhere. He'd send it through one of his cousins or somebody, I been thinking."

"Humph!"

She turned pleading eyes to Frances. "I can't do it, Mama. Can't send Spurgeon off. And Robert, he's a good boy, and Papa's gonna get him into law-breaking."

Frances threaded the needle for stringing leather britches. "You need to think real clear. We ain't no better off than you and Elias. Only difference is he's gone and got hisself owing money he can't never pay back."

"Mama, I can't." Her voice faded. "I can't," she whispered.

Two weeks later Spurgeon sat in the wagon bed, nestled in Emma's arms, her chin resting on his head. Amos drove the horses up the Lattimores' long, winding lane. The log house was a simple structure, a little larger than the Broder home, to its east a barn of generous size with a tin roof. She told herself the boy would be improving himself, and being here was better than working at the still.

Slowly, Spurgeon climbed from the wagon, then, like the gentleman she'd taught him to be, he held out his hand to help her down. She did not let go of it once they stood side by side.

"I'll take him up to the house," Amos said. "I think it best you stay here."

Emma could not release the boy's hand. Spurgeon looked up at her, his eyes pleading. He rushed into her embrace, clung to her as they both wept uncontrollably.

Finally, Amos came between them. "I'm sorry, son. None of us want things to be this way."

Spurgeon seemed to understand. He straightened his shoulders, bit his lower lip, and without looking back, followed Amos to the door. Emma held her apron to her face and sobbed into it.

On the return trip to the Broder house, Emma sat on the wagon bench next to her father. He reached over and patted her knee. "I wish it wasn't so, darlin', but remember many a young boy has done the same and been a stronger man for it."

"But will he . . . Papa, when he becomes a man, will he ever forgive me?"

Elias stood on the schoolhouse steps and watched the twelve pupils prepare to enter the building, the girls forming one line, the boys another. It was the first day of his third year teaching in Aquone. He had learned not to expect a thirst for knowledge among any who stood before him.

He was about to clear his throat as a signal that conversation was to cease, when it did of its own accord. All eyes turned toward the road. Facing the school but not approaching was a boy. And his mother. A colored boy. A colored mother.

The mother gently nudged her son toward the schoolhouse, toward the children, toward Elias. He was eleven or twelve years old, maybe thirteen, slightly taller than his mother, with long, gangly legs. The book satchel he carried gave him a studious appearance. Like the other pupils, he was barefoot.

Elias descended the schoolhouse steps and approached the two. "Uh—this is a white school."

The woman kept her eyes downcast. "Yes, sir. I know, sir, but my boy—he wants schooling in the worst sort of way, and there—there ain't no colored school around these parts."

"Well, we don't take your people."

But something about the way the boy, unlike his mother, looked directly into the white schoolmaster's eyes led Elias to engage him in conversation.

"So, why do you want to attend school?" Elias asked.

The youth spoke with confidence, though his voice had the wavering pitch of a boy on the verge of manhood. "I already know how to read, sir, but I want to read what men with great minds have wrote. And I want to learn how to put my ideas into words. Good words."

"What's your name, boy?"

"Micah, sir. Micah Burdick."

Elias quickly decided that anyone who valued learning should be granted the opportunity. He beckoned with a jerk of his head. "Come, Micah Burdick."

By now the pupils were chattering among themselves, wondering what to make of their schoolmaster leading the Black boy in their direction.

"Quiet!" Elias demanded, as he and Micah climbed the steps of the building. Looking back toward the road, he saw the mother bring a handkerchief to her eyes. He nodded his head, an attempt to assure her that her son would be safe, then led everyone inside. He assigned Micah a desk in a back corner of the room.

The following morning, Mr. and Mrs. Cunningham met Elias at the schoolhouse door, Mr. Cunningham in his canvas pants, she with a light jacket over the same blue cotton dress she'd worn when first interviewing Elias.

She put a hand on her hips, thrust her face toward Elias's, and said in a high-pitched voice, "Whatever do you have in mind, Mr. Muller, bringing that Black boy into our schoolhouse?"

He took a step backward, creating more distance between them. "Mrs. Cunningham, ma'am, there's no school for 'em in these parts, and I figure that as long as he doesn't make trouble, I'll take him on as a student."

Mrs. Cunningham reclaimed proximity. She placed her face nearer to Elias's and waggled her finger.

"Why, in no time he'll be thinking he's as good as the white young-uns."

Elias kept his voice calm. "I won't allow that, Mrs. Cunningham, and neither will the other children. I plan to keep him separated from them. Sort of as if he was in his own school."

Mr. Cunningham nudged his wife, seeming to signal that there was more she should say. Which she did. "Our government in Raleigh, they're plannin' a law to keep the n——s from taking over again. To vote, a body's gonna have to be able to read. You want that boy to vote someday so he and them others can put their own in charge of runnin' our state like they did after the war? You're working 'ginst your own people, Mr. Muller."

"Mrs. Cunningham, he already knows how to read. I'm sure it won't upend our democracy if I teach one colored boy. Now, if you'd be so kind, I'll get on with my day."

He left Mrs. Cunningham with mouth agape and went to the head of the two lines of children.

"Well, you'd best make sure he don't!" she called after him. "Make trouble, that is."

In the days that followed, Elias heard but chose to ignore the younger students' curiosity about the dark-skinned boy in their midst.

"Are you really kin to a monkey?"

"Why's your skin so brown?"

"My papa says God cursed your grampa, that's why you're so brown."

One day, seven-year-old Mamie sidled up to Elias's desk while the others were at recess. With freckles and pigtails, missing both upper front teeth, she lisped, "Thir, the boyth ain't lettin' the n—— use the outhouse, and they beat him up yestherday on the way home from thchool."

Two days later, she again reported in private conversation, "Thir, I don't think it's right that the big boys are thpittin' on the n—— and callin' him names."

After recess Elias summoned Thomas Abbott and Hadley Cunningham up to his desk. "I'll see you two after school." His flat tone of voice signaled that the future conversation would not bode well for them.

Three hours later the schoolhouse was eerily quiet, except for the creaking of the wood floor. While Thomas and Hadley remained seated in their desks, Elias paced in the aisle beside them, his chest inflated, chin lifted. Back and forth. Not speaking. Back and forth.

A loud slap of the ruler against the palm of his hand startled them. "I do not like what I hear about the way you're treating the colored boy. He is a child of God—"

Both boys snickered.

"I will not allow you or any other students to treat him unkindly!" Elias shouted.

He raised the ruler and brought it down on Hadley Cunningham's back. "Ouch," Hadley said in a mocking tone, which so aroused Elias's ire that he hit him again, this time with greater vigor. He hit Thomas Abbott's back with equal firmness.

Walking the three miles back to the cabin, he fumed. Mrs. Cunningham would be angry, but he didn't care. Of course, Micah shouldn't be in a white school, but there wasn't anywhere else for him to go. Elias admired the boy's quick mind and the extent to which he'd already mastered reading and writing skills the four older students lacked. Maybe the boy's abilities and drive in pursuit of knowledge antagonized the others as much as, or more than, the color of his skin.

He remembered a boy back in the piedmont. A white boy about Micah's age, devouring Miss Pritchard's books, memorizing the map and dreaming of all the places he would someday go. Devastated when Papa made him quit school. Elias recalled his own persistence in reading the Bible and the only other book in the house.

In Samuel's novel the hero never attained his ambitions, but his son did. What if the one who lived out Elias's dreams wasn't a son but—he struggled to imagine it—might an intelligent colored boy—might Micah someday achieve greatness and tell all, *I owe my success to Elias Muller?*

By the time he approached the cabin and Smidgeon raced to meet him, yapping at his heels excitedly, Elias had made a decision: If that boy wanted to learn, by gum, Elias would do all in his power to make that happen.

"It goes against God's plan. Why do you suppose he put us on different parts of the world? To keep us separate, of course."

"They git all that larnin' and think they're equal to the white man."

"Larnin's for the white man. God made the heathen of Africa ignorant, and they're supposed to stay that way."

All winter long, Elias heard such remarks. From tobacco-juice-spitting men in the church yard, wearing Sunday store-bought suits that would do double-duty as their eventual burying clothes. From Laura Jacobs, who rued the day she'd made lodging available to him. From Mrs. Cunningham, who kept threatening to withdraw her four children from school but never did.

"Well," he finally told Mrs. Cunningham, "when I was hired, nobody said I was only supposed to teach white pupils."

"It didn't cross nobody's mind that a white man wouldn't know."

The more people condemned him, the more determined Elias became. "I see a boy who wants to learn, and I'm going to do what I can to make that possible," he more than once said aloud to himself.

Micah had an eager mind and was quick to memorize facts, whether of a historical or scientific nature. Within six months he'd surpassed Elias in mathematical understanding.

Finally—and Elias was grateful—Hadley Cunningham quit attending school. "He ain't spending time with nobody but the n—— ," Hadley complained.

Mrs. Cunningham let it be known that she was unhappy with the schoolmaster and raised the issue: Might it be better to have no schoolmaster at all than have a n—— lover? Though she kept her youngest children in school, two other families withdrew theirs.

Elias was no longer asked to preach at church. No longer did the unmarried women flutter their eyelashes, and when he approached a cluster of men after services, they stood mute until he walked away. He continued to attend, no longer out of a desire to worship but to spite members who shunned him.

Now his sole companions were Sassafras, who'd burrow into his coat pockets for apples, and Smidgeon, who daily raced down the road to greet the returning schoolmaster.

Chapter 15

"Come along now," Emma urged Leo, who stopped every time an object along the narrow dirt road captured his notice: a sparkling sliver of mica, a turkey feather, a stick to wave in the air. At this pace half the day would be gone before they reached their destination. She picked him up and carried him piggyback, making determined haste to Minnie's.

It had come upon her suddenly, surprisingly, then not surprisingly at all. She'd caught glimpses, like something lurked around a corner, whose presence, if she didn't see it, couldn't be there at all. Recently, she'd come to staring it squarely in the face: Fury. Yes, she was furious. Some of it was directed toward her parents, their deciding what she should do with her boys, taking a mother's rights away from her. But mostly, she was furious at Elias.

She came within sight of the lane leading to Minnie's house. From over her shoulder Leo pointed down at fallen tuliplike blooms of a poplar tree. Balancing him on her back, she reached down, picked up a blossom, and handed it to him.

"Ooo," he said. "Boo-tee-ful."

Focusing on her anger wasn't fair to the boy. She forced a gentle voice. "Hold it easy now, so we can draw it when we get back home."

Making her way up the lane, she tried to calm her thoughts, concentrate on being polite instead of right away seeking Minnie's counsel. She needed to acknowledge that several years had passed since they last spoke, and how good it was to see her again.

"Why, glory be!" Minnie exclaimed when she opened the door. The comforting smell of frying chicken poured outside.

Though her body was not as willowy as it once had been, more rounded but in a pleasing way, Minnie still had her girlhood sparkle. Her eyes expressed delight upon seeing Emma, and her smile made her cheeks puff out like they were filled with chestnuts.

She held onto Emma's hand then reached up and chucked Leo's chin. "Hello there, little fellow." Leo handed her the poplar blossom. "Why, thank you. Here, let me help you down." To Emma, "We was just fixin' to have dinner. Please sit a spell and eat with us."

She led Emma and Leo to the table where her husband, Floyd, occupied a chair at the end and five children sat on benches. "Oscar, honey, move over a bit so Mrs. Muller and her boy can fit in there next to you." Before Emma and Leo were situated, Minnie had already set two places for them.

As if on cue, all heads bowed. "Our heavenly father . . ." Floyd began. His prayer was short and to the point: "Thank you for this food and your many blessings. Amen." In an orderly fashion, dishes were passed to Floyd, then around the table. There was a platter piled high with chicken parts and bowls of mashed potatoes and collard greens, cornbread served in a basket.

Rather than be seen but not heard, the children laughed and talked among themselves, even initiated conversation with Emma. "Where do you live?" "Over yonder, on the other side of the ridge." "You got other young-uns?" Could she honestly claim to have three sons in all when she had given one to the Lattimores?

As if she sensed Emma's discomfort, Minnie said, "That's enough now. Who wants vanilla pudding?"

"Me, me!" Leo called out, waving both hands. Everyone laughed.

Emma marked how kindly Floyd spoke to his family and how generous he was toward them: sugar for pudding, real coffee, shoes on the feet of all, a new Home Comfort cook stove for Minnie. Emma envied not only the abundance that came with being well provided for, but also the abundance of love and respect in the home.

After the meal Floyd returned to the field, and the children went their separate ways, except for Lily Ann, who led Leo by the hand outdoors. She soon had him giggling and chasing after her.

Emma had a knack for knowing what to do in another woman's kitchen. She poured water from the kettle on the stove into the dishpan. Soon she and Minnie had established a rhythm, Emma washing and rinsing the dishes, Minnie drying and putting them away.

"A body doesn't just one day come knockin' on a door only to say hello," Minnie said. "I'm thinking you came with something on your mind."

Emma took her hands from the dishpan, shook them to remove the excess water, dried them with her apron. She faced Minnie. "Looks like Floyd treats you right good."

Minnie reached to put a dried plate up on a shelf. "He surely does, he surely does."

"Here's why I come to see you." Emma took a deep breath. "I find myself in the same situation you was in a while back. A husband who's gone off, Lord knows where. Now one of my boys is a blockader—please don't tell nobody—the other living over with the Lattimores, working hard, real hard, but not going to school as Elias would want him to. Mama and Papa, they don't got no money. Leo and me, we're two mouths to feed that don't do nothin' in return."

"Ah, I understand. Yep, it's the same kind of situation I found myself in. Daniel, he took off, leaving me with two little ones. Ain't seen hide nor hair of him in over six years. I 'spect, though, he run off with a lady from up near Morganton. He was all the time going up there. For business, he said. Humph!"

"You done all right though. You found you a good man. I want to do likewise so I ain't such a burden on my ma and pa. That's why I'm here. I want to know what I can do."

Minnie took Emma's hand and led her to the table. "Yes, I learned a heap. I learned you got two options: you can get a divorce or you can swear he's dead."

"Oh, I couldn't do that, swear he's dead, as I don't—maybe he is, maybe he ain't."

"This may be the time to break the commandment, the one about not bearing false witness. We're lucky in these parts. The arm of justice, as they say, it ain't long.

Now, if we was over in Charlotte or up in Raleigh, we'd have to pay one of them lawyers. Round these parts, though, the county people—they'd just as soon a woman says her husband is dead or she has a good reason to want a divorce. If she finds her another man, she and her young-uns won't be a burden to nobody.

"A man like my Floyd. His wife died of diphtheria, and he needed a woman to care for his children. Justice Hull, I reckon he's got a soft spot in his heart—maybe it's the missus who tells him to go easy on women. I went, me and my two young-uns, and I said, 'Your honor, I want a divorce.' It was that easy. 'Your honor, that man went off and left me with these two little ones, and I ain't seen hide nor hair of him, nor did he give me a cent.' How long's Elias been gone now?"

"Three years, coming up next month."

"Probably dead. Yep, I'd tell Justice Hull—say Elias took off for Texas and you heard he got killed in a gun fight." Said with a smile of satisfaction over her creative solution.

"And then?"

"You find you a man who lost a wife and he needs a woman to keep house and take care of his children. They're around. A good man, though, who'll treat you real fine."

It was late afternoon when Emma headed back toward her parents' home. On her back Leo, arms around her neck and legs around her waist, chattered giddily while she considered Minnie's new life. And her own options.

Hiram Hoover's wife had died in childbirth. The same with Joseph Armbuster. Men were helpless creatures who couldn't get along without a woman to fix their meals and keep house.

Chapter 16

Crockery shattering on the floor. A roar like a train passing.

Elias leapt from bed, groped his way through the darkness, and opened the cabin door. After five days, rain still poured. Smidgeon ran up to him, whining, rubbing his wet fur against Elias's legs. The shaking and roaring gradually diminished then stopped altogether. All that could be heard was Smidgeon's whimper and raindrops slapping the ground.

The next morning, Elias, a rain slicker over his suit, stepped out of the cabin into the dim light. The rain had weakened to a drizzle, accompanied by a moaning wind. Facing into the wind, he took long strides toward the lane.

"No!" he shouted.

He sank into mire up to his knees. The lane, his garden, the orchard, the field he'd planted in wheat—mud inundated it all. "Damn those loggers!" The naked mountainside, the days of heavy rainfall. Perfect conditions for a massive mudslide.

His thoughts were jumbled. Dismay, disappointment, despair. He slogged back onto the porch, took off his boots, and once inside dropped onto his rocking chair. He dared not approach students in this frame of mind. Eyes closed he rocked and rocked, trying to calm himself as one would calm an infant with the back and forth. "Dear God, why hast thou forsaken me?" he cried out.

He took a deep breath and experimented with gratitude. His life had been spared. As had the cabin, the farrowing shed, and the shed with his tools, where Sassafras spent her non-laboring hours. Of what value were tools, though, when the land they were used for was hopelessly submerged in mud? Hopelessly submerged. Hopelessly. Hopelessly.

Hope. He had to hold on to it. Hope for what? There could be no harvest this season. Nor for the next year. No redemption for the beans and tomatoes and yams and squash he had planted in his garden. No redemption for the orchard that would have produced a decent crop for the first time since Elias's arrival.

To combat the dampness and chill hanging over the April night, Elias let a small fire continue to burn in the cook stove after supper. He sat at the table, the oil lamp illuminating his Bible. His head was bowed, his hands tightly clasped. Before the mudslide he'd anticipated a successful growing season that would allow him to pay his debts and return to his family. But now . . .

Dear God, I hear you say, 'Gird up thy loins like a man.' I cannot. I'm a failure at being a man. I cannot provide for my family. I'm a failure at my job. I do not like the students. The young ones are wiggly, and the older ones, the boys especially, they don't— and there is all the hostility over Micah—

"Damn you, dog, interrupting my prayer!"

Better, though, to check on the ruckus Smidgeon was making than wallow in self-pity. Lantern and gun in hand, Elias stomped out the door, down the three steps, onto the spongy ground. He stopped abruptly and gazed upward. For the first time in more than a week, rain clouds had vanished, leaving the sky sparkling clear. The hazy belt of the Milky Way swept across it. Nearer Earth individual stars bid, *Look at me! Look at me!* Constellations leaped out: Ursa Major, Ursa Minor, Cassiopeia. *When I consider thy heavens, the work of thy fingers, the moon and the stars* . . . For the first time in days, weeks even, Elias invited calmness and gratitude. The tension of recent days left his arms and shoulders.

Shrill barking brought him back to his reason for coming outdoors—whatever the reason might be. Walking toward the farrowing shed, he heard Smidgen's barks become yelps then turn into weak guttural growls. Elias lifted his lantern to see inside. A red wolf standing over Smidgeon's writhing body paused to stare warily into the brightness. Two dead piglets lay nearby. In one swift, smooth motion Elias put down the lantern, brought the gun to his shoulder, and fired. The wolf yelped then folded.

Smidgeon was whimpering, blood flowing from his neck. Elias knelt and stroked his head. "Well done, thou good and faithful servant." He had no choice but to end the dog's misery.

Lantern and gun on the ground, he started to drag the wolf carcass out of the shed. A flash of light. Bright orange. He turned toward the cabin. Through the window came the glow of a flame. Briefly, he stood immobile, his mind struggling to understand.

His books! He ran in the darkness, twice tripping, pulling himself up, running again, until he burst in the door. Thick smoke pushed him back outside. He took off his shirt, half covered his face, took a deep breath, and reentered, groping his way toward the bookcase. He had arranged his books deliberately and knew the placement of each. He grabbed the two at the far-left end of the top shelf: *Young's Analytical Concordance to the Bible* and *Christian Research in Asia with Notices of the Translation of the Scriptures into the Oriental Languages.* With them in hand he ran to the door, his lungs desperate to inhale.

Away from the cabin he collapsed on the ground, clutching the books, panting for air. The smell of smoke, carried by a gentle breeze, hovered in the air. The crackling sound of burning wood drowned out nighttime noises. He watched hypnotizing flames reach skyward, engulfing the roof, exposing rafters. Orange streaks lapped at the outside walls. Then all that remained crumbled inward. His money was in there, as was his Bible, his other books, and only suit. Everything he had worked for these three years.

He wept.

Aug. 8, 1985

Dear Lydia,

I can't for the life of me understand you and Steven driving across the country in late June (and camping besides!), nor the sirenic lure of an ecclesiastic gathering. My other reaction: envy. I remember how you and I unsuccessfully begged to go to Annual Conference when it was finally held in the West. No matter that it was 1000 miles away!

It sounds, though, like your trip wasn't so much about singing "A Mighty Fortress Is Our God" with a thousand other Brethren, than about retracing two chapters of our lives. Your details (5 single-spaced pages!) got me into my own reminiscences of visiting Mother's family in Missouri and living in Phoenix.

So, your trip to the Vernon County courthouse paid off. Papa and Mother really did get married, and we weren't bastard daughters. (Ha, ha!)

Thanks for including the photograph of Cousin Prudence's house. I'm impressed by how much effort someone put into restoring its Victorian features. You and I spent hours on that porch swing fighting over whose turn it was to look through the stereoscope at her huge collection of cards.

I also have vivid memories of sitting in a corner, pretending to read a book but listening intently to the adult conversation. I was fascinated by their special relationship. The three of them had known each other somewhere else, I think up in North Dakota.

It's not surprising that nothing in Phoenix looked familiar. Good grief, we lived there in 1925! Our little house out in the desert is probably part of a mall by now. A Phoenix memory your letter evoked: My little pocketbook decorated with Indian beading went missing, and I was confident that "some Mexican kid" had stolen it. Papa sat me down at the kitchen table and lectured me about prejudice. He said Mexican children were just as good as I was, then made me stand and sing, "Jesus loves the little children, all the children of the world." Four times!

I also have a vague memory of him helping a Mexican man build an addition onto his house. I was scared Papa would fall off the ladder. He tried hard to bring

Mexican families into the church. An impossible goal: mixing Mexican culture with staid German Brethren.

It's strange, isn't it, what events stay lodged in our minds?

I always enjoy hearing from you. It's about time you and Steven make the trip up to the Northeast.

Love,

Dorcas

Chapter 17

The train crew shouted, horses neighed, the steam engine hissed. The clock in the nearby tower made its half-hour gong. Elias stood on the Morganton platform carrying a burlap bag containing his two books and the clothes he'd worn the night of the fire. His appearance bore witness to his deplorable situation: baggy pants, shaggy hair hanging over his collar, and a week's growth of beard. Laura Jacobs had sent him off with train fare, three dollars, and a shirt and pair of pants that had belonged to the late husband of someone she knew. More to rid Aquone of Elias than as an act of kindness.

Across from the train station a red and white striped pole spun around. He could at least show up clean-shaven and with a fresh haircut. Dodging buggies, oxcarts, and mounds of fly-covered dung, he crossed the street. A poster on the door advertised John Rudisill's ability to cut hair according to the customer's physiognomy. Peering through the window, Elias was relieved to see no other patrons.

He was leaning back in the barber chair, white lather covering his chin and jaws, when another customer entered. The man carried a newspaper and wore a vested suit of quality and shoes of finely polished leather.

"Mornin', John," the man said.

"Mornin', Mr. Hudson."

As Mr. Rudisill's razor deftly removed swaths of lather and beard, Elias stole fleeting glances in the mirror. The customer propped an ankle on the opposite knee, unfolded his newspaper.

"I say, John," the man said after a while, "ain't that a mess down in Cuba? What do ya wanna bet Cleveland's gonna change his mind?"

Elias cleared his throat, intending to say that the United States shouldn't stay neutral, what with Spain moving Cubans into reconcentration areas. He stopped himself. Engagement would draw attention. He silently stared into the mirror as the other two men discussed current affairs.

Once Elias was clean-shaven and his hair *physiognomically* groomed, Mr. Rudisill removed the barber cloth and shook it, letting a mass of dark brown hair fall to the floor. He turned the chair away from the mirror so that Elias might step down.

Mr. Hudson set aside his newspaper and stood. Only then did he seem aware of Elias's presence. He squinted. "Hey, don't I know you?"

"I doubt that you do." Elias picked up the burlap bag to signal that he was a country bumkin, unlikely to know a man of Mr. Hudson's stature. "I just arrived in town." He paid Mr. Rudisill twenty-five cents and rushed out the door, leaving behind the fragrance of men's cleanliness products.

He crossed back over to the train station, where men were loading crated goods onto wagons. He found a teamster heading south: a driver more boyish than adult in appearance, but who was heaving weighty bags of fertilizer onto the wagon bed as if they were stuffed with feathers.

"Been long in these parts?" Elias asked once they were on their way.

"No, sir. I moved up this way from Kings Mountain. Married me a local girl."

Elias filled his lungs with the loamy smell of freshly ploughed soil, the green scent of spring plantings in other fields. The wagon passed rows of young tobacco plants, cattle grazing on a knoll. Now and then, a stand of trees. In the distant west the Blue Ridge mountains glowed in the late afternoon sun. Only yesterday morning he'd left their betrayal behind.

"I've been away for a spell," Elias said. "When I left, the Alliance was getting some influence in these parts. You involved in the Farmers' Alliance?"

"Oh no, sir, my father-in-law, he ain't got much use for 'em. Says they're too tight with the Republicans, who're too tight with the Blacks." He thrust back his shoulders and added proudly, "We're Democrats." Elias held his peace.

By the time they got to the Casar turn-off, it was late afternoon. Elias grabbed his burlap bag and jumped to the ground. The young man continued on his way.

A tightness gripped Elias's stomach. He did not move. Could not move. Hymns had been written about going home, but they referred to heaven, where there was no ambiguity about meeting God and loved ones face to face.

Doubt, the word that hammered against his skull. Why return to a place that did not value his mind, a place that offered no nourishment for a man's intellect? His friendship with Samuel had proved that kindred spirits existed.

Doubt about how his arrival would be received. Should an apology accompany his entrance? But why apologize when debt had left him no choice? Or should he just walk in and assume a man's right to his wife's and sons' allegiance?

Doubt about the future. Once back in the family circle, he would never be able to break free.

For half an hour he stood in the same spot, sometimes kicking at the reddish-brown clay, at other times gazing in the distance without taking notice of what lay out there. Finally, his attention was drawn to dark clouds hovering over the distant mountains. If he didn't hurry and take that first step toward Casar, he'd get wet.

He stood at the foot of the porch steps. A sudden change of heart gripped him, confidence he had made the right decision. It was as if he'd been on a spiritual pilgrimage, as had Christian in *The Pilgrim's Progress*, and arrived at the Celestial City, except it wasn't heaven itself but the nearest place to it on earth. He entered his in-laws' home without knocking, stood in the doorway waiting to be welcomed.

The family sat at the table eating supper. Conversation halted, mid-sentence it seemed. Eyes turned to him. Gasps. As he approached the table, no one stood. Brows were furrowed, lips pursed.

"Well, I'll be damned," Amos finally said.

"Well, well, well," Elias shouted jovially. He stepped closer, placed a hand on Emma's shoulder. She swiped it away. He placed it there again, this time in a firm grip. She forcefully removed it.

Amos motioned for one of the boys to make room on the bench. "Sit down, son. Francie, bring the man a plate."

Elias dropped his burlap bag against the wall and took a seat across from Emma. He'd forgotten what an attractive woman she was, with her auburn hair and freckles. An awkwardness hovered. She still had not spoken, wouldn't even look at him, staring instead down at her plate. He studied the boys. There were only two, and they had changed so much that he wasn't sure who was who. Defiance was in the eyes of the older one; the younger boy, with Emma's coloring, would not look at him either.

"Spurgeon?" he asked the defiant-looking one.

"Robert," the boy said.

"Leonidas," Elias said to the younger.

Dread overcame him. "Where's . . . where's Spurgeon?"

"There's much to discuss," Amos said. "Fill your belly first." With his fork he transferred a slab of cold pork from his own plate to the one in front of Elias. "Robert, pass the cornbread down this way for your papa."

"First, tell me about Spurgeon," Elias said. "Did he die? Did my boy die?"

For the first time Emma spoke, her gaze still fixed on her plate. "We had to farm him out. He's living with the Lattimores."

Elias put both hands on the table and half rose. His tone was angry. "Why did you do that?"

Emma looked up and glared at him through piercing brown eyes. "Because you wasn't here and we got no money."

"Well, I'm here now, and we're gonna go get him."

"Not so fast, son," Amos said. "As I said, there's much to talk about." Elias's and Emma's eyes locked. There was neither affection nor joy in hers.

"You never did write," she said accusingly.

"I did too," he lied. "Sent some letters through—" he searched for a name— "through your cousin Leonard."

She scoffed. "You did not. You let us think you was dead."

"Well, I'm home now. And I've got plans." He manufactured one on the spot. "Plan to ride up to Dorothy Jane's and ask Peter to let me manage his farm up a piece from here. There's a house with it."

Amos spoke. "Things ain't that simple. Circumstances have changed. You see—"

Emma gave him a cold stare and lifted her chin in defiance. "I got married again," she announced triumphantly.

Elias looked at Amos, seeking confirmation or an explanation.

"That's right," Amos said. "When she didn't hear from you, we all thought you was dead. A new man to the area, an Ezekiel Powell, they got hitched."

"You got married? I told you I'd come back and get you."

"I didn't know where you was. Maybe out in California or Utah with that Mormon cousin of yours and another wife or two. Or up north. When I didn't get a letter or nothing, I thought you was dead."

"Well, where is he? Where is this Ezekiel?"

"He—he—he didn't stay around. He took off too."

"So you ain't—you aren't married anymore."

Quiet settled over the room, everyone engaged in their own struggle with events.

"Powell," Emma said softly. "Powell's my name now."

"Is that legal?" Elias asked.

"Justice Hull, he said it is because you was dead. But now you ain't."

For the first time Robert spoke. "Folks, we got us a resurrection!" He laughed raucously.

Next to him Leo giggled.

"Robert!" Emma said sharply.

"Yes, ma'am."

Suddenly, Elias felt exhausted. He pushed away the uneaten meal and stood.

"Reckon I'll have to sleep in the barn, think all this over." He picked up his burlap bag and walked out the door into the dark night.

Part II:
Lee

Chapter 18

October 1896

The snoring kept him awake. Twice he got up, walked over to the bed William and Matthew shared, and clamped William's mouth shut.

Snoring and the cesspool swirling in his mind. This was not where he wanted to be: sharing a room with three strangers, smelling the rancid odor of male sweat, defecating in the same outhouse as ten others. Samuel had lodged among men, with their foul language and drunkenness, but he'd gone there with the purpose of writing a novel, confident in his future return to civilized Cincinnati.

Anger, it kept him awake too. Hadn't he promised to return? The idea of Emma sharing a bed with another man riled him most. An adulteress, that's what she was, raising his sons in an environment honoring neither God nor marriage.

Anger at himself, as well. He should have found a way to send at least a small amount of money. But had he not imposed frugality even on himself? Except for the purchase of four books. He'd assumed Emma's willingness to sacrifice, too, and trusted Amos to provide the boys' basic needs. Certainly not farm Spurgeon out.

The anguish of loss. His sons . . . he wanted to take them hunting and teach them the ways of the Lord. To spend winter evenings seated by the stove, discussing theology and literature, he explaining the fallacies of Darwin's conclusions. They would look up at him, eyes filled with admiration. Evenings that were not to be.

The anguish of failure. That's why he needed to start a new life down here in South Carolina. A new life required a new name: Lee, short for his middle name, Leander.

He'd barely drifted off to sleep when there came a pounding on the door. Beside him in bed, Cletus groaned. Sluggishly, without exchanging words, the four men rose and donned work pants. The stairs creaked as they, joined by seven men from two other rooms, went to Mrs. Sheets's table. The aroma of biscuits fresh out of the oven greeted them.

The room, barely large enough to hold the long rustic table and eleven chairs, possessed neither decoration nor charm. Standing behind their chairs, the men bowed their heads as Mrs. Sheets lifted her squeaky voice to thank the Lord for her generous spirit. Amen, the men said in unison. Chairs scraped across the wood floor as they sat, reached across each other for biscuits, and devoured eggs and gravy and grits. At the sound of a factory whistle, they rose as one and headed out the front door, the others toward the cotton mill, Lee in the opposite direction.

He'd found employment in the wood department of the Anderson Buggy Company. *The largest buggy factory in the South. One buggy every twenty-five minutes.* The company claimed its one hundred twenty-five employees were highly skilled and called them *carriage mechanics*. In fact, they—and Lee—did little more than tend machines, each one performing a single task.

A noontime whistle interrupted the grinding sounds of steam-driven lathes. Men set tools aside, carried their dinner pails to outside tables. Rain had started to fall, its pings landing on the tin roof.

"Lee," he said, joining five men. "Name's Lee Muller."

Seated on opposite benches attached to a long oak table, they carried pails made from tobacco tins, their meals identical to the one Mrs. Sheets had prepared for her boarders: ham biscuits and an apple. Leaning on their elbows, they chewed their biscuits and talked with mouths full, white crumbs landing on black or brown or red beards.

"You gonna vote?" one across from Lee asked another.

"Course I am. It's a white man's duty."

"Had me worried at first, all them new rules. I can't read or write, and if I had me three hundred dollars' worth of land I sure as hell wouldn't be workin' here." Grunts of agreement. "Old Oliver Wilson, though, he winked at me and said—Wilson says a white man walks into the polling place and he'll be guided in his understanding. A n——, though, he's up shit creek."

A hefty man with a shaggy beard bit into an apple. He turned to Lee. "You're a Democrat, ain't 'ya?" He flashed a snaggletooth grin. "Round these parts we string up n——-lovin' Republicans."

This election, Lee's sympathies were with the Populists, who were supporting the Democrats. He was able to speak truthfully: "I'm one-hundred percent behind Bryan, him standing with the farmer and supporting free silver."

Returning to the rooming house in the encroaching darkness, drizzle-soaked hair hanging in his eyes, he gave thought to what it would mean were he to make South Carolina his home. The state's politics were brutal. It was impossible for a Republican to push against the system and win. No, this was not his destination, merely a stopover on his way to—he had no idea where to.

Surrounded by the grating sounds of steam-driven motors and the smell of sawdust, Lee operated a piece of machinery twice his height. All day long he stood by a monster of belts and gears, which produced up to eighty hubs an hour. Though it was automatic, its sharp blades and an occasional malfunction required concentration.

As a boy he'd resented his father's corrections and admonitions to be more attentive to the task. Here he begrudged even more the supervisor's reprimands. He felt the strain of standing in one place all day, of devoting all his attention to a machine that might at any moment go haywire. He dared not allow his mind to meander into satisfaction over the recent election completely stripping Democrats up in North Carolina of power.

Lee doubted he and God could meet right now, given his present state of mind. His soul was in a dark place. An isolated and isolating cavern.

Instead of attending church on this Sunday morning, he walked along a dirt road leading out of town. The cerulean blue sky stretched overhead. Cotton fields extended as far as the eye could see, bushy gray stalks with random tufts of white still clinging. In some fields, plants had already been plowed under.

Human voices. Singing, loud and energetic. Back from the road stood a small building of gray clapboard perched on slender piles of rock.

Curiosity led him to the door. The room overflowed with colored folks, their singing the most joyous he'd ever heard.

He took tentative steps inside. Believers were in the aisles and the pews, heads rolled back, stamping their feet, some slapping tambourines. He considered himself a *calm* Baptist. Even when the Spirit had come over him at age fifteen and led him to the mourner's bench, he'd not shouted as others did. Now, though, he was drawn to the melody the congregation sang, to the insistent rhythm. A hand reached out to him, an invitation to set his discomfort aside. Soon he was tapping his foot. Then clapping his hands and singing heartily.

As on cue, everyone sat. The preacher addressed the worshippers. "How can we sing the Lord's song in a strange land?" At first his words were slow and measured, the congregation affirming him with *Amens* and *Halleluiahs*. Like an insistent drumbeat, his cadence increased in volume and speed, those present staying with him, shouting now, standing up and waving their arms.

Lee was standing, too, shouting *Oh Lord*, grieving over his self-imposed exile. When the sermon ended and singing resumed, he moved into the aisle, not self-consciously, but overcome by the spirit of the worshippers. Suddenly, as if all had heard a signal, the room quieted. Women gathered their purses and rounded up their children; men slapped each other on the shoulder as they headed for the door. Inquisitive eyes turned toward Lee.

A broad smile came from a place within him. A place that grieved his exile but was leaving with hope.

Outside in the warmth of the sun, people greeted each other. Reverend Jones introduced himself to Lee. Other men shook his hand and said what a pleasure it was to have him worship with them. Lee sensed caution, most conversations limited to the beauty of the day and how God provided all good things.

Several families headed back toward town, children skipping ahead, women talking among themselves. Lee walked alongside the men, matching his stride to their unhurried gaits. He didn't grasp all of what they said to each other, much of their conversation in a dialect he didn't understand, but he recognized they were discussing the past election. One man owned the requisite three-hundred dollars' worth of land but had been denied the vote anyway. Several who could read and write had studied the state constitution, but the white people at the poll asked a question then said their answer was wrong when it wasn't.

At the fork in the road, the families went to the left, Lee to the right. "So long," they sang out. "Nice meetin' you. Come worship with us any time now."

Mrs. Sheets's mustache and muscular build were incongruent with a maternal nature that considered the men living in her boardinghouse as sons. Sons she urged to be clean and presentable when they left for work. Sons she strove to rescue from Satan's clutches.

She expressed concern about her own salvation as well. "Get thee behind me, Satan!" could be heard as she scurried down the hallway, or "Lord, give me strength!"

"Thou shalt not live by bread alone," she'd boom when men returned from their workday. She considered the pail of ham and biscuits an inadequate substitute for the hearty noontime dinner *her boys* would have eaten back home on the farm. In the kitchen she was assisted by a Black woman—from down around Charleston,

Lee had heard—who prepared stews with fish from the Catawba, everything seasoned with exotic spices. Harmony between taste and smell, a treat for the tongue.

After supper the men would congregate in what Mrs. Sheets called her parlor: a ten-foot square room with eleven ladder-back chairs. Embroidered maxims hung on the walls: "Think often of your death and your accountability to God" and "Never listen to loose or infidel conversation." On a corner table stood an electric lamp, of special interest to the boarders, Lee included, who had never seen electricity in a home.

Among the tobacco users Dan Palmer was the only one who rolled and smoked his. The others kept a wad tucked inside their gums. A reticent man, Palmer had a fragile build—the belt at his narrow waist tightly cinched to hold up too-big pants—a sallow complexion, and straight black hair cut just below the ears and parted in the middle. His matching beard was neatly trimmed. When questioned he never said more than *yep, nope,* and *I reckon.*

Lee would lean back in his chair, arms folded, feet stretched out and crossed at the ankles, as he listened to the men bemoan their present situation or tell stories respectful of neither women nor men of influence.

"I was farming with my brother," one boarder said. "This here agent come by and says he'll pay off all our debt if the whole family—me, my brother, his wife, and their young-uns—if we all move up here and work at the mill. I'll be damned if I'm gonna live in one of them mill houses with the slew of 'em. I'll just keep my body here a spell and see how it goes."

"It's a trap anyways, living in a mill house. You gotta trade at the company store, and before you know it, you owe more'n you make."

"This one man, I heard he owed so much that him and the family snuck off in the dark of the night, but the mill powers-that-be sicced the sheriff on them and forced 'em to come back to work off their debt."

About his own past Lee offered no details. He'd come from the mountains, he said, having given up farming, the economy being what it was. He'd never married, finding marriage too restrictive. He liked to go where the spirit led—a reference to his own spirit, not the Holy Ghost.

Dan Palmer had no story to tell. He just sat stiffly in the chair, feet flat on the floor, silently smoking his rolled cigarettes.

At around 9:30 Mrs. Sheets would bustle into the parlor, take a hurried glance around as if checking roll, then remind *her boys* that tomorrow was another workday. Saturday evenings after work, even though darkness had already set in, the men—except for Lee and Dan Parker—headed for the countryside to visit family. To return late Sunday night.

On a Sabbath afternoon, after he'd again worshipped at the colored prayer house, Lee rapped on the door of Dan Parker's room. Dan Parker answered, a book in hand.

"Ah, a fellow reader," Lee said. "Might I interest you in a walk? Perhaps we can discuss books."

"Thank you, I prefer being alone," Dan Parker said.

"That's fine. On the Lord's Day a man must seek solace according to the dictates of his soul."

Lee's ear had become accustomed to the worshippers' dialect, and though he did not—could not—keep up with their fervor each Sunday, he recognized that his emotions had long been trapped. In his gritted teeth. Tight shoulders. Clenched jaw.

He'd believed dancing was a sin—not to the degree of stealing, killing, coveting anything belonging to your neighbor (especially his wife). But here, dancing was for the Lord, certainly not a worldly sin. Did the Psalmist not say, *Praise him with the timbrel and dance?*

One Sunday, as the group walked back to town, he overheard a man say to another, "I surely would praise the Lord if I could read and write." The man's children were attending the Friendship School for Colored Children, and while he was pleased about their getting an education, he also wanted the opportunity for himself.

"I can teach you," Lee blurted. "You and anybody else. You've gotta be able to read if you're gonna vote."

From behind him a deep voice scoffed, "They ain't gonna let any colored man vote, no matter if he can read or not."

Lee knew that to be true. Yet if the men wanted to learn to read, he'd teach them. In the weeks and months that followed, five men stayed every Sunday after worship services. All ardent students. All faithful in attendance. The Bible was their text. Reverend Hall at Friendship School provided slates for writing.

Three men sat in the front row of the prayer house, Bibles on their laps, slates beside them on the bench.

Lee paced, eager to begin the lesson. "Where are Thomas and Ezekiel?" he asked.

The three stared down at their Bibles.

"Well, sir," Brother Williams said, "the circumstances, the circumstances . . ."

Throats cleared. Brother Anson, the oldest of the group and born into slavery, finally volunteered, "I'm afraid we ain't gonna see the young fellows anymore. They, uh, they left the county."

The story unfolded. When two white men ordered them off the sidewalk, Thomas and Ezekiel had refused to walk in the street. One of the white men hollered "Constable!" Thomas and Ezekiel took off running.

Ezekiel's mother gave them a loaf of bread and told them to hightail it out of town, or they'd end up on a chain gang and she'd never see her son again.

The Republican Party held the position that colored prisoners contracted out to factory owners and road-construction crews took jobs from law-abiding white citizens. But these two young men were not criminal types, Lee now saw. They certainly did not belong in prison or on a chain gang.

The atmosphere at Mrs. Sheets's boardinghouse drastically changed when a fellow named Leonard, from down in Chester County, took the bed of a boarder who'd returned home. Leonard was as vitriolic in demeanor as he was ugly in appearance, with a permanent snarl and a voice as grating as a rusty gate hinge.

On a typical evening the parlor was lit by the single electric lamp on the table, supplemented by glimmers of streetlight entering through two windows. Men leaned against the wall, their chairs balanced on two back legs. A cloud of sweet-smelling chewing tobacco and Dan Palmer's rolled cigarettes hung over the room.

"They're animals," Leonard said, his jaw swollen with a wad. "That's why we gotta protect our white women. Let one get anywhere near, and before you know it, he's on top, forcin' his pisser in her."

Men took turns telling of hangings down in Fairfield County or down in Richland "for takin' liberties with a white girl."

"Can't wait to git my hands on one," one said. "That big oak tree on the road over to York, the one on Horace Peters's land, it'd make a perfect hanging tree."

Lee was afraid to speak out in disagreement. Neither did Dan Palmer utter a word.

Having prayed over his noontime ham biscuits, Lee lifted his bowed head to see the approach of two men he usually ate with coming toward him.

"N—— lover," one muttered, then walked past, over to another table.

Another stopped and leaned into him. "Teach them Blacks to read, and 'fore you know it they'll be votin' and takin' over our state."

Lee took a bite of ham biscuit and chewed deliberately, trying to give the impression that he was content eating alone. In truth, he was starting to get scared.

He'd known angry men his whole life. Milford Hughes, for example. As stubborn a man as ever lived, who got so mad at his mule that he shot it. When spring planting came along, he was furious because he didn't have a work animal. But the anger Lee had been witnessing at the buggy factory and at Mrs. Sheets's felt different.

Papa used to ask, when he analyzed a confounding situation, "Who benefits?" Who did all this rage against colored people benefit? Certainly not these white men, who were poor and likely to stay that way till the end of their days. Men with power were manipulating these suckers, creating a scapegoat so poor white men would blame someone else for their low wages and dangerous working conditions.

The boardinghouse was strangely quiet. Lee marked the absence of the cook singing in the kitchen and the spicy aroma of supper that always greeted men returning from work. The silence was broken by wails of despair coming from Mrs. Sheets's quarters. Should he knock and ask the cause of her distress or go up to his room?

Before he had a chance to decide, boarders who worked at the textile mill entered the house, Leonard ahead of the pack. Immediately Mrs. Sheets came out of her quarters, her face swollen, her eyes red.

She looked to Lee as she spoke, as if pleading for him to understand. "He didn't go to work today," she said through tears. "Told them he was sick and wanted to sleep."

"Who?" Lee asked.

"Us," Leonard and another boarder said in unison. "He told us," Leonard said.

Lee was confused. "Mrs. Sheets, what are you talking about?"

"Men busted into the house," she said. "They had guns, and they—they hollered, 'Where's Dan Parker?'"

Her face was contorted in fury. She shouted into Lee's face, "He's a n——!"

"What do you mean?" Lee asked.

"The constable came to arrest him because he's been pretending to be white, and—" she spoke between barred teeth—"he's—married—to—a *white* woman." She shook her head in consternation. "To think I had that devil in my house. He ate at my table. He sat—"

"So where is he now?" Lee asked.

Mrs. Sheets wiped her eyes with the hem of her apron, then crossed her arms in satisfaction. "He got what's coming to him. They pushed him down the stairs then hauled him off to jail. Good riddance, I say." She resumed sniffling. "I run a reputable house. I am kind to my boys. But Dan Parker is *not* one of my boys!"

"We gotta get the son of a bitch," Leonard snarled. "Sleepin' beside us, eatin' with us."

"And married to a white woman!" Cletus shouted in disgust.

"Come on, Lee!" someone yelled as the group headed for the door.

Lee had no soft place in his heart for a colored man who married a white woman, but he wanted no part in administering justice. That was up to the law.

"I'll come along shortly!" he called back as he placed a hand on the staircase newel, signaling a need to go to his room first.

He paused at the top of the stairs. The house had again turned eerily silent. Had Mrs. Sheets gone to her room? Or had she followed the men out? Where was the cook? During his six months in Rock Hill, he had not been in an upstairs room other than his own. He opened the door of the one where Dan and two others slept, tentatively entered, paused when the floor creaked.

A smell hovered, the pungent odor of lint-covered clothes seeped in the mill's humidity. There were no pictures or Bibles. It was as if each man's identity had been subsumed by the machine he operated. Lee didn't understand how, but he sensed that their extreme hatred toward a quiet colored man who rolled his cigarettes was somehow linked to what they'd lost when coming to this place.

When the men returned late that night, drunkenly whooping and hollering, Lee pretended to be asleep. "Damn, how that n—— screamed and twitched." "Lord-amighty, he shat in his pants." "We should 'a cut off his pecker."

They had hanged Dan Parker from the big oak tree on Horace Peters's land.

Wearing jean pants as if he planned to go to work, Lee ate breakfast with the others. Eyes lowered, he appeared to concentrate on mixing his eggs into the grits. Everyone ate quietly, slurping coffee, their forks and spoons scraping plates. Once, the chuckle of one of the men seemed to call for a chorus of chuckles before everything returned to quiet.

Most mornings everyone left together, Lee and another boarder turning toward the buggy factory at a cross street, the others continuing on to the cotton mill. But this morning he said he needed extra time in the privy. Then he hid behind the ancient live oak tree in Mrs. Sheets's backyard, waiting for her to go on her morning errands. Once she was out the door, he climbed the stairs to his room. He hurriedly stuffed his carpet bag with razor, black gum toothbrush, the extra pair of underwear, the second work shirt, his Sunday suit, and his two books. He placed the two dollars he owed for a half-week's stay on the table where meals were served and walked out the back door of the house. Each movement made in a frenzy, his mind darting to keep ahead of any who might decide to search for him.

One last stop was necessary.

Hand grasping the door handle, he paused before entering the prayer house. Except for the squeaking of his footsteps on the wooden floor, the room was quiet. He took a seat on the front bench, bowed his head, closed his eyes. A mournful melody came to him, enveloping him in the spirits of those who worshipped of a Sunday. Eyes still shut, he stood and began to sway to the slow rhythm, taking deep breaths, releasing them slowly. He was overcome by a swirl of dizziness that caused him to stumble and fall. He landed on his knees. Before the altar.

He reached out and ran his hand along the sacred table. A master craftsman had recognized the potential in a walnut board; shaped, smoothed, then polished its surface.

Something ordinary transformed into the holy.

Lee prayed. He prayed for the good people who worshipped there. For Thomas and Ezekiel, that they would be safe. For the other three pupils, that their lives would be transformed by knowledge. That the men at the boarding house who'd done such an evil deed would repent and never again take the life of a human being. He prayed for the soul of Dan Parker.

He left the church and crossed an expanse of dirt. Along a walkway of flat stones, narrow green leaves of bulbs were breaking through soil. The windows of the house were open, a woman's voice singing "Everybody talkin' 'bout heaven ain't goin' there. Heaven, heaven." He knocked.

Reverend Jones came to the door, not wearing the suit Lee was accustomed to seeing him in, but work pants and a denim shirt. His demeanor, too, was different; his Sunday energetic escalation of fervor replaced with an unenthusiastic "Come in, young man."

"I haven't the time, Reverend Jones. I'm thinking that for my own safety I need to leave town."

"I assume you were not among last night's evildoers." Spoken somewhere between a statement and a question.

"Be assured, I was not. Please tell the men that I'm terribly sorry. I pray that they will learn to read and write, but it won't be through me. I shall be forever grateful for the hospitality y'all extended to me. God bless you."

October 30, 1985

Dear Lydia,

My, but you and Steven have squeezed a lot of travel into this year: west, north, and south. I assume you'll stay home over winter and try to make sense of your research.

I'm impressed by all the information you found up in North Dakota. So, our uncle was a Confederate prisoner of war who had to join the Union Army and was sent all the way up there! And you actually found the place and circumstances under which he died. Imagine how our grandmother felt, losing her boy to war—a useless war at that. (Admittedly, from my Yankee point of view.)

Through my memories, I accompanied you as you zigzagged across the Midwest on your way north and stopped at all those towns our family lived in. I can still picture the parsonage at Council Bluffs, that cramped bedroom you and I shared. I hear us whispering our secrets before we fell asleep. Right now I also find myself retracing our walk to school, past the rickety house where that old lady sat on her front porch every morning and greeted us. Oh my, once I get started . . .

I'm glad you made it up to Fargo, too, though I can't think of a single pleasant memory of the place. The parsonage was drafty and we were always cold. Papa had spent some time up there in his younger years and already knew what the weather was like. That was one time you and I didn't object to his decision to move again.

Mama never complained, though I suspect it was hard on her, too, having to make new friends everywhere we moved. I doubt that even in the privacy of their bedroom she ever spoke her mind. A true saint she was, to live with a man as strong-willed as our father.

It's strange that you've found more documentation about his brother, who died before Papa was even born, but still aren't having much success locating Papa. I assume you're planning another trip to North Carolina. I still think you should pursue the Elias angle. You're getting nowhere searching for Leander.

My greetings to Steven.

Love,

Dorcas

Chapter 19

"You look like you could use a ride, mister." A man in overalls held the reins to a team of horses pulling a wagon. The color of his short beard matched the knotted blond hair leaking out of a straw hat. He appeared to be older than Lee, probably in his fifties. "I'm only going a few miles to pick up some baby chicks, but it'll give you a resting spell."

Lee squinted into the afternoon sun. He tossed his bag on the wagon and climbed up beside the driver.

"Heading to Yorkville?" the farmer asked.

"So far, that's my plan."

"So far? Doesn't sound like much of a plan if you've got to say 'so far.'"

"Just striking out for a little adventure. They've got a new cotton mill coming in, I've heard."

"Yep. On the small side, as mills go. Quite an accomplishment, though, for Yorkville. Locals being the ones to raise the money, not outsiders planning to get richer off the hard work of poor Southerners."

The man presented himself as a son of the South yet spoke with an exact pronunciation that belied his ties to the region. "Me, though, I don't understand a man tradin' the natural world—" he waved his hand over the landscape as if blessing it— "all that blasted noise of machines, lint flyin' everywhere. Why?"

Shame if he went home, Lee thought but did not say, and death if he stayed in Rock Hill.

"This your land?" he asked instead.

"More or less. Used to be part of Old Man Wallace's before he broke up his plantation. We farm nearly two hundred acres."

"Far as I can tell there's been no planting."

"Yep, cotton should be in by now. We got rid of the scraggle back in February, but it's been too wet to plow. A farmer always seems to get rain when he doesn't need it and doesn't get it when he does."

"Isn't that the truth?"

"Where you from?"

For once Lee saw no reason to shy away from fact. "Up in North Carolina. Farmed up there but things didn't work out for me. You say you grow cotton?"

"Mostly. That and millet. We keep some animals too."

The farmer introduced himself as Mr. Northrop, not offering his given name. A talkative man, he let it be known that he believed women should get the vote. Lee argued that as head of the family, a man voted on behalf of the household.

"Say," Mr. Northrop said when he arrived at his destination, "seeing you haven't got definite plans and we can always use more help—like I said, it being late to get cotton in, there's gonna be a lot to do in the coming month or so. You look strong of body. I'm offering you work for a spell. You'll find our little community an amiable one."

"That's mighty kind of you. Give me a few minutes to think it over. By the time you get the chicks loaded—"

"—You'd have a place to lay your head at night. At no cost, I might add. And some good eating."

When Mr. Northrop climbed down from the wagon, Lee saw that walking was an arduous task for him: dragging one leg, marking the effort with a scraped trail in the soil. Yet it seemed not to slow him down. He headed at a swift pace toward an outbuilding, shouting, "Hey there, Wheeler, you out here? I came for my birds."

It was true. Lee had no plans. He hated farming but the men in the boardinghouse complained plenty about the mill: the lint, the noise, the danger, the pressure to produce. He knew nothing about growing cotton. Mr. Northrop, though, would be the one making the decisions, and the work would be temporary, five or six months. During that time Lee would have a chance to consider what to do next.

"I'll take the job," he said, when Mr. Northrop returned to the wagon carrying a crate of chicks.

Wagon boards groaned, and baby chicks peeped as the pair of horses turned down a lane so long that Lee could barely discern structures at the end. There appeared to be several small buildings, most likely former slave quarters, and two sizeable ones, most likely barns. Peach trees in their spring pale-pink array lined the lane, emitting an intoxicating perfume of oversweetness. Goats with straggly beards grazed in an enclosed field.

The wagon came to a halt in the center of a prosperous-looking complex. Seven slave cabins had been refurbished: whitewashed, with tin roofs, windowpanes, steps of new lumber leading up to a sturdy door. One of the large buildings was indeed a barn, with a wagon ramp leading up to wide double doors. The second large building was a hen house. Both appeared to have been recently constructed, the siding not weather-warped but neatly aligned and, like the cabins, whitewashed.

In the center of everything, a pavilion sheltered a partially enclosed kitchen where a colored woman vigorously stirred something in a crock. She looked up, smiled broadly, and waved. Beyond the pavilion, a garden, four acres or so, much of it of reddish-brown dirt not yet planted. At the nearest end, though, there were straight rows of bright green lettuce, feathery carrot tops, and cowpea vines climbing stilted pyramids.

A colored man came out of the barn. "Mr. Hawkins," Mr. Northrop called down from the wagon, "meet Mr. Muller. Mr. Muller will be helping us out for a spell. I thought we'd settle him in over yonder." With his head, Mr. Northrop indicated the cabin on the end. He stepped to the back of the wagon to unload the crates of baby chicks.

Spectacles gave Mr. Hawkins a learned and earnest appearance. Probably no more than twenty years old, he was a head shorter than Lee, and while not frail, he didn't look strong enough to toss a bag of fertilizer or seed up onto a wagon.

"I hope you'll find our community a welcoming place." Mr. Hawkins spoke in a clipped, cultured voice.

The interior walls of the cabin were newly plastered and whitewashed. There was a feather mattress, a chest of drawers, a table with two chairs, and a rocking chair next to the fireplace. Most surprising was a single bookshelf bolted to the wall. It held seven volumes, Robert Lewis Stevenson, Nathaniel Hawthorne, and Herman Melville, among the authors.

A colored man introduced as *Mr.* Hawkins? Books on a shelf? A clean, attractive living space? What kind of place was this?

Lee put his few clothes in a drawer and hung his Sunday suit on a hook. He was placing his two books alongside the ones on the shelf when a bell clanged insistently. He looked outside and saw that Mr. Northrop, Mr. Hawkins, and three other dark-skinned men, were gathering at the long table in the kitchen pavilion.

"Time for supper!" Mr. Northrop called out to him.

The table had been set with six plates and bowls, a tureen of bean soup, and a plate stacked high with cornbread. One by one Mr. Northrop introduced the men: Mr. Bailey, Mr. Arnold, and Mr. Baldwin. Mr. Baldwin appeared older than the others, in his sixties, Lee guessed, a large man with a shiny pate and intense dark eyes. Each man extended a welcoming hand. Colored and white men eating at the same table?

Conversation was lively and, to Lee's delight, political in nature. He expressed his opposition to President McKinley's determination to stay with the gold standard. To which Mr. Hawkins expressed his disapproval of Democrats. To which Lee said he was a Republican, but he'd voted for Bryan because he was a friend of the farmer. To which Mr. Arnold joked about such logic being a privilege of a white man, who got to vote.

Lee grimaced.

When the table was cleared, the cook served bread pudding. She looked at Mr. Northrop as if seeking permission, more a playful look than one of subordination, then, seeming to get approval, took a seat alongside him and ate dessert with the others. Miss Iverson, her name was. She had a relaxed way about her, an infectious smile. A strikingly beautiful woman—as tall as Lee, and slender—who allowed her hair to hang in long ringlets instead of wrapping it in a scarf as many Black women did. She spoke with an unfamiliar accent, a lilting sound, and had a beguiling lisp, so that *mister* came out as *mithtuh*.

The following day, Mr. Northrop, Mr. Hawkins, and Mr. Arnold stood side by side in a fallow field. Each sifted a handful of soil through his fingers and agreed it was finally dry enough to plant cotton. Mr. Northrop announced that he and Mr. Arnold would drive the two teams of horses, plowing the fields, breaking up the soil with a disc. Mr. Bailey would continue to be in charge of the livestock: eight goats and five kids, three sows with piglets. Mr. Baldwin carried out the responsibilities of smithing and general repairs.

Lee was to assist Mr. Hawkins in the garden. With a wheelbarrow the two men transported starts of broccoli, cabbage, and cauliflower from the cold frame, then placed the fragile young plants in holes and patted down the dirt. Moving along parallel rows on their knees, they carried on an animated conversation, skipping from topic to topic. Mr. Hawkins skillfully making a case for why the United States should not declare war against Spain on Cuba's behalf, Lee saying they should. Lee arguing that Jesus was coming again—probably at the advent of the new century— Mr. Hawkins arguing that the departure and arrival of other centuries had brought no Day of Judgment, so why should this one?

Three days following Lee's arrival, after all had gone to their separate cabins for the remainder of the evening and Lee was reading *Pilgrim's Progress*, there came a knock at the door. Mr. Northrop entered. He wore no hat, and for the first time Lee saw that his blond hair only grew along the fringes of his head. The skin on a large bald area was many shades whiter than his arms.

"I want you to take over delivering the eggs," Mr. Northrop said, "and the vegetables as soon as they start comin' in. I've been doing it, but now that we're working cotton, you're the only one who can carry on."

"The only one?"

"If I send one of my other fellas into town, chances are he won't come back. They see a colored man pausing—even if only for a minute—and before you know it, they got him wearin' a striped uniform and shackles, leasing him out to work on the roads. I'll take you along on tomorrow's run, so you can learn the route."

Lee didn't question this rationale, but Mr. Northrop's reference to my fellas didn't go unnoticed.

Early the next morning, wagons were already in town, delivering and collecting goods, creating a chorus of creaking wheels and rhythmic clomping. Lee and Mr. Northrop sat high on the wagon bench, Lee's hands relaxed as they held the reins of Ulysses, a horse too old and lacking in energy to work the fields. Behind them, baskets of eggs were nestled in a bed of straw.

They stopped in front of two-story clapboard houses with wide front porches. While Lee carried baskets of eggs to doors, Mr. Northrop remained seated on the bench, waving a friendly greeting to housewives in aprons. At kitchen entrances to the Rose Hotel and the Female College, Lee introduced himself to the colored cooks.

"So how did you and the folks on the farm come to know each other?" he asked along the way.

"Well, Mr. Hawkins and Miss Iverson were students of mine when I was teaching agriculture at Benedict College. The three of us became friends. They're both very capable, which you've surely noticed."

"So, you—what made you start this venture?"

Mr. Northrop motioned with his thumb to turn right at the next corner. "Gee," Lee commanded Ulysses.

"What made us . . . we'd probably had too much to drink, so the impossible seemed possible. Not that I'm doubting our decision. The idea came to us that white and colored could live together in harmony, own all things in common, like the church did in the book of Acts. Mind you, though, our religious views don't agree with the Apostle Paul. They brought along two people they knew."

"Mr. Bailey and Mr. Baldwin."

"That's right. Mr. Baldwin—you can see he's older than the others. He was a slave working as a smithy on a plantation over in the Tidewater. Had him a wife who got sold before the war was over. He's pretty sure she was brought to these parts, so he still, after all these years, posts notices."

"The name of the farm. Peniel. I assume there's a connection to Jacob wrestling with the angel."

"Yes, 'face of God,' it means. Our little group sees the face of God in every person. We believe in the equality of the races, and promote education and intellectual pursuits for all."

"A religious name, though you say you don't agree with the Apostle Paul. Yet you pray before every meal. A religious act, is it not?"

"We believe that we must live in a constant state of gratitude. We do not endorse any particular belief system, such as what Baptists, Methodists, or Presbyterians practice. Turn left at the next corner. . . . I take it you're a religious man, Mr. Muller."

"Yes, I am. In fact, I used to be a preacher, along with farming." He chuckled. "And I was a teacher for a spell. Now here I am farming again. Keep thinking I'm getting to the age where I oughta settle into something more permanent."

By the time they returned to Peniel, Lee was thinking that maybe his arguments with Samuel had prepared him for living among—not exactly atheists, but people aligned with freethinkers. Surely, God had led him to this place. A haven that combined hard work and intellectual stimulation. Yet it seemed unfathomable that he should again be in the company of colored people. Young Micah out in Aquone. The men he'd been teaching to read and write over in Rock Hill. And now here he was in this strange place where everyone was addressed as Mister and Miss, where the opinion of each person was respected.

Lee was becoming the public face of the Peniel community. When delivering eggs, he took time to talk with Yorkville housewives about the weather and inquire about the well-being of their children. Sometimes he held the hand of a bereaved woman and prayed with her. At the Rose Hotel and the Female College, as well as at the back doors of wealthier homes, he visited with the colored cooks. White women complained that the new mill was bringing the wrong kind of people to Yorkville. He nodded in agreement, ashamed of his cowardice. Mill workers were, in fact, of his own ilk, farmers who could no longer sustain a family on income from their acreage.

He considered himself an astute observer of human interaction, of hierarchy and resentments. Yet he was taken aback one Saturday while removing Ulysses's tack.

Mr. Hawkins approached. "I'll be frank with you, Mr. Muller. You go ridin' around town every Saturday, sittin' high up on that wagon, taking all the vegetables to white and colored ladies. You smile at them and talk about how hot it's been and when's it gonna rain."

"Uh-huh," Lee said cautiously, "that's kind of the way it goes."

"And what do you think the rest of us do while you're gallivanting around?"

"Well—uh—"

"I'll tell you. We're out in the damn sunshine hoeing cotton."

"Now see here, I do my share. I've been working plenty in the fields. And the garden."

"The main purpose of Peniel's supposed to be witnessing to colored and white being equals. Yet we send a white boy to town so no white folks'll be offended. Of what value is our conviction that white and colored faces reflect the face of God if no one sees colored faces?"

"It's not my decision. It's probably for your own good. I've seen for myself the animosity a lot of white folks have got 'ginst your people. Like getting lynched just for talking with a white woman."

"You're soundin' like Northrop. Everything's for our own good, as if we don't know what's for our own good. Lucy May Henderson says you stop by, smile that big smile of yours, and lean against the doorframe just chatting away. Don't see you getting in any sort of trouble talking with a colored gal."

"Oh, so you know Lucy May?"

"She says you flirt. You think you've got a right to our girls, but we don't dare deliver eggs and vegetables to a white housewife."

After the confrontation, Lee sometimes caught bits of conversation among the others: Mr. Northrop's name spoken with acerbic tongue. What did they say about him?

They were rude noises, roosters' crows at the crack of dawn, urging human sleepers of Peniel, wake up! Interrupting dreams haunted by Emma and Dan Parker and students at Aquone and President McKinley. Scenes in which Lee stood to preach all tongue-tied, or failed to rescue one of his boys from the waters of the Catawba.

Cotton was laid by, its canopy shading the soil, making hoeing unnecessary. For five or six weeks, all cotton farmers could do was pray for enough but not too much rain and plenty of warm days. Not a spell for relaxing, though. Practically every garden vegetable ripened at the same time—beans and tomatoes and strawberries— requiring the men to assist Miss Iverson in the pavilion. Canning, the new method was called, sterilizing jars with lids that sealed out bacteria. Canned vegetables would not only feed the Peniel community but could also be sold in town.

The kitchen was clearly Miss Iverson's domain. Her glare demeaned them all when she shouted, "That's not how you string a bean!" "That sauce's got to be stirred constantly. Constantly, I said!" "You're gonna scald yourself and everybody around you!"

Lee resented doing women's work, especially being bossed by a woman. But at night, in those few moments before exhaustion of the day overtook him, he'd think about Emma, his mother, and Dorothy Jane in sweat-soaked dresses, wiping their brows with their aprons while gliding heavy irons over his shirt sleeves and collars. All the windows open, flies coming in while the oven pumped out heat for baking bread. He'd always felt sorry for himself, having to steer a plow and dig out tree stumps, never fully appreciating the work women did. "Forgive me," he whispered aloud. Not to God, but to the women in his life.

∞

He had never picked cotton, but by late September, when cracked-open bolls revealed puffy clusters of white, the others warned that if his back ached from hoeing, the worst was yet to come.

They were right. He dragged along a six-foot bag and tore cotton bolls determined to stay attached to razor-sharp claws. His back ached from all the bending over. Evenings, he daubed turpentine on cuts.

Meanwhile, Mr. Northrop was frequently away on business in Yorkville or up in Charlotte: to see a lawyer, purchase tools, find a better market to sell the cotton. To himself, Lee justified the absences. Someone had to be in charge of an operation such as Peniel, and Mr. Northrop was certainly the most qualified.

Come supper time one late October evening, Mr. Northrop energetically spoke about news he'd gleaned that day: There was unrest among coal mine workers up in West Virginia.

Suddenly, Mr. Arnold pounded his fist on the table. "See here, Northrop, while you're away, we're out in the field picking cotton just like our parents and grandparents did. This is not a community of equality but one of slave and master."

Mr. Northrop's gaze moved from man to man, his tone mollifying. "Friends, remember how we worked together last year? From the beginning we agreed to grow cotton because that's a crop we've all had prior experience with. This is always the hardest time, the picking, but I've been keeping track of prices in Rock Hill, and it promises to be a good year. When we're under such stress—let's not let our emotions turn us against each other." His command of the situation seemed to calm the waters.

Tensions decreased over the winter months, the men finding solace mostly in repairing equipment or chewing the fat around Mr. Baldwin's smithy works. The goats and chickens still needed tending. Meals were eaten in a cleared area of the barn, kept warm by a wood stove. Lee continued his egg and canned-vegetable routes in Yorkville, read in his free time. Mr. Northrop took frequent trips to Charlotte, where he managed the sale of cotton that the Peniel community stored there.

In early January the apron over Miss Iverson's dresses could no longer conceal her expanded waist, and her stride was awkward, her toes pointing outward as she lumbered along. Lee made several guesses as to which of the men was father to the child she carried. Either no one else cared or everyone already knew, for no mention was made of it.

By the time he'd completed his first full year at Peniel, Lee saw cracks in the façade of the "face of God" community. He tried to initiate discussions at the supper table: Should colored and white be allowed to marry? No one spoke on the matter. Should infants be baptized, or was it an adult decision? No one seemed to care. Who would run against McKinley the next election? No one seemed to care.

Right in the middle of cotton planting, Miss Iverson gave birth to a son. A light-complexioned boy with an oval face like Mr. Northrop's and a small mouth like Mr. Northrop's and deep-set eyes like Mr. Northrop's.

Three days later, Lee packed his clothes and two books in his carpetbag. He took off by foot for Yorkville.

Chapter 20

It was not where Lee wanted to be, but there was no place he *wanted* to be. Not up in Burke or Cleveland County, where his reputation had been sullied and Emma's mere presence was a reminder of her perfidy and, yes—he sometimes, but not often, admitted to himself—of his own failure as a husband and father. Not out west in Aquone, where Mrs. Cunningham and her allies were out for his blood for teaching a colored boy to read and write. Certainly not in Rock Hill, where white men staked their manliness on killing colored men and white sympathizers. And not at Peniel, an upside-down community that pretended to be one way but was, in fact, another.

"Don't tell the others, but I'll only charge you two dollars a week," Mrs. Cornwall said when he appeared on her doorstep. He could pay her once he found a job.

To which he replied, "Don't tell anyone I'm here. The circumstances under which . . ." A clearing of the throat signaled his reluctance to say more.

For a year he'd made regular deliveries to her Yorkville rooming house. In exchange for a cup of coffee and a large square of fig, hickory nut, or other kind of cake at her kitchen table, he'd listened to her talk. About how, after thirty-five years, she still missed her husband, Floyd, shot by Yankees at Shiloh. And how her son, Jasper—in the grave but two years—once rescued a neighbor boy from a rabid dog—including details about the boy's mother, father, and each of his five sisters, and the dog itself, with a brown rump and short ears that stood up like sentinels. She'd informed Lee about neighborhood gossip: what women weren't speaking to each other, who snuck out of a Saturday night to dance at the Rose Hotel, and who had poisoned her first husband so she could marry the second.

The room he now shared with three other men was slightly more pleasing than Mrs. Sheets's place over in Rock Hill. A bit larger, with a chest of drawers for every occupant. Every man had his own bowl and pitcher, Lee's with a design of purple grapes and green vines. A chipped spout.

Chances were that Peniel members had gone their separate ways, leaving Northrop to manage the cotton-growing season by himself. Maybe Miss Iverson had stayed behind. Lee's disgust went to his very core. White and colored were two separate races and should not be producing half-breeds.

And there had been the Great Confrontation. Mr. Arnold, in his husky voice with perfect enunciation, yelled, "You're no different than the slave master, raping a colored woman because she's his property. I tell you, Betsy's not your bitch!" It was the first time Lee had heard a reference to anyone's given name.

To which Mr. Northrop had yelled, "I did not rape her. Our feelings toward each other are mutual." Yet Miss Iverson made no effort to confirm his defense.

In Yorkville Lee had found employment as a loom fixer at the cotton mill. But after a week of training and the supervisor's almost continuous curses about his ineptitude, he was transferred to the carding room. Twelve-hour days out in the field were bad enough; twelve-hour days inside a building, breathing hot, humid air, were intolerable. He quit.

"Word's around that Mr. Daly needs a man," Mrs. Cornwall told Lee. "It was just him and William Stevens, then last week Stevens got hisself kilt by a lightning strike while he was out fishin.'"

She gave Lee her deceased son's bowler hat and narrow four-in-hand tie. He put on his only suit, wet his hair down, shaved, and walked the mile to Daly Buggy Sales and Service. He figured he knew a lot about buggies. Besides, Samuel had once said that being a politician and a minister were similar in that both were trying to sell something.

Lee was the right man for the job. With the well-to-do he used correct grammar and displayed his intellect. He brought innovations to their attention: improved shock absorption and the excellent quality of the russet leather interior. Pointed out the polished fenders. With the less affluent he'd throw in an *ain't*, said *hunnert* for *hundred*, *hit* for *it*, and *garteed* for *guaranteed*. With this group he emphasized the economy of the vehicle, the ease of handling. He didn't mention that they could buy an open buggy from the Sears catalog for less.

Recently, as he read his Bible by the light of the oil lamp, he'd probed what Holy Scripture said about divorce. Had Jesus not said, "If a woman shall put away her husband, and be married to another, she committeth adultery." Nowhere did he read that if the wife divorced her husband and she was the one to commit adultery, the husband couldn't remarry. Besides, God said, "It is not good that man should live alone."

If he again married, it would not be coerced or rushed but approached with a rational mind. He would choose a wife of steady disposition, not given to mood swings and not headstrong, a nurturing woman rather like Mrs. Sheets before the debacle in her boardinghouse, only younger and more attractive. He certainly did not want a strong-willed wife like Mrs. Cunningham. Foremost on his list of qualities was a woman committed to God.

What better place to find such a woman than at church?

As if competing for proximity to heaven, every Yorkville church—Presbyterian, Methodist, Baptist—tried to outdo the others in splendor. Spires had replaced simple belfries. Instead of clear-paned windows, the most prominent churches boasted stained-glass windows financed by the town's wealthiest citizens. Lee chose to attend a Baptist church housed in a modest but sturdy structure of brick.

It was the church where Charity Alexander and her four daughters, all of marriageable age, were members. Three of the daughters approached Lee the first Sunday he attended. They tilted their heads in feminine playfulness. They fluttered their eyelashes. They laughed at his witticisms.

The fourth, after staring him boldly in the face, walked away with cool indifference.

Chapter 21

Charity Alexander determined that Lee would make a suitable husband for Gladys, her oldest daughter. He was pleasing to the eye, with a slender yet sturdy build, dark hair that he habitually swept from his face with a brush of the hand, and intense translucent blue eyes behind spectacles. He walked with confidence. His smile came easily.

For the purpose of bringing Gladys to his attention, she invited Mr. Muller for Sunday dinner. Conversation around the dining room table was lively. Mr. Muller listened attentively. Upon careful study, Charity determined that he was older than she'd first thought. Not a sapling, for sure. When he didn't make his availability or unavailability clear, she decided that he'd likely lost a wife, a child, too, perhaps, to influenza or diphtheria. Maybe the wife had died in childbirth, the newborn along with her. Clearly, he was an educated man from a good family.

She was concerned that whenever he spoke his glance most often turned to Mildred. Of Charity's daughters she was the least interested in marrying, the gift of flirtation beyond her understanding. Of the four girls, the least venturesome, the one least likely to abandon the family fold.

Yes, if Mr. Muller was searching for a wife, he'd best set his sights on Gladys. Who, over dinner, with her cleverness and lilting laughter, nearly met Charity's expectations—though she could have been a trifle more attentive to when Mr. Muller's plate was empty, so that Charity had to be the one to offer him another piece of chicken.

And there was the way Gladys couldn't stop prattling on and on about her and her sisters' ancestry, speaking too long and with too much detail, going through a sequence of great-great-greats and the Battle at Kings Mountain and the seventy-six slaves her grandparents had owned—here she brought hand to heart to emphasize that she hadn't been born yet when the war was going on. All narrated with animation, for Gladys did like to be the center of attention.

"So, did your father fight in the war?" Mr. Muller asked Gladys.

"Yes," Gladys said. She lowered her head in reverence. "He lived through it. Mama's only brother, though—my uncle—he died up in New York."

A pall lingered over the table.

Mr. Muller turned to Charity. "I'm terribly sorry. I had a brother I never knew—I wasn't even born yet—he was killed in the war too."

Gladys lifted her chin and arched her back, drawing attention to her bosom. "Arthur volunteered. A true patriot." All of a sudden her pride seemed to collapse, and she slumped. With a weak smile she said, "My goodness, so here we are more than thirty years later still talking about the war. What's done is done."

"I'll tell you what," Charity said after an awkward pause, "let's go over to the big house."

Charity often led her daughters on what was for her a sentimental excursion to the house where she'd spent her youth. She would narrate scenes of parties and her days with a private tutor, Miss Agnes, and her riding lessons with Mr. Branson. Today's tour, though, was to impress a potential suitor.

She was disappointed that the girls chose to walk in pairs, their clasped hands swinging as they chatted among themselves. Mr. Muller had little choice but to walk alongside Charity.

They approached the house from the east, passing through a copse of longleaf pines to reach the columned portico. Mr. Muller admiring the grounds, she apologizing for the thickened undergrowth.

Then it was in full view. Mr. Muller gasped as she hoped he would. Despite years of neglect, the house retained its aura of magnificence. They climbed rickety steps leading to enormous double doors. Upon entry Mr. Muller spoke in a whisper: "I bet you have some wonderful memories."

"Indeed, I do. The first time I met Mr. Alexander, he came through this door. We were both children, mind you, but we played together so joyously. Mama and Papa—my, what parties they had, friends came to Avalon from miles around."

"Avalon," he repeated.

She led the way to the dining room. "We had a table that could seat fifty people. The china plates had gold rims, and over there, silver pitchers and a silver tea set were on the sideboard."

"Fifty," he said in awe, like he could picture himself at the table, making a toast to—she remembered a toast to Jefferson Davis himself.

They entered the library, which had once held a thousand books. "A thousand!" Mr. Muller nearly shouted, obviously impressed.

Charity laughed. "For show, I think. I don't remember ever seeing Papa with a book in hand. The men would come in here to smoke and play cards."

The shelves were covered in grime. Here and there a book lay flat. Mr. Muller picked one up and blew a layer of dust off it. "Ah, *Pickwick Papers*." He turned the pages reverently.

"You may have it if you like. You can see it's not doing anyone any good here."

It was just a book, a battered one at that, yet his face lit up as a boy's would upon being given a peppermint stick.

Yes, he definitely was a suitable match for Gladys.

There were other invitations to the Alexander table. Sunday afternoons, when Mr. Muller became increasingly comfortable, entertaining the women with colorful stories of getting into mischief as a boy and seeking protection behind the skirts of his mammy, who had chosen to stay after the truce. He spoke of a comfortable and happy childhood and the inspiration of his teacher, Mr. Talley, at Amherst Academy. He'd been blessed to attend Rutherford College, where he boarded with Mrs. Sheets.

It was becoming apparent that Mildred, not Gladys, was the daughter whose approval he sought. But Mildred showed no interest. As if mute, she spoke with her eyebrows when in his presence: the right one raised in mocking; the left one to show doubt; both raised to indicate boredom. When Mr. Muller came calling, she would flash an eyebrow signal then whisper something to one of her sisters, which led to a round of giggles and the four of them staring at their guest. He tried to hide his agitation, but Charity could tell by the way he bit his lower lip that their behavior riled him. Any other man, Charity thought, would have given up.

On a Sunday afternoon in late October, it occurred to Charity that perhaps it all was a game. Mildred was leading him on, and he knew it, and she knew he knew. Then, as the 1900 election approached, she and the girls learned the worst.

Mr. Muller was a Republican.

Some among Charity Alexander's circle of acquaintances pitied her. So much loss, so much humiliation. During most of the war, she and other daughters of wealth had maintained a life of gaiety, traveling from home to home, mingling with young officers on leave. Her heart, though, belonged to Lieutenant Henry Alexander.

Three days before General Lee's surrender, her only brother, seventeen years of age, died in Elmira Prison. Her father, Colonel William Drummond, survived the war, but upon his return to Avalon was shocked to discover no crops planted, no laborers, and that his wife had regularly welcomed one of the slaves into her bed. The colonel immediately dropped dead of a heart attack, leaving Charity's mother free to take off with her Black lover for parts unknown.

At age twenty-four, Charity owned 870 acres, five barns, fourteen slave hovels, the overseer's house, and the planter's residence. In 1867, in a quiet ceremony, she and Henry married. Without slaves the main residence was more a burden than a comfort, so Henry set about transforming the overseer's house into a suitable home for his new wife. He covered the walls with floral-patterned wallpaper, repaired the shutters, and rebuilt the seven steps up to the wide front porch. Three dormers allowed light into two upstairs bedrooms, later occupied by the four daughters Charity gave birth to. Like many planters, the family found themselves land-rich but money-poor. The day before their twentieth anniversary, Henry fell from the roof he was trying to patch and died.

So how was it that after all those losses, she still maintained the demeanor of a Southern woman of means? A prideful erect posture, a feminine tilt of the head when engaging in conversation, a perfumed lace handkerchief. Every Sunday she wore the soft suede gloves given to her upon her seventeenth birthday, with pearl buttons extending from wrist to elbow.

Charity was one to move on. She survived by renting out much of the land she'd inherited from her mother's side of the family to sharecroppers, and paid twenty Black men to work the remaining cotton fields. Her four daughters were not at all a burden, but a blessing, dearer to her than life itself. Unable to offer the luxuries she'd had in her youth, she could, through savvy business practices, provide a comfortable life. She inspired them to make the best of their circumstances, to find in each other deep friendship and happiness.

Her wish to find husbands for all four was not based on her need to reduce the fold but to increase it, to welcome into the family orbit men, if not of prominence, at least of upright character. She wanted her daughters to experience the joy she had found in her love for Henry.

There had been a time when any man would have felt privileged to have Charity by his side. She'd made sure the same favored status held true for her daughters. She'd done all she could to instill in them the qualities of the finest in Southern womanhood.

But time was passing. Gladys was already thirty-four, and the number of eligible suitors had diminished. Perhaps the time had come to find a widower for her. Lovey and Judith, too, were getting past their prime.

So, what was she to do about Mr. Muller's obvious interest in Mildred? He seemed a proper man—intelligent, college-educated, from a highly-regarded family, he said. But she'd questioned him as subtly as she could, how it was that he now lived a distance from his kin and sold buggies for a living. He was trying to make it on his own, he said, to prove that he need not rely on the wealth of family. Yet his single pair of brogans with scuffed leather provoked a bit of doubt.

And there was his unrepentant identity as a Republican. To welcome Mr. Muller into the family seemed a betrayal of Henry, who had worked tirelessly to elect Wade Hampton governor and rid South Carolina of Federal troops. Henry had been an esteemed member of the Klan and strategized on restoring the power of white landowners. Efforts that had met with success. The Democratic Party now ran the state.

One Republican voter could do little harm. Besides, the womanly charms of the Alexander family would surely change Mr. Muller's sympathies.

"It's been two years," Charity said. Arm-in-arm, she and Mildred took matching strides along the moss-draped path between the overseer's house and the main house. Their free hands lifted their skirts above the ankles. "Hasn't he asked you yet?"

"Yes, several times." Mildred faced her mother, lowered her chin, and raised her right eyebrow. "Especially after you announced you'll give all us girls a hundred acres when we marry."

"And?"

"Doesn't it worry you just a little that he might want to marry me for the land that comes with my hand?" Mildred giggled. "Hmm, land that comes with my hand. A rhyme."

Charity ignored the attempt at humor. "A little incentive doesn't hurt."

"Oh, Mama, I don't want to marry. I'm happy as a bug in a rug. You and Lovey and Judith and Gladys. And me."

"Why do you think I'm giving a piece of land as a wedding gift? To keep my girls nearby. You know, much pleasure comes from being married to a good man."

Mildred stuck out her tongue. "Ugh. Good man. I wish he wasn't so—he's *too* good. All the time talking about God's will this and God's will that. He's decided it's God's will that we get married. How about my will? And he's got our future all planned. Says I'll make a good politician's wife. Like he thinks this state will ever elect a Republican." She smirked. "A Republican who's divorced. Many would think him a libertine."

Both women stopped abruptly, waiting for a reddish-brown snake to slither across the path. "Just a corn snake," Charity said. "A justified divorce, his wife being an adulteress. Still and all, you'd have to go all the way to Charlotte to find a man of his quality."

"What appears as quality isn't necessarily. Not that I've uncovered any specific flaw—well, as I said, I find his self-righteous attitude irritating." Mildred pulled Charity's arm tighter to herself. "I want a man I can love the way you loved Papa. No sparks fly when Lee touches me, and his kisses—they're so—there's a hole in his heart I don't want to be responsible for filling."

"As dear as you are to me, I know you well, Mildred. A more obstinate girl, there isn't. Anywhere. Take my word, many a woman has learned to love her husband. So can you. And you'll love the babies that come from being his wife."

"I want babies without being anybody's wife."

"Mildred! Surely, you don't mean that."

Mildred pulled away from her mother and laughed. "Of course not, Mama. Just said that to rile you. It doesn't seem fair that I should get a husband sooner than the others."

"You're just making excuses. Their chance will come."

The two came to the end of the wooded path, out into the bright light. The big house loomed before them. Weeds hid any evidence that there had once been a track where they stood, but Charity remembered white-gloved slaves stationed at its edge, helping visitors alight from carriages. Oscar. That was the name of the one her mother had run off with.

"Do you ever think about leaving this place?" Mildred asked.

"Now, why would I? This is home. Where my mama and her father before her lived. Where I first saw Henry and knew my heart would belong to him for the rest of my days. No, I can't think of any reason why I would ever leave."

"Then neither shall I."

On March 23, 1902, the clock in the courthouse tower tolled two o'clock as the party—Charity, her three daughters, and Lee—climbed the flight of stairs and entered the massive red doors. All four women wore bell-shaped skirts and white ruffled bodices that enhanced their already ample bosoms. Hats were their main extravagance. Charity's was high-crowned with a rolling brim covered in folds of blue velveteen, with three quills dyed blue. Her daughters had chosen variations of wide-brimmed hats with low crowns, trimmed with clusters of flowers or fruit.

Lee Muller wore his only suit, wrinkled and appearing to have been made for a larger man. The cuffs of his white shirt were frayed.

That afternoon, more as protocol than celebration, taking fewer than eight minutes, Mildred Alexander and Lee Muller were united in marriage before the Justice of the Peace. When Mr. Muller vowed "Till death do us part," Mildred raised her left eyebrow and winked at Judith.

For a wedding gift Lee's employer presented a two-person gig at a discounted price. Charity came face-to-face with the nag pulling the gig, gazed into its pathetic eyes, and thought, *Surely, upon marriage, Lee Muller will use some of his family's resources to buy a decent horse.*

As promised, she gave the newlyweds a hundred acres: prime land along the creek, a lovely spot for a house, good soil for cotton. She sent letters to her male cousins, urging them to come once the cotton was laid by and build a house on the property. Until then Lee and Mildred would live with her in the overseer's house.

On a knoll overlooking the plantation, a wrought-iron fence surrounded the final resting places of Mildred's forebears. Lives memorialized by engravings in stone. Outside the fence, a little to the east, slabs of decaying wood marked the graves of unidentified slaves. On warm Sunday afternoons, Lee often sat with his Bible beneath a poplar tree near the gate to the enclosure, sometimes reading, sometimes just thinking. As he read sagas about the patriarchs—Isaac, Jacob, and Joseph—he wondered about the stories of those buried on the knoll, both inside and outside the fence. He thought of Samuel, a collector of stories and the dearest friend he'd ever had.

Lee remembered his father telling of German ancestors and generations who'd come down the Great Wagon Road. Their stories buried with them in the cemetery at Sinai Baptist Church.

And his own story?

Like Jacob, tricked into marrying Leah, Lee was convinced he had been trapped into marrying Emma. Mildred, though, was a wife of his choosing, a woman who could read and write—confirmed by her and her sisters' framed common-school diplomas hanging on Mother Charity's parlor wall. That Mildred had challenged his advances, resisted his every effort to charm her, had only made her more desirable. He'd won her through persistence. His marriage to the granddaughter of a wealthy family had increased his status, made him less of a yokel, more of a gentleman. "And they twain shall become one flesh." His and Mildred's stories had merged.

Chapter 22

"Damn!" Mildred yelled as she entered the outside door to the kitchen.

"Don't slam the door," Charity said. "It'll make the cake fall."

An excuse for her inevitable failure. Growing up, she'd assumed she would always have a slave to prepare her meals. Nearly forty years after war's end, she reminded herself that culinary skills were not marks of a real lady, anyway.

"And mind your mouth, young lady," she added.

"You won't care about your cake—or about my cussing—once I tell you this." She kicked the table leg. She kicked the wall. Judith, holding a needle midair over her embroidery hoop, came into the kitchen to see what the ruckus was about.

"Darlin', whatever's the matter?" Charity asked.

"He's gonna separate us."

"What?"

"He's taking me away." Feet planted apart, hands on her hips, Mildred announced, "Lee sold the land."

Charity shook her head in confusion. "Sold . . .? Why it's only been two months since . . ."

"He was just at the courthouse, signing the land over to Elbert Handley. Seven hundred dollars he got. Says we're moving up to North Carolina, over by Pineville."

She buried her head in Charity's bosom. "Mama, I don't want to leave you."

Mildred stood an arm's length from the stove, creating distance between her belly and the heat. "After the ball is over,'" she sang with gusto. She stirred the grits, shoulders swaying to the rhythm. "'After the break of morn/After the dancers' leaving/After the stars are gone.'"

Lee looked up from his newspaper. "Where'd you learn that song?" his voice soaked in disapproval.

At his words Mildred stopped singing and put down the stirring spoon. She stared back at him, her chin lowered, her right eyebrow raised mockingly. "You find fault with what I sing? Seems to me you should be glad I carry a song around in my heart."

He stood, fingertips pressing against the table as if suppressing anger. His tone was measured. "I merely asked where you learned it."

She turned her back to him and resumed stirring. She did not raise her voice. "Lee, I've sung that song pert-near every day since you met me. I'd say that shows how much attention you pay. If you must know, Myrtle Richards's mama and papa have a gramophone. Lovey and I used to go to her house. It's a catchy song, wouldn't you say?"

She began to sing, louder this time. "'After the ball is over, after the—'"

"I won't have my child hearing such songs."

She again turned to face him. "You druther I sing 'Rock of Ages'?" Her eyes had a glimmer he never liked, as if she knew she was getting the better of him.

"It's a song one hears in a beer hall and obviously refers to dancing."

"Now I've never pretended to be someone I'm not. If you wanted a girl who scorns fun, you knew I wasn't the one for you."

"I have nothing against pleasurable pastimes, but I will not allow music of the dancehall in my house."

"In *your* house. Let me remind you that Mama pays the rent here. She sacrifices so that I don't have to live in that hovel across the road that comes with the land you rent. Now go sit in the main room until I call you to dinner."

Newspaper in hand, he stomped out of the kitchen. Maybe she'd get over her obstinacy once she became a mother.

He didn't anticipate Mother Alexander's intrusion. With a flurry she arrived during the last week of February and took over housekeeping—Lee's life, in fact. Her cooking was no better than Mildred's. Unseasoned potatoes, dry biscuits, scorched pudding. Overly solicitous of Mildred's every discomfort, Charity encouraged the expectant mother to remain in bed and contended that only a doctor was worthy of delivering her first grandchild. Her argument offered her the opportunity to retell—how many times had Lee heard the story of Henry's friendship with Dr. Bratton, who had hosted Jefferson Davis when fleeing Richmond. Jefferson Davis himself! She would search for someone as qualified as Dr. Bratton.

Lee argued that giving birth was a natural event. All around the world women did it without a doctor present. He himself had assisted in the births of cows and goats, and a woman was no different.

The small town's only doctor turned out not to measure up to Charity's scrutiny. Finally, she approved the midwife Mildred had already selected.

Lightning flashed, thunder rumbled. In the glow of the oil lamp, Lee tried to read but was unable to mute the incessant moaning and screaming from the bedroom. Not like the shrill squeals and whinnies of sows and horses and goats, but of human torture. During Emma's labor he'd always been sent to the shed. This time the weather had trapped him indoors. He brazenly questioned God's punishment for Eve's disobedience, then muttered under his breath, "Forgive me, heavenly Father, for questioning your wisdom."

Hours later, when he returned with the midwife, both of them soaked to the bone, Mother Charity wrapped the midwife in a blanket and served her a cup of sassafras tea. Lee was left on his own to dry off. "Boil a kettle of water," the midwife told him as she left the room to attend Mildred. More screams, the midwife's soothing voice assuring Mildred, "We're about there. Give it another push." Silence. Total silence. Dear God, Lee prayed, please, please, please . . .

A faint whimper. Another.

When he entered the bedroom, Mildred was sitting up in bed, her disheveled hair wet with perspiration, clasping the newborn to her breast. He leaned over and kissed her damp forehead, then stepped back. Madonna and child.

Mildred's affectionate gaze went to her mother. "We're naming her after you, Mama. Charity. Charity Louise."

Did a father not have a say in naming his own offspring?

Mother Charity took her namesake from Mildred, turned, and with a generous smile placed the swaddled baby in Lee's arms. "Here," she said, "meet your daughter."

His daughter. This beautiful baby girl. He rocked her gently in his arms, his voice laden with emotion: "Dear little . . . little Charity, I shall shield you from all harm as long as I live, so help me God."

Gladys arrived by train, bringing with her a tiny pink sweater and matching bonnet, apparently such a remarkable accomplishment that Mildred and her mother couldn't praise it enough. "Your stitches are so even." "Such soft yarn." A return to "Your stitches are so even."

L'il Charity's birth coincided with cotton-planting time. Despite his lifelong hatred of farming, Lee suddenly looked forward to being out in the field. Looked forward to escaping women's prattle. Looked forward to being alone in his thoughts.

But when he came indoors, there were the three women. Over dinner and supper they incessantly gossiped about people over in York County Lee neither knew nor cared about. "Remember when Papa . . .?" "Remember when Herschel Peterson . . .?" They would laugh or touch each other's hands in understanding. They complained about Pineville, insinuating that Lee was cruel to bring Mildred to this one-horse town. Younts's General Store didn't carry Senger's Baby Powder, and no stores carried suitable fabric needed for a new dress now that Mildred would return to her previous size.

"For the love of God," he shouted when he could no longer restrain his anger, "can't a man have a little peace and quiet? Can you women just quit your yacking while I eat?"

Charity slammed her fork on the table. "Well, I know when I'm not wanted." Her back stiff, nose in the air, she stomped out of the kitchen, followed by Gladys, who huffed and puffed.

Mildred sat there nursing L'il Charity and glared.

Lee removed his glasses, wiped them with his handkerchief as if to clean them, and put them back on. His appetite was gone. He stood, the chair scraping the wood floor as he pushed it out of the way.

He slammed the door behind him and headed down the road, not with a destination in mind but to clear his head. Papa wouldn't have spoken that way, and he shouldn't have either. He wanted them to like him, wanted to be part of their close-knit group.

Was there a way to undo the alienation he'd just increased? It wasn't yet finished, but . . . For months, each evening after dark, he'd escaped to the lean-to, where he'd set up a simple woodworking shop. By lantern light he'd connected the bottom to the sides with mortise and tenon, sanded the surfaces, and meticulously carved a facing with images of apples, pears, and grapes. All that needed to be done was rubbing beeswax into the wood.

In the lean-to he removed the canvas and picked up the nearly finished cradle. As if it were fragile, he set it at Mildred's feet. Without speaking a word, he leaned over and kissed L'il Charity's forehead.

November 1, 1985

Dear Lydia,

Yes, we were always on the move. I don't think it was because Papa couldn't get along. Around others, he was quite an amiable man, with a clever sense of humor and a yarn for every conversation. Only at home did he brood. I'm guessing he had a restless streak and couldn't bear to stay in one place more than two or three years. Or maybe he just wanted to help a congregation get started, then head on to the next one.

He was an excellent preacher, which from my adoring child's vantage point was his strength. Every time I heard him, I was ready to turn my life over to Jesus. I was probably the only person he ever talked out of getting baptized. I would have been seven or eight at the time. He reminded me that it was an adult decision.

Mother was like the assistant pastor, doing everything from cleaning the church to leading the singing. She was the ideal preacher's wife, wasn't she? I never heard her complain, but surely, she disliked pulling up stakes so often. Remember our move from Iowa to North Dakota, how she cried because Papa made her leave her piano behind? Meanwhile, he'd always take along his bookcases and countless boxes of books. It's hard these days to imagine moving all of one's possessions by train.

My next-door neighbor was an "army brat." We've compared notes on what it was like moving a lot as children. No wonder I've lived in the same house ever since Walter and I married.

Keep digging. I'm fascinated by all your findings.

Love,

Dorcas

Chapter 23

King Cotton. King in the sense that those who farmed it were its subjects, forced to make cotton's whims a daily priority, from removing dried scraggle in February through harvest time in October.

A worrisome crop. A cotton farmer worried before he planted it, the cotton seed being particular about conditions. The soil couldn't be too cold; moist, but not too wet. A seed couldn't be planted too deep. Once in the ground it needed plenty of water, leaving a farmer to worry if the rains were late in coming. Every day, Lee looked to the west for forming clouds. He worried about weeds. Pigweed would take all the moisture and starve the cotton plant. He worried about insects, about the boll weevil in particular, which hadn't yet made it this far east—but it was coming, local farmers feared. Granulated cutworms, breeding nonstop, their little white eggs resting on the tops of leaves, but before you knew it they were larvae hiding during the day, coming out to munch all night long. Gnawing right through the stem.

Muscles taut, bulked from years of chopping wood, heaving logs, making sure the plow followed the rows, he worked from sunup to sunset. With a soiled handkerchief he wiped sweat pouring down his face. A farmer. Not a livelihood where a man could apply his intellect.

Oh, blessed Lord, I confess I cannot find contentment. I need a home for my soul.

He left his manure-covered boots on the back stoop, stripped off his mud-splattered coveralls, and opened the back door into the kitchen. Mildred bolted from a chair at the table to a standing position. Like a magician's sleight of hand, she slipped something inside the cupboard.

He already knew her answer to the question he was about to ask: "What're you up to?"

"Oh, just resting a spell while Clarinda takes a nap."

"She was readin' a book," L'il Charity said from the corner where she presided over a tea party with her doll.

"Child," Mildred said, "he didn't ask you."

Lee opened the cupboard and took out the offending book. "Grapes hanging from a vine. The cover says it all. A novel about forbidden fruit, I reckon. Why don't we just sit down and give this novel-reading habit some thought? Again."

At first he'd appreciated being married to a woman with a good mind, had anticipated evenings spent reading aloud to each other by the kerosene lamp. His plan had survived but one evening. "'Call me Ishmael,'" he had read from the book, his tone sonorous and dramatic. "'No, when I go to sea, I go as a simple sailor, right before the mast, plumb down into the forecastle, aloft there to the royal masthead.'"

He'd not even read all of page two before Mildred stopped him. "This whole book's just about men, isn't it? Frankly, I find it tedious." She refused to participate in any more nightly readings.

With Emma, all he had to do was cite the Apostle Paul telling women to be submissive to their husbands, and she acquiesced to his demands. Mildred's streak of rebelliousness often led to the opposite of what he wished. If he said *It's important that we leave for church early,* she'd deliberately make sure they were late. If he said *I want my eggs fried runny,* she'd make them hard. For her, communication between them was a game. As for himself, he sometimes took pleasure in her unconventionality.

Except when it involved reading novels. Women's novels. He'd find them under the bed, behind the chest of drawers, out in the henhouse even. They were responsible for her neglecting her responsibilities. Like her mother she didn't put much effort into being a good cook, and she'd done such a poor job with the laundry—allowing grime to work its way into the fabric of his work clothes—that he'd had to hire a colored girl.

Now he took hold of Mildred's hand and tried to speak in his smoothest and most endearing tone. "Any of those books over on the shelf would be better for your relationship with God than what these lady novelists write."

With her free hand she wiped a stray lock from her face. Smiled a Mildred-smile, which always left him guessing what lingered behind it. "You know I don't want to read your stuffy books."

He resisted a lecture on the gifts of the Spirit. "I've nothin' against novels, if they're of an edifying nature."

"Do I have to keep telling you? Your writers are men, and men all the time have gotta be huntin' or killin' something."

If he lost an argument with her, he felt emasculated; if he believed himself victor, he felt guilt over being an overbearing husband.

He thumbed through *The Awakening* and read aloud. "'But among the conflicting sensations which assailed her, there was neither shame nor remorse. There was a dull pang of regret because it was not the kiss of love which had inflamed her, because it was not love which had held this cup of life to her lips.'" He slammed the book shut. His tone jumped an octave to mimic a woman's high pitch of emotion: "'It was not the kiss of love.'"

"You have no right telling me what I can and cannot read." She stood and started to leave the kitchen. L'il Charity called out, "Mama, Mama, wait for . . ."

"Where do you get these books?" Who was to blame for bringing disharmony into his household?

She faced him, hands on hips, her body seeming to increase in stature and strength. "The women at church. The church, Lee. The women at church. We exchange them."

"So, who owns this trashy one?"

"I'm not saying. You'll tell her husband. And it's not trashy."

"Instead of reading the Bible, y'all are passing smutty novels among yourselves and subverting holiness."

"A lot more holiness comes from our side of the curtain than from the men's side. Brother Allen mumblin' over on y'all's side."

During Sunday school the women's and men's classes were divided by a floor-to-ceiling curtain. Lee often eavesdropped, mainly so he could identify Sister Morrison's misconceptions about the meaning of a certain scripture. As when she said that women should be allowed to preach, when clearly the apostle Paul wrote against it. Not infrequently did someone from the men's side have to stick his head through the curtain gap and tell the women to quiet down.

Clearly, Sister Morrison was a bad influence. But what could you expect of a Yankee? Her education at one of those female colleges up North and her having married the mayor's son made all the church women think she was the nearest thing to God-almighty. She had to be supplying the novels, and Mildred was under her spell. This had to stop.

The train carrying Judith from Yorkville was late. Heat poured out of the potbelly stove into the waiting area crowded with trunks and restless passengers anxious to be on their way south to Charlestown or north to Charlotte. Behind the bench where Lee sat waiting, whiffs of cold air slipped through a rattling window, offering relief from the heat of the stove and human bodies driven inside by rain. In front of him mothers held onto the suspenders of little boys trying to escape. Men hid their faces behind newspapers.

He would have preferred Mildred's mother and sisters not visiting so frequently. Over the course of the marriage's seven years, they had come to recognize the nonexistence of the wealth he'd claimed his family possessed. They made no effort to hide their judgment that Mildred had married beneath her. If he was in the kitchen, they went into the front room. If he was in the front room, they went into the kitchen. If the weather was suitable, they escaped to the outdoors. Wherever he was, they made a point of being elsewhere.

Nearby stood two women of elegance. They'd refused when he and other men offered a seat. Sisters, he guessed them to be. They stood next to a tower of new leather suitcases and round millinery boxes. On the hat of one woman, a stuffed hummingbird made its nest. The hat of the other sister flaunted a cluster of purple plumes. While Lee couldn't resist eyeing the scene with fascination, he disapproved of the extravagance. He suspected these were the kind of women portrayed in the novels Mildred read on the sly. Women more interested in worldly matters than in spiritual ones.

Still, no trains passed through the station. There were whispers of a collapsing bridge, of a buggy stuck on the track, of a man jumping in the path of an engine. Dread permeated the crowded room.

Near one of the doors, Lee noticed a display of religious tracts. Having read the entire newspaper tucked under his arm, he selected "The House We Live In" from the display rack. Eight pages containing the tenets of faith of a religious group he'd never heard of.

"The Brethren preach the Gospel," the tract said. "The Brethren never go to war." "The Brothers and Sisters adorn themselves in plain and modest apparel and utterly repudiate the vain and ever-changing fashions of the world." The tract cited scripture to support every belief. These were serious students of theology, it appeared, the kind of men with whom he'd like to sit down and engage in discussion.

The screech of brakes and bustling inside the station interrupted his reading. All the reasons for the delay had been rumors. On his way out to the platform to meet Judith, he picked a tract from every slot on the rack, seven in all.

Back at the house L'il Charity ran out to greet Aunt Judith, squealing her delight. Mildred, with Clarinda on her hip, took Judith's hand and led her indoors. Knowing his presence was not welcome, Lee remained outside.

The rain had ended but dark clouds raced overhead. To keep his hands warm, he thrust them deep into his coat pockets. His steps were heavy, his head bowed. He followed the ruts in the road, careful to avoid stepping into ones filled with rainwater.

He'd walked about half a mile when he looked up and stopped abruptly. From where he stood on a knoll, he could see beyond the grayish-red flat fields of plowed-under cotton plants. To the north the heavens were the color of slate. To the west there were narrow openings of blue peeking through. He faced south; he faced east. He stood in awe of the vast panorama with its variegated shades of gray and blue.

Across the road stood a solitary oak tree, its ancient branches stretching in multiple directions, its narrow leaves a drab green. On a low branch, in plain sight, a mourning dove perched. Gray and slender, with a peach-colored breast, the bird's beady black eyes met his. For a moment they stared at each other, until the dove took flight.

Old folks said a dove was a sign that somebody was about to die. Mother Charity had reported that on the day of her husband's death one had landed on her clothesline post. Lee's pulse quickened. Who was in danger? L'il Charity? Baby Clarinda? Mildred? Himself?

He crossed the road, sat on a raised root beneath the tree. Though the dove had flown away, its spirit remained. Suddenly, he felt his body drop, as if suspended from a hangman's noose. He was surrounded by walls of dirt. Trapped in a grave, in darkness, he gasped for air. Gasped again. And again. And again.

Minutes earlier he had been studying the sky. But the answer to his unspoken question was not in the heavens. It was in the depths. He resisted making the journey, trying to shoo the spirit of the dove away. Instead, the echo of its coo lured him deep, deeper, yet deeper. Until he occupied a shadowland, where he saw into his own soul.

His soul was empty. It was dead.

Leaning against the tree, eyes closed, he remembered his boyhood. He thought of the men in Mr. Gruen's store, heard them praising his intellect. Other people praising his soul-saving preaching.

For forty years the Israelites had wandered in the wilderness. Forty-one years he'd been wandering Earth. He'd dreamed of being a politician, but Democrats now controlled the state. He'd dreamed of being a minister, but divorce had silenced his voice. He had no future in politics. He had no future in ministry. His mother-in-law paid rent on the house his family lived in.

He leaned forward and clasped his arms around raised knees. He bowed his head. He tried to muzzle the emptiness and hurt. *Every man has his burdens,* he told himself. Had the Lord Jesus not been born in a lowly stable? Had he not lived at the edge of society instead of among the powerful? Could he, Lee, not be content simply farming and being a faithful servant of God?

They came without warning, beyond his control: tears. Tears for the young boy with expansive dreams. Tears for the young man who had aspired to enter politics or ministry. At first he tried to muffle the sobs, then gave in to them. His shoulders shook, his chest heaved, and his breathing was jerky. His deep, throaty wails of sorrow sent a nearby squirrel scurrying up the tree.

He lifted his head and, to the west, saw increasing swaths of blue. Somewhere the sun was shining. Somewhere he could rise from the grave of despair and live in the light of possibilities.

He must find that place.

∞

He addressed a postcard.

General Missionary and Tract Committee, Elgin, ILL.

Dear Brother in Christ,

I have come upon your tracts and desire more information about the Brethren.

I would especially appreciate any document indicating whether there are congregations in my area.

Yours truly,

Leander Muller

∞

Three weeks later, Mildred dropped a large envelope on the table. "Leander Muller, it says. Assume that's you. Church of the Brethren. What's that?"

"A strange sect that offered free reading material. I'm mainly curious."

The envelope contained a recent edition of *The Gospel Messenger*, a periodical. On the first page was an advertisement for fifteen theology books. The back pages listed the name and address of every ordained minister in the denomination. Lee put a faint pencil mark beside churches in North Carolina. Twenty-seven congregations in the whole state, most of them up near Tennessee, none anywhere near Pineville.

The periodical included news from what they called *The Brotherhood*. Sister Brubaker departed this life . . . Brother Kreider led a revival . . . Love Feast was held in this place . . . Sister Hollinger had gallbladder surgery . . . The Ladies Aid of White Branch Church held a successful bake sale to raise money for the mission in China.

Lee mailed the Brethren $1.50 for a one-year subscription.

From the women's side of the curtain, Lee heard Sister Morrison say, "Now, I've taken it upon myself to write a piece that I'm going to read to you today. We can all name the disciples, the men. But Luke, in chapter eight, tells us about three women: Mary, called Magdalene, Joanna, and Susanna. They were disciples too. They ministered to Jesus. Of their substance, Luke says."

I've taken it upon myself to write a piece. I've taken it upon myself to write a piece. Sister Morrison's audience was a Sunday school class of ordinary women. Lee could not be a politician; he could not be a preacher. But no one could deprive him of putting on paper words God placed on his heart.

A writer of theological reflection needed legitimacy. Little chance that the Baptists would publish anything he wrote. What about those Brethren folks? Their congregations were widely dispersed, the nearest one more than a hundred miles away. If his writing appeared in one of their publications, there would be no one to question his legitimacy. But first, he needed to establish a connection.

What would prevent him from starting a Brethren congregation on his own? Not in Pineville. None of the Baptists in town would join a church he was starting. This left him a leader with no followers.

If his goal, though, was to write, not preach, what would be the harm in creating a congregation that only existed on paper? Who would know, given there were no Brethren anywhere near? Where to locate it? Up in Catawba County. What to name it? The Downs family used to live up near Camp Creek before they headed out West. Had to be at least thirty years ago. Downs Chapel, he'd call it.

He began to submit news items to *The Gospel Messenger.*

April 18. NORTH CAROLINA. Downs Chapel church met in council with our elder Leander Muller presiding. We had a pleasant meeting, this being the first council held since Bro. Muller has been ordained elder. Bro. Leander Muller changes his address from Aquone to Pineville, NC. Route 3—R. Thos. Downs, Chestnut, N.C. April 9.

June 13, NORTH CAROLINA. We held our communion service May 30 at 6 P.M. at the close of the week's meeting, conducted by our elder, Leander Muller. Previous to the Love Feast three accepted Christ and were buried with him in baptism. Our church was greatly strengthened and much good has been done.—R. Thos. Downs, Chestnut, N.C. June 2.

In August, when cotton was laid by, he finally had time to write. At the kitchen table he took pen to paper. He printed the title in the center of the page: "Importance of Right Thoughts."

"Thoughts are the indexes of the soul within. If the thoughts are dreamy or ignoble or impure, the life is sure to correspond. We become like the things we habitually admire. By thinking of only the best, we come one step nearer our divine nature."

The editor published his article.

September 12, NORTH CAROLINA. Eld. Leander Muller recently held a series of meetings near Highlands, N.C. and baptized eight. We believe that many revivals might be held in this area with like results.—R. Thos Downs, Chestnut, N.C. September 4.

Word came by telegraph that Mama had died. Without consulting him, Dorothy Jane had her buried in the cemetery among Lizzie's in-laws. It didn't seem right, graves scattered like that. Andrew up in Dakota Territory, Pinckney over in Rowan County with his wife's people. Now Mama at the far end of Burke County, not anywhere close to Papa and Johnny. Lee considered his own burial. He didn't take to the notion of his body being laid to rest someplace where he didn't belong.

For more than a year he sent news items and articles to *The Gospel Messenger*. Until he thought of himself as one of the Brothers. Elder Leander Muller, tied to them by a common theology and by their accepting his words on a page. The fellowship up in Catawba County was growing larger and larger by the month. He was holding evangelistic meetings and baptizing scores of newly saved souls. If something *seemed* true, he decided, and he could convince others that it *was* true, it *became* true.

But sometimes reality smacked him in the gut. He was just a farmer. And not a successful one. He couldn't pay his bills. He couldn't support his two daughters and a wife whose tastes and needs were worldly like her mother's. Even at marriage, a union in which a man was supposed to be the head of the family, he was a failure.

Chapter 24

Mildred had baked sugar cookies—a third of them burnt on the bottom—so that Charity, as she had done her whole adult life, might have a sweet to accompany afternoon tea. For this daily ritual Mildred spread a crocheted tablecloth, a wedding gift, over the small round table in the main room. Seated on the dark green velveteen sofa Charity had given the couple, mother and daughter sipped tea and conversed.

"I have found a worthy cause to devote myself to," Charity announced on the first afternoon of her weeklong visit. Teacup in hand, she beamed a closed-mouth smile. "I and other ladies of influence have organized Rock Hill's chapter—" She set her cup in the saucer. "We're organizing a chapter of the United Daughters of the Confederacy."

Alternating between nibbles of sugar cookies and sips of tea, she expressed contempt for Yankee writers who spread lies about how evil the Southern way of life had been, not even recognizing men like Mildred's grandfather, who'd brought his slaves to Christ. The Daughters were raising money to pay a real historian to write the truth about what it was like before the war, the bravery of Southern boys in battle, and the courage of women left to manage the homeplace.

Mildred confessed to the restlessness stirring within her. She yearned for a cause, too, one worthy of her energy. By the time the teapot was empty and only crumbs remained on the plate, Mildred had decided to organize a Pineville chapter.

The redbud's cheerful blush challenged winter's drabness. Cottonwood pollen floated through the air. The Muller family was taking a Sunday afternoon buggy ride, L'il Charity tucked between her parents, Clarinda on Mildred's lap. Lee held the reins loose in one hand; in the other, his handkerchief was on the ready to cover pollen-induced sneezes.

Mildred had on suede gloves with pearl buttons, a gift from her father to her mother before the war, and the hat she'd worn on her own wedding day: wide-brimmed with a low crown and a cluster of waxed fruit. She was, after all, Charity's daughter and wouldn't think of appearing in public any less stylish.

All was not at peace in the Muller household. Mildred argued, "It's a way to honor our Southern heritage."

"But it pays tribute to the wrong thing," Lee said through a stuffy nose.

"Honoring my father and grandfather and Uncle Arthur, who by the way, gave his life."

"I lost a brother, too, remember."

Mildred scoffed, "After he pledged allegiance to the Yankees."

"To the *United States*. Face it, we lost the war. The heritage you speak of was the one your mother—the memory of all those magnificent parties she still clings to. Do you think poor farmers who fought your war would think it a worthy heritage to honor?"

"Why, Lee Muller, you're a traitor, you are."

"Papa spoke plenty against the war. He was none too pleased that Andrew joined up."

"They're the very ones we're honoring, the soldiers who fought. And I'll have you know our family—most families, I might add—we took good care of our darkies. They loved my grandpa."

"Your granny, too, one of them did. A little too much."

"Ooo, I never should have told you about that. It's the organization's purpose to honor the devotion of Southern women too. The ones who—they had to stay home and . . . Yes, my granny ran off with that, with that—I won't even honor him by calling him a man—but all the time she kept the plantation going. Women suffered, too, and we want to recognize their efforts."

A series of sneezes kept Lee's face in his handkerchief. "Gesundheit," L'il Charity repeated each time. A word Lee had taught her, his having long ago learned it from Herr Gruen.

By now, the fruit on Mildred's hat was bobbing up and down with every shake of her head. "And if we don't write the history—would you have Yankees deciding for future generations what's true and what's not? Our cause was just, and the truth must be told."

Her jaw was firm, her eyes locked into his. She grabbed his arm, clutched it firmly. "Did you know they're building statues of, of—" she spat out the rest of the sentence— "their despicable generals." She lifted her chin in defiance. "I promise you, Pineville will have a statue dedicated to one of our own."

"In that case, let it honor the poor farmers who died and not the generals." He stopped talking to blow his nose. "Anyway," he mumbled, "seems to me your time would be better spent doing the Lord's work."

"Defending the honor of the South is the Lord's work!"

"Pee-yew!" L'il Charity squealed, holding her nose.

"Pee-yew!" Clarinda imitated, also pinching her nose.

The family laughed. Lee applied the whip to urge the horse to move faster past the hog farm. The tension was broken.

For the time being.

The sputtering hickory log in the fireplace, its sweet smell like ham cooking, lessened the December chill. The rocking chair squeaked as Lee bent forward then back, forward then back. Mildred sat on the green sofa, ankles crossed, crocheting a doily, green and white, with extensions like octopus legs. On the hooked rug at her feet, Li'l Charity alternated between tickling Clarinda to make her laugh and pinching her to make her cry. Clarinda pulled Big Sister's braids for revenge.

From the corner of her eye, Mildred saw Lee reach for one of his thin church magazines on the table next to the rocker. "A new life . . ." he mumbled, whether to himself or for her ears, she couldn't tell. For hers, she concluded, when he leaned toward her and pointed to words inside a dark ink square. "See, here's . . ."

Words tumbled out of his mouth. *Jawin'*, she called it, the way he could chatter non-stop like a gurgling spring. About farming: whether the cotton was in bloom or was ready to pick, or how much he expected to get paid per bale. About politics, which Mildred found both boring and disturbing. About God and Jesus. What a certain word meant in Greek.

"They call it church extension by colonization. There's this group of Brethren going to North Dakota, buying land up there and starting a congregation. A mission effort. They've done it before. A while back more than three hundred went by train— even took their livestock and equipment—the whole lot of them moved from Indiana and started a church. This says wheat grows abundantly there." On and on he went.

Until she interrupted. "Too cold up there for me."

"You're a reader of novels. Do they not revolve around someone's unhappiness, and that person goes forth seeking . . ." His voice faded.

Mildred raised her left eyebrow. "I thought you didn't approve of my novels."

"I don't. They stir up women so they're not happy with their circumstances." He reached down to separate the girls. "Y'all stop the fighting now, ya hear? What I'm talking about is different. My dissatisfaction comes from reality, and I see a way out."

"So?"

She was humoring him, letting him get this crazy notion out of his system. As when he wanted to join Cousin William in Texas, then found out the boll weevil was bringing ruin to all the cotton farmers out there. Or when he wanted to move her and the girls to the Oklahoma Territory, then news came that a series of tornadoes had killed more than fifty people.

Now as he talked, her mind wandered from passing L'il Charity's winter coat down to Clarinda—would it fit?—to Mama's forthcoming visit, which would surely include a train trip into Charlotte, where the two would shop along Tryon Street. On the last trip Charity had bought her a hair barrette of silver.

Lee interrupted her meandering thoughts. "Mildred. Mildred. We could buy land real cheap. It's never been farmed, so the soil's rich. And—" he raised both hands, as in a halleluiah gesture "—I could preach."

Mildred tried to conceal a smirk. "These people'll let a divorced man preach?"

He rolled up the publication. Tighter and tighter he rolled it. Finally, he spoke. "I plan not to tell 'em."

"That's lying."

"The way I think of it, Jacob pretended to be Esau because he knew God had chosen him." Lee rose from the rocking chair and came to sit beside Mildred on the sofa. She put down her crochet hook, let the doily rest on her lap. "I believe with all my heart that God has called me to preach." She could tell from the confident tone in his voice that he'd given this careful thought. "You know, God gave Jacob a new name after they wrestled at the Jabbok. God said, 'Thy name shall be called no more Jacob, but Israel.' The Brethren know me as Leander Muller."

Mildred shook her head and scrunched her eyebrows in resignation. How was it that he could always explain away any obstacle to his desires? She picked up her crochet hook and half-completed doily. She'd lost count of the rows.

He'd paced so much over winter that Mildred feared he'd wear a path on her new lattice-patterned linoleum. He said he was praying. She told him to go kneel some place real still-like. He kept on pacing.

One night after they'd just engaged in intimate activity, she rolled onto her stomach, her head turned away from him.

"Mildred . . . Mildred." His mouth was to her ear and he was nudging her shoulder.

"Lord's sake, Lee. Please. Spare me your jawin.'"

"But we need to talk." Not in his demanding *I'm-in-charge* tone, but a plaintive appeal. He had an uncanny way of throwing her off guard that way, so that she wouldn't know whether to respond with resistance or empathy.

But she was tired. "Can't it wait till morning?"

"No. Sit up." She didn't move. "Please."

They sat in the dark, leaning against the headboard, Mildred reluctantly letting Lee hold her hand as he talked. "It'll soon be time to plant cotton, so we can't put off the deciding. I've been praying fervently, *Not my will but thine be done.*"

"And?"

He sounded melancholy, as if he wanted Mildred to share the intensity he felt. "He's calling me to move up to North Dakota. It's fertile territory for mission work." As if an afterthought, "And farmland is cheap."

"Did God say what I'm supposed to do?" Her tone was edgy.

"He always wishes man and wife to be together. So I'd say, yes, God wants you and the girls to come along." He added, "I want it too. I want you there with me."

She would let him say his piece, act like she was genuinely interested. "So, is this church—are they like those Holy Rollers?"

"Everything I read makes them sound like a thoughtful, quiet people."

She yawned. "They like that peculiar group you were part of?"

"I see a resemblance, the way they live in close-knit communities."

"Like those Shakers up in Kentucky?"

"Maybe, a little. But the Brethren marry and have families. Look, Mildred, far as I can tell, they're not all that different from Baptists. They baptize in a stream, like we do, only they get dunked three times. I'd never join them if they baptized babies."

She'd been born a Baptist and planned to die a Baptist. There was no way on earth or in heaven or in hell that she was going to move up to North Dakota and be anything but a Baptist.

Mildred wanted to leave the scene, walk out of the house, and catch the next train to Yorkville. *Home* to Yorkville. She tried to block out Clarinda's high-pitched screams as she thrashed in her highchair and threw black-eyed peas. For reasons Mildred didn't understand, L'il Charity sat back in her chair, tears rolling down her cheeks, arms folded in a refusal to eat.

Oblivious to all this, Lee was mopping up gravy with a slice of bread. "I wish you felt the same commitment. I should have—"

"Lee! Can't you see now's not the time? You've got a way with Clarinda. Please clean her off and calm her down. I'll see what I can do with L'il Charity."

Lee charmed Clarinda into cooperating while he washed her face and hands, then put her down for an afternoon nap. When he returned to the kitchen, Mildred was washing dinner dishes. He took a cotton towel from the rack and started drying them.

"About our earlier conversation at the table . . ."

"As I recall, there was no conversation. The baby was screaming and I was on the verge of losing my mind."

"Well, what I was about to say, I've been praying about our future, and I should have invited you to pray alongside me. Then you'd feel this—"

She took her hands from the basin and placed them on the washstand. She turned to face him. "Do you think I don't pray? That I don't pray every day for my daughters, for Mama and my sisters, that God will keep 'em healthy and protect 'em from harm? Do you think that I don't pray for you, that you will be satisfied?"

"But do you pray that our family will faithfully serve God and do his work? That God will guide us in deciding whether to go up to North Dakota? Here, join me now." He took her wet hand, pulled her toward the table. "Let's pray together over this matter."

She jerked her hand from his, met his pleading gaze with crossed arms. Yet her tone was gentle. "Lee, I can't leave my family. Mama acts real independent, but she needs us girls to stay nearby. It would break her heart for me to take her only granddaughters that far away. You're more like those Bible men who just packed their tents and went all over the place. Me, I like to stay put. This is the farthest I've ever lived from where I was born."

"Does that mean you won't go?"

"Yes, that's what it means. Maybe God's called you, but he did not call me. You're free to make a decision for yourself, though. I won't stand in God's way."

Nov. 30, 1985

Dear Lydia,

It sounds like your trip to the Brethren offices and archive in Illinois was productive. I'm amazed that you found so many references to Papa in "Messenger." Your discovery of the announcement about his daughter's death gripped at my heart. A few times he told me about the sorrow of losing his family. When I asked questions, he'd just hang his head and not answer.

Now we have a name to go with that photograph: Clarinda. And a lovely name it is. Next time you travel back down to North Carolina, I hope you'll be able to find her grave. We can assume, can't we, that it will be near the church he was so active in? Just think, we had a half-sister.

Other than finding her grave, I don't envy your trip. I can think of few things more boring than hanging out in the dark corners of a library and getting a cramp in my neck from staring into a microfiche machine. You always were the more studious and persevering of us two.

I'm not surprised to read that Papa was recognized for his temperance work. He'd turn over in his grave if he knew I keep a bottle of chardonnay in my refrigerator.

Love,

Dorcas

Chapter 25

He'd never been north of Tennessee. Now he was speeding along at forty miles an hour over the prairie, no elevations for the train to ascend and descend, no curves or tunnels, just miles and miles of flat land. Occasionally, he caught sight of a desolate homestead with a small house, a barn, and a windmill. This far north, the occasional tree was still leafless.

Three days of travel. Listening to the hypnotic clickety-clack of train wheels as they scraped against the rails, the penetrating, lonely whistle of the engine, shrill brake squeals as the train came to a stop at a station. When he wasn't napping or conversing with other passengers, Leander read his Bible or gazed out the window in contemplation.

It had all been part of God's plan: the delay in Judith's train arriving; Brethren pamphlets with their clear statements of belief; his articles getting published in *The Gospel Messenger*; news about the mission effort in North Dakota. Now this journey.

Escape, a word that kept coming to mind. He'd wanted to escape farming, but like Baptists back home, the Brethren tended to pair farming and ministry. An honorable way to provide for one's family, he'd finally convinced himself. Did not a clump of soil in hand and song sparrows along fence rows connect a person to the Creator?

By going to North Dakota he'd at least escape a politics he could no longer tolerate. Escape ignorance too. Mildred said he was a snob. He admitted to holding in disregard any who lacked intellectual curiosity.

He'd escaped to Aquone, to Rock Hill, to Peniel, and Yorkville. His experiences in those places had made him a wiser man. So maybe escape wasn't the right word. He was not escaping the past as much as he was embracing a future that offered the chance to serve God. Like farming, a man's life was a sowing and a reaping. Sowing something for the future, reaping something from the past.

"Welcome to North Dakota, Brother Muller."

Brother Jacob Showalter, in a broad-brimmed hat and a heavy black overcoat, was a tall, bulky man with a bushy light-brown beard extending half the length of his belly. Brethren from Pennsylvania, along with their belongings, had arrived by train only weeks earlier, six households in all.

From the train platform Leander looked out over the wide expanse of snow. His teeth chattered and his toes became numb. The Brethren elder took his satchel and guided him to a sleigh pulled by a Morgan mare so splendid that Leander couldn't help but run gloved fingers over its muzzle.

Covered with a pile of blankets, the two men headed out over the plain. Brother Showalter swept his hand across the landscape. "Unfortunately, all this snow covers last year's corn," he said. "Locals couldn't get it all in before winter set in. The fields are going to be too soft for plowing for a spell."

The sleigh pulled in front of a frame farmhouse in the middle of the prairie. Perched on blocks, the house had recently been abandoned by homesteaders who had given up and returned east. They'd also left behind a sod barn now sheltering the Showalters' three cows and more than a dozen chickens.

"Welcome to our humble home," Sister Showalter said as Leander entered the front door. A heavy wool sweater covered her dark woolen dress. A bonnet of white netting covered braids coiled around her head.

"Ma'am, you feed your family mighty fine," he said of the spread Sister Showalter later served for supper. "What do you call this soup?"

The children giggled. The oldest, a girl of about twelve, scoffed, "You never had chicken corn soup? Wait till you've had it a slew of Mondays."

"And Tuesdays and Wednesdays," a boy said.

"Mister, why do you talk so funny?" a young one said.

"Wilma! That's not polite."

"It's all right. What do you mean, young lady?"

"You say y'all, and way-ul for well, and day-owln for down. Your voice, it sounds—it's like you're running a bow real slow over a violin string. You know what I mean, Papa?"

"Well, now, I'm sure we sound funny to Brother Muller, too, seeing your mama and me grew up speaking German."

In truth, they didn't sound funny at all. Their use of *sehr gut* and *Gott sei dank* reminded Leander of boyhood hours spent in the Gruens' General Store.

April 18, 1909

My dear Mildred,

I have arrived safely. The journey, though long and exhausting, was also exciting. I refer to no specific instances, no train robberies, collapsing bridges, or anything of that nature. Often, the view out my window was nothing but flat grasslands. I did, however, have many interesting conversations, as those who travel to this distant state tend to be colorful and ready for adventure.

I am pleased to report that the Brethren here in Englevale have welcomed me with open arms. They have purchased farms abandoned by settlers who were neither as robust nor as committed as they are. The Showalters, with whom I am staying, have seven children, so the only place for me to sleep is in a minuscule room off the kitchen. They are tolerating me until I make a decision about buying or renting land.

While we wait for the ground to thaw, we repair houses. Once we have built barns, we will begin to replace flimsy houses with sturdier ones. All of this work is done cooperatively, each man assisting others in creating a new life here.

How are you? I grow ever more confident that you will be greeted as a Sister in Christ.

Please write to me too. I am anxious for you and the girls to join me here.

Love,

Lee

A misstep would give him away. A hesitation here, a wrong word there.

Members of the well-established Cando fellowship were hosting families from neighboring congregations—*neighboring* encompassing Brethren living as far away as Englevale, a day's trip by train. It was the weekend of Love Feast, an event Leander had read about in *The Gospel Messenger*.

Friday evening, the frame meetinghouse was crowded and noisy. On opposite sides of the center aisle, Sister greeted Sister with the Holy Kiss; Brother greeted Brother. They spoke of the journey's ease: smooth roads, clear weather. Or travail: a child falling out of the buggy, a broken wheel. When three elders separated from the crowd and stood behind a long table in front, a hush fell over the room. Even crying babies calmed.

The quiet didn't last. "All hail the power of Jesus' name, let angels prostrate fall," worshippers sang. Leander joined it with gusto, unable to hear his own voice amid the robust basses and baritones surrounding him.

Then Brother Brumbaugh preached from behind the Elders' Table, holding his Bible in the left hand, stroking his long gray beard with the right. "In First Peter we read, 'But ye are a chosen generation, a royal priesthood, a holy nation, a peculiar people.' Brothers and Sisters, we gather here as a peculiar people. Not conformed to this world but transformed by the renewing of our minds."

Peculiar in garb, Leander mused. Women wore prayer coverings of white netting—black bonnets when worshipping—and modest dresses, all of them cut from the same pattern, while men wore the tieless *plain coat* that buttoned to the neck and had a narrow stand-up collar. Prior to leaving Pineville he'd purchased such a coat through a tailor who advertised in *The Gospel Messenger*.

Mildred was not likely to take kindly to wearing the prayer covering required of women from the time they awakened in the morning until they slept; nor would she exchange a fashionable hat for a black bonnet on Sundays.

". . . with the Lord and with our fellow man," interrupted his thoughts. Brother Brumbaugh paused for dramatic effect, lifted his index finger as if scolding a child. "If there is among us one who would deceive, let him confess his sins." All eyes turned to Leander.

Lord, you know I'm no Judas. I don't deceive for thirty pieces of silver nor to gain any advantage over others. No, that was his imagination.

Brother Brumbaugh had moved on. "It blasphemes the very name of God if we partake of the Lord's Supper without first making peace with all we have harmed."

All? Leander pressed the palms of his hands together, leaned forward, and bowed his head. Over the years he had left plenty of ill will behind him. He had left three boys fatherless. Even when he'd fallen to his knees and cried, Emma had not forgiven him. Now Mildred and the girls were dependent on her mother's largesse.

Had others not betrayed *his* trust? Emma's father had not taken good care of his boys. Mr. Northrop had bedded Miss Iverson at Peniel. Mrs. Cunningham and the residents of Aquone—they had mistreated him.

So much in his past stood between him and God. Between him and others. He feared there was no way he could participate in tomorrow's sacrament in good conscience.

Like many Cando Brethren, the Everharts had built a house for hosting out-of-town guests. Two separate flights of steps led to a divided upstairs, one area for men, the other for women. Leander was to share a large room with four men. Mothers and children, plus two single women, would sleep on the women's side. Others who had traveled a distance were staying in similar homes.

In the Everhart parlor there were no ceramic statues or paintings or mirrors in gilded frames. No bric-a-brac of any kind. While frugal, Cando Brethren had built sturdy houses and barns. Interiors were clean, organized, and practical.

Sipping cups of Sister Everhart's hot chocolate, a cluster of men guffawed, while the women caught up on each other's lives. Children were released from the obedient quiet they'd sustained in the meetinghouse.

A group began to gather around the piano. It was a fine instrument, a Steinway of finely polished rosewood. A young woman sat on the swivel stool, energetically pounding out "Are you Washed in the Blood of the Lamb?" She had removed her black bonnet, wearing instead the white prayer cap that tied beneath her chin. Her green eyes reflected the dark green of her dress. Her plainness reflected a piety Leander felt drawn to.

He enthusiastically joined the singing. But later, upstairs, while bursts of wind slapped the windowpane, he tossed and turned on the pallet. "Is there among us one who would deceive? Let him confess his sins," Brother Brumbaugh had said. If these people knew of his unworthiness, that he was divorced and remarried; that he had created a fellowship on paper only and had no history with this circle of believers . . .

But what choices did he have? Was it not a sin to waste the gifts of intellect and oratory God had given him? Finally, his spirit calmed and he fell asleep.

At a table where several without family were eating together, he set down his plate stacked with scrapple and syrup, fried eggs, and biscuits. The pianist of the previous evening sat across from him.

"Leander Muller," he announced. "Elder Leander Muller. From over in Englevale." To the pianist he said, "And you might be . . ."

"I might be Queen Victoria, but I'm not." A blush came over her face. "I'm Evalina Baker." Her nod to the left invited another woman to introduce herself.

"Prudence Petry."

"Where y'all from?"

"I'm from over near Carrington," Prudence said.

"I'm from Missouri," Evalina said softly. A nervous downward glance had replaced her sassy tone. "Prudence is my cousin. I've been staying with her a spell."

A beguiling smile, his Southern drawl—he used them to advantage. "And you, Sister Petry? You originally from Missouri too?"

"Please, call me Prudence. No, I came out with two families from Ohio. I've got a claim. A hundred and fifty-seven acres in all."

Sisters were not to draw attention to their physical features. Prudence, Leander noted, did not have much to display, at least not as far as femininity was concerned. She had the stature of a man, large and muscular, with traces of a mustache. A woman of the outdoors, whose hands resembled his own, calloused and rough from working the plough and digging in the soil, browned by the sun's rays.

Evalina, on the other hand, did not resemble her cousin. Of womanly proportions, she had intense eyes that assured him she was listening. He watched her hands as they buttered a biscuit, the fingers long and agile. The night before, they had moved up and down the piano keyboard. Graceful, yet strong in conveying the Spirit of the Lord. She wasn't shy, not overly assertive either.

Leander offered an abridged version of himself. "I read in *The Messenger* about our people"—he deliberately chose the word *our*— "starting a new fellowship up here." He pushed a bite of scrapple around to absorb a puddle of syrup, not looking at it but shifting his glance from cousin to cousin. "Down in North Carolina I've been holding revivals, and we're making great strides there. I came north to use the gifts God has bestowed upon me."

"And family?" Sister Prudence asked. "Did you bring family up here?"

Mildred. What to do about Mildred.

His eyes reflected an intense sadness. His chin quivered. "I have a daughter I hope to bring up here as soon as I'm settled."

The cousins both clasped their hands as if in prayer and shook their heads in sympathy.

"The Lord's will be done," Sister Prudence said.

"The Lord's will be done," Sister Evalina repeated.

The soft glow of candle flames. The comforting fragrance of beef that had cooked all day. Seated at separate tables, Brothers and Sisters reverently sang "My faith looks up to thee" in four-part harmony.

Head bowed, Leander took surreptitious glances to his left, to his right. In the sacredness of the moment, he listened to the gentle scraping of the basin against the wood floor. By the time it was passed to him, he knew to kneel and wash the feet of the Brother beside him.

Once the basin for washing hands was passed, everyone turned toward the table for the feast of beef, broth, and bread, symbolic of the fellowship among them. Then Holy Communion—This is Christ's body shed for you and This is Christ's blood shed for you. By the close of Love Feast weekend, Leander felt right with God and with all present. He felt as if he belonged.

As farewells were being said, Prudence Petry approached him. "Come late September we'll be holding a week of revival meetings up our way. I'm inviting you to be our preacher. Would that suit you?"

"Why, I'd be honored." Yes, indeed.

May 2, 1909

My dear Mildred,

Spring is becoming more evident. The ground has thawed enough that we can now plough and ready it to plant wheat. Pale blue prairie crocuses are in bloom.

Brother Showalter reminds me of my father. You were not blessed to know him, but he was a gentle, God-fearing man who would have fit well into this remarkable group of people. They are honest in all their dealings. They are knowledgeable and hard-working farmers as well.

I continue to rejoice over how warmly they have received me. I have twice been called on to preach. Both times my words were well received.

I will say again how happy you will surely be among such kind people. I also think you will find North Dakota an agreeable place to live. Spring temperatures are quite pleasant. I pray to God that in the not-too-distant future I shall be able to fetch you and the girls.

I remain your,

Lee

What he did not tell Mildred was that as much as he shared Brethren beliefs, and as kind as they and others in Englevale were, he often felt at odds with northern ways of social interaction. For him, a son of the South, there were no strangers. But try to engage in friendly banter at the post office or apothecary, ask Brethren or other settlers *How's it goin'?*, and he'd receive a cool reply.

He did not tell Mildred a truth of which he was already certain: she would not be happy among Yankees.

While Leander's knees complained about the hard wooden floor, Brother Martin thanked God for sending His only begotten son, for the salvation bestowed on the believers gathered there, for the rain, for the sunshine, for the birds of the air and fish of the sea. He beseeched God to bless the efforts in the fields of grain and all efforts to win souls to Christ. Finally, to return harmony to the fellowship and "help our dear Sister see the error of her ways."

"Amen." Fourteen worshippers rose from a kneeling position to hear Brother Martin expound on Holy Scripture. Though his appearance and demeanor were austere—a bushy beard of charcoal black and the requisite plain black coat, a sonorous voice—Leander knew him to be a man of humor, whose banter outside this room could create boisterous laughter among the Brothers.

"'But every woman that prayeth or prophesieth with her head uncovered dishonoureth her head: for that is even all one as if she were shaven.'" Brother Martin's gaze went to the women's side of the center aisle. "Should we not all be in a constant state of prayer? And are we not called to witness to our unbelieving neighbors the love and sacrifice of our Lord and Savior?"

Leander also looked in that direction. Sister Neher, a baby on her lap, sat with chin lifted, peering straight ahead. Instead of reflecting a sense of shame, her demeanor appeared self-assured. Reminding Leander of Mildred.

Following the worship service he pulled Brother Showalter aside. "Am I the only one who doesn't know the cause of dissension among us?"

Brother Showalter raised his eyebrows in astonishment. "Have you not heard? An unfortunate situation, indeed. Pray for Sister Neher. We have handled it all according to Matthew eighteen. Just this past week—I was among the three Brothers— we rode out to the Neher place. We prayed with her and Brother Neher, who has tried to persuade his wife as well, but she will not bend. We are left with no recourse."

No recourse? "What, may I ask, is the problem?"

Brother Showalter shook his head in resignation. "She refuses to wear the prayer covering."

"But she had her head covered today."

"Yes, yes. She wears the bonnet on Sunday but refuses to wear the covering at other times."

Would Mildred join the church if membership required her to wear the little white cap day in and day out? If she were to stand out, she'd much prefer it to be over a fashionable hat with feathers or a cluster of fruit on top.

In a letter he tried to open her mind to Brethren virtues. "They are strongly committed to living peacefully with others. They do not swear, they speak the truth." He did not mention the prayer covering. Or Brethren opposition to all war. Mildred was still determined to defend the last one.

As for himself, there was one belief that, like a blister on the heel, rubbed him the wrong way: Brethren did not vote. They did not accept the state as having any authority over them. Neither did they approve of running for public office. Wasn't it a Christian duty, he wanted to argue, to challenge the state, to guide it toward higher values?

May 20, 1909

Dear Leander,

I hope this letter finds you well. You will notice that my address has changed. Mama has been feeling poorly for quite some time and needed extra help. Don't worry, I moved your books here, too.

Mama is taking much delight in having the girls nearby. I find comfort knowing that she is well cared for. Gladys, of course, has been with her, but the two of them do not always get along. I make jokes about their conflicts and am sort of a cushion between them.

I left my work on behalf of The Daughters in good hands. We already had collected money to build a monument across from the train station to honor men from the area who fought for the cause. I will, of course, continue here in my efforts, so that the full story (the true story) is told.

Your,

Mildred

June 24, 1909

Dear Prudence,

I pray that you are in good health and that your work for the Lord is going smoothly.

218

I have yet to determine where to settle. I find that fertile ground along the Sheyenne River has been taken. Anyone selling is asking more than I can afford. I hear land up in Eddy County is going for 20 dollars an acre. Also, your work at Carrington sounds like you might be in need of more workers on His behalf.

Might I visit you so that I can look at land up there and evaluate possibilities for my future? Now is a good time, as the seeding is finished.

Yours in Christ,
Leander Muller

From the other end of the station platform, Prudence and Evalina enthusiastically waved and rushed toward him. Sister Prudence's yellow cotton dress seemed to have been tossed over her head with little attention as to how it might land. Evalina, though, had taken care, her dress crisply ironed, every fold resting as it should.

The journey by wagon to Prudence's claim followed a bank of white cloud feathers in a vast caerulean sky. Now and then a ridge crest looked out over a flat, treeless expanse of green native grasses. On Prudence's tract there was a tarpaper-covered shack, a barn more substantial than the dwelling, and a corral with several head of cattle and calves. Near the barn the metal blades of a windmill whirled.

"You're the first guest we've had in quite a spell," Prudence announced as the wagon came to a halt in front of the shack.

Though the outside was crude, the interior had a homey feeling. Prudence had fastened newspapers to the walls, whitewashed them, then decorated with large swaths of calico. Open windows invited a pleasant cross-breeze, making the gauzy curtains flutter. The single room contained a range with a coal bucket beside it and furnishings she'd brought west by train: a sturdy bed, a long oak table, four chairs, and a large chest of drawers. Her other belongings were stored in a narrow bumpout, where everything had been pushed together to allow room for the pallet Leander would sleep on.

Immediately, Evalina poured three cups of hot coffee and, with a wave of the arm, invited Prudence and Leander to sit at the table.

An awkwardness hovered. The cousins fidgeted with the ties of their prayer coverings. Leander ran a finger around the rim of his cup, took a sip, ran his finger around the rim, took a sip.

"So, Leander, how are you finding North Dakota?" Prudence finally asked.

"The temperature's been quite pleasant." No more words came to him.

Evalina made an effort. "And the meetinghouse. Has construction begun yet?"

"I expect we won't have time to start on it till fall. First, we had to get everybody's wheat planted."

Most likely the caffeine took effect, for he suddenly felt a surge of energy. He straightened his posture, made sure his Southern drawl conveyed charm. "We only just got started replacing our people's sod houses and shacks. The pounding of hammers can now be heard far and wide. I regret that to make this journey, I left the work to others, but this seemed the best time, given the growing season."

He took a deep swallow of coffee. "So, Prudence, what are your plans for the future?"

A gust of wind whistled through the room and sent papers on top of the dresser flying. Prudence and Evalina scurried about collecting them. Leander, as if in his own house, took a bowl from the cupboard to use as a paperweight.

When everything was back in order, Prudence said, "You asked about my plans. Winter was harder than others we've had. Thank the good Lord, Evalina was here with me."

"Why, for days at a time," Evalina said, "we couldn't even get out the door to feed the animals. There was so much snow, we went a whole month without getting any mail."

Once the thought occurred to Leander, it wouldn't leave his mind: Neither of these women had ever been with a man. Prudence probably never would, but Evalina . . . A woman without guile, gentle in spirit. Sisters' dresses had extra folds to conceal the curvature of their breasts, but he was certain that beneath those folds, she had . . .

"My plans," Prudence said. Louder, as if aware of interrupting his thoughts. "You asked what my plans are. Well, I feel called to help the mission effort up here. I also have to support myself. Figured land that's worked for the buffalo will work for cattle, so I brought along a bull and six heifers. Now my herd's grown to eighteen." She shrugged. "For the time being, God's placed me here, so this is where I'll stay."

"And the church? What's happening with it?"

"We're growing. Slowly but surely, as they say. We just took in a Lutheran family from back in Pennsylvania. Trouble is . . ." She placed her elbows on the table, leaned forward, and grimaced. "We've had this happen more than once. A family moving here needs fellowship and, if need be, somebody to lend a hand. But as soon as they get settled and don't need us anymore, they . . ."

"Now, Prudence," Evalina said, "you know that's not the Brethren way. We're about serving God and our fellow man, not thinking about what we'll get in return. Ours is a heavenly reward."

"And you, Sister Evalina?" Leander asked. "You plannin' to stick around?"

"Oh, I've never intended to stay. One winter up here's plenty for me. I'll be going home—probably in November. Prudence and I have always been close, and I felt myself in need of adventure." Her laughter was like her fingers gently racing up the piano keyboard. "I surely got that. Yes, I did."

After supper, Leander helped feed the animals. Homesteaders in Englevale had built on adjoining corners of their land so they could be near others. Not so up in Eddy County. He looked out over Sister Prudence's parcel, tumbleweed rolling by as if it were lonely and in search of other clusters. The vastness of the landscape absorbed the cows' moos, the horses' neighs. He couldn't understand an unmarried woman settling in such a desolate place.

Perhaps it was darkness not setting in until close to nine o'clock. Or, given the isolation, the pleasure the cousins found in having company. Or Leander being enthralled by the women's strength and piety, but mostly by Evalina. In any case, the three overcame their earlier shyness and talked late into the night. These two women were different from any Leander had known. Adventuresome, yes, but also committed to the Lord's work. And they enjoyed rigorous conversation about theology as much as he did.

"Hey, you two ought to be preachers," he said when the evening was over. He laughed at how preposterous the idea was. The cousins smiled weakly.

Leander spent a week in their company. Riding Prudence's horse to several farms, he questioned the feasibility of settling this far north.

Besides, if Evalina didn't intend to stay . . .

He could start a herd of cattle, like Prudence. But except for having kept a few pigs, a cow, chickens, and a mule, he didn't know much about working with animals. Fields of wheat could be ignored for a week or two; animals needed daily care.

If Evalina didn't intend to stay . . .

Mildred's happiness. That must be considered. Even though they had no money to spare, she liked to take the train to Charlotte just to look in store windows. Her starting a chapter of The Daughters had shown him the importance of her having a project.

Nor was he likely to find satisfaction living such an isolated life. He was a social being.

And if Evalina didn't intend to stay . . .

July 12, 1909

My dear Mildred,

It's been a spell since I last wrote. For that, I apologize. Summer being the season of productivity, we're all working long hours. The right amount of rain promises a good wheat crop, and the corn is doing fine. When we men aren't in the fields, we're building houses and barns with wood brought in from over in Minnesota.

The Sisters are equally industrious. Sister Showalter nurses her newborn, bakes bread, ham loaf, and shoofly pie. With the children's assistance, she's put in a garden large enough to feed half of Ransom County.

Our fellowship continues to be strong. I have already preached several times. Everyone expresses appreciation for my thoughts and my ability to articulate the teachings of Jesus. Two new families from Ohio have joined us, and we are reaching out in friendship to our neighbors. Two weeks ago the home of a Norwegian family burned to the ground. With wood intended for our meetinghouse, we built them a house in three days. Windows have yet to arrive from Fargo.

I think you will find the weather here quite agreeable. The days are fourteen hours long and, for the most part, cloudless. I do wish that I might occasionally luxuriate during the long period of dusk, as it is such a lovely time.

Summer's work demands have left little opportunity to search for a place for our dear family. In my mind, I see a homestead that has good soil and is located in a setting of natural beauty. Cottonwood trees all around it will provide shade, and I shall plant lilac bushes so you can inhale their sweet fragrance in the spring. We may not have the house we want at first, but I promise to eventually build you one that suits your desires, for a woman spends many hours of her day inside.

Be assured that God has answered my prayers for a new start. Again, I will say that I'm anxious for you and the girls to join me here.

Your,

Lee

What he did not tell Mildred was that most houses were shacks. That they looked out onto grassland, not lilac bushes and cottonwood trees. That winds strong enough to blow a man over whipped across the prairie, their constant howling keeping him awake at night, fearful his little side room would be picked up and hurled to kingdom come. He did not complain about the stuffiness of the small space he occupied off the kitchen, nor that Brother Showalter could sometimes be overbearing. He did not tell her that, in truth, though summer temperatures did not reach South Carolina's threshold, the humidity was just as sweltering.

Answered prayers? Partially. The settlers were too busy tending crops and building new barns to seek details about his past. Besides, the Brethren assumed basic honesty in others.

Answered prayers? No. He'd wanted to be in the company of those of a scholarly bent. Like the men who wrote articles in The Gospel Messenger. Apparently God willed otherwise.

Meanwhile, God was not answering the prayers of the Glick family. A well driller went down more than 175 feet on their land and found no water. A tornado came through and destroyed their tar-paper shack. After they moved in with the Herschburgers, their infant son died of dysentery.

Leander walked three miles to visit the Glicks. "I, too, once lost an infant son," he said. "I understand the sadness that has entered your life. It's a pain that only God can heal. In God's time." He knelt with them and prayed.

He walked back to the Showalters' with eyes downcast, hands thrust deep in his pockets. In God's time, he'd told Brother and Sister Glick. How long had it been, how many years since the wagon ride in the early morning, when he'd heard Emma scream and felt the stab in his heart? To this day, the sorrow of losing his sweet little boy stayed with him. God's time for healing hadn't yet arrived, it seemed.

Two teams of horses pulled reapers across Alvin Aurbach's fields. Behind them, Leander was one of eight men stacking sheaths into stooks, now and then raising his forearm to wipe beads of sweat onto his already soaked shirt.

Back in North Carolina wheat was grown for family use, some for trading. Up here it was a business. In total, eight Brethren families owned a little over two thousand acres. Now they were racing against time to cut the wheat immediately after it matured.

Without warning, the blistering sun disappeared. Overhead loomed a dark, angry cloud. There was a sudden drop in temperature.

"To the barn!" They all dropped their pitchforks and ran.

Lined up at the barn door, the men peered into darkness like that of late evening after the sun had just set. Lightning lit up the greenish–gray sky. Rain fell in torrents. Hail pounded the earth, balls of ice the size of plums.

"Oh, dear God!" Alvin Aurbach groaned.

Ruined crops. Violent weather. Physical exertion. Numbness of the mind. Leander was reminded that he did not want to be a farmer.

The last week of September, when the wheat harvest was on its way to Minneapolis flour mills, he set out for Carrington. He carried with him his leather folio holding fourteen sermon outlines. As before, the cousins met him at the train station and brought him back to Prudence's ranch.

"Looks like you enlarged the corral," Leander observed.

"Only until fire season passes," Prudence said. A plowed expanse around her shack and corral was charred, the grass deliberately burned. "It's to protect the stock—and me—from a brush fire." She pointed to the east. "Look over there. One's burning as we speak."

In the distance a thick layer of black smoke hung over the land.

Prudence and Evalina had enthusiastically promoted the two-week revival meetings. Fliers announced Leander's sermon titles and there were articles in the *Carrington Weekly Independent*. The meetinghouse was packed on the first night. As word spread of his inspiring sermons, meetings had to be moved to the larger Baptist Church.

During the day Leander helped around Prudence's homestead. He'd like to think he did work a woman couldn't handle, like lift heavy bundles of hay, but there didn't seem to be much that Prudence couldn't do. So, it wasn't surprising when she declined his offer to help her pick up a new kitchen sink at the train station.

"You'd best be devoting time to prepare for tonight," she said. "Not that I'm suggesting your sermons need improving." Already, eighteen new believers and backsliders had come forward during "Just as I Am Without One Plea."

In her absence Leander sat at the table, his Bible and sermon outline in front of him. Nearby, Evalina was preparing a cinnamon and sugar loaf. He found her presence distracting. Despite the extra fabric over her breasts, her wide belt suggested a shapely woman. Her erect posture indicated a sense of dignity, not a haughtiness like that of Mildred's sisters, but a confidence in her good stead in the Lord.

He couldn't help himself.

He stood and approached her, placing his hand at her belt-cinched waist. She turned to face him, and when she did, he lowered his head and kissed her. Full on the mouth.

She drew back, horror written across her face. "Why, Leander!"

"M—m—my sincere apologies, Evalina. My sincere apologies. I don't know what came over me."

He peered deep into her eyes staring up into his. Such beautiful green eyes. Like those of Sassafras, over in Aquone, when Leander placed the harness around her neck. It was not an insult to be compared with a mule, rather, a compliment. For often he'd considered Sassafras's affection for him: the way she nuzzled at the pockets of his overalls in search of an apple or carrot. In fact, after Samuel left, Sassafras had been the only one he could talk to.

"I understand." Which confirmed his associating Evalina's eyes with those of his beloved mule.

A westerly wind carrying smoke from a distant prairie fire forced Leander to hold down the pages of his Bible with a firm hand. "Then cometh Jesus from Galilee to Jordan unto John, to be baptized of him."

He handed his Bible to Prudence and stepped into the stream. The pebbles beneath his feet were sharp; the water reaching his waist was frigid. He extended a hand to welcome the repentant sinner into the water.

He'd mentally prepared himself to baptize the converts: three dunks forward, not one backward, as Baptists did. But when the first person knelt in the water, a girl of fifteen, he nudged her to lean back. She refused. She hunched her shoulders forward. He pushed them back. Then he remembered. "In the name of the father . . ." Forward, "The son . . ." Forward, "And the Holy Ghost." Forward.

Twenty-seven souls were saved that day.

October 15, 1909

Dear Evalina,

Again, I want to apologize for taking liberties the week before last. I do not know what came over me. I greatly value your friendship and that of your cousin. I want you to be able to trust that such impulsive behavior is not in my character and that you need not fear being in my presence.

I find much comfort in your and Sister Prudence's company, as you both follow the examples of virtuous women of the Bible. I am reminded of Naomi and Ruth.

Sincerely yours,
Leander

October 19, 1909

Dear Leander,

Please give no thought to what happened. I understand that a man who has long been deprived of a woman's affections might on one occasion yield to temptation.

All in our small congregation were greatly inspired by your presence among us. Last Sunday the meetinghouse held more worshippers than usual, though I must say there were far more on the women's side. Where would the Brethren (or any other church) be without women workers on behalf of our Lord? I cannot help but think it quite remarkable that you have committed your life to serving the Master.

My plan is to leave Carrington during the first week of November. I will continue to pray for the church at Englevale and for your success in finding land that is both productive and affordable.

Yours sincerely,

Evalina

Leander wrote to Prudence and Evalina: "Might it suit you if I visit again before winter sets in?" What he did not say: *Before Evalina returns to Missouri.*

October 26, 1909

Dear Leander,

I am glad to report that L'il Charity has learned her numbers to ten. I think Clarinda has inherited your gift of gab. I wish you were here to answer all her questions. Why, why, why all day long can make a body grow weary.

Since I last wrote, Mama has taken to her bed. Dr. Cooper says she suffers from a weak heart. I have not told you yet that Judith is expecting a baby in March. Doctor Cooper fears she will not be able to carry it that long, so before Mama's illness Gladys was staying with Judith and William. Now she divides her time between Mama and Judith. Lovey has offered to return from California, but Gladys and I are certain we can handle everything.

I am still able to stay active with the UDC. The Yorkville chapter has already raised a significant amount of money to build a monument, but there is some disagreement about who to honor. I have stressed the value of honoring the memory of local boys who died. Several of the other members want to dedicate it to General Daniel Harvey Hill, as he came from these parts. I have also been putting great effort into organizing essay contests for students. Their work will be judged by how accurately they tell the real story of Southern life before the war. As you know, I consider it important that we not let the Yankee version of events go unchallenged.

I shall close for now, as I have many tasks ahead of me today.

Your,

Mildred

Conversation between Prudence, Evalina, and Leander flowed comfortably at the table spread with pork loin, baked beans, and broiled cabbage.

"I wish you'd go back to Missouri with me," Evalina told Prudence over the dessert of apple pie.

"And forsake our mission efforts here? The harvest is plentiful, but the workers are few."

"I worry about you, a woman alone out here in the middle of nowhere. I saw for myself how cruel winter is."

Leander nodded. "You've gotta respect Old Man Winter."

Evalina's smile implied her gratitude for his support. "Mr. Nilsen told me how he once got caught in a blizzard and got all disoriented and couldn't find his way back home and would 'a died if somebody hadn't found him. He said it happens a lot, folks getting confused."

Prudence scowled. "I suggest you listen less to Mr. Nilsen and his grim stories."

"What if you run out of coal?" Evalina asked.

"I'll use cow chips."

"You could run out of food."

Prudence stood and started to clear the table. "Come now. A body can hardly make it down the cellar steps, so many baskets of beets and potatoes. And there're all those jars of beans and pickles we canned." She reached over to pat Evalina's hand. "Don't you worry. This is where the Lord wants me to be. Now, that is that!"

Besides preserving food in preparation for winter, the cousins had built an enclosed entry to block the cold from entering around the door. They had chinked the chimney and nailed wood strips around the door and windows.

There was work yet to be done. Leander helped pack a thick layer of horse manure and straw up to the eaves of the shack's north-facing side. Along other walls they stacked layers of sod. Their weariness of an evening sent them to bed early.

The wind had picked up. Dark clouds gathered in the west.

"Leander," Evalina called from the foot of the ladder, "you should come down. Prudence says it feels like snow's moving in. We need to put all the tools away and get everything cleaned up."

Suddenly, a gust carried off a strip of tar paper he was trying to fasten to the barn roof. He scurried down the ladder and took off after it. Evalina joined him in the pursuit, one hand holding her skirt above her knees. Whipping about, end over end, the strip skipped across the prairie, Evalina and Leander chasing it until both were winded. Panting, they stood next to each other, leaning over, hands on their knees, watching the tarpaper become smaller and smaller.

Leander stepped closer and placed his hand at her waist. Evalina did not protest. They remained that way, still trying to catch their breath.

Finally, he removed his hand. Slowly, wordlessly, they walked back to the shack.

Snow began to fall before dark. At Sister Prudence's insistence, Leander brought the pallet, quilts, and buffalo cover into the main room, near the stove. All night long he was kept awake by the wailing of the wind, the slap of snow against the outside walls, the shack trembling on its fragile foundation. Morning brought no relief. The windows were encrusted with ice.

"I'll go out to the barn and take care of the animals," he volunteered.

Prudence chuckled. "You really are a Southern boy. You're heading out into— we don't even know how deep the snow is—but you plan to head out there without boots on? And all you've got is that coat that wouldn't warm a dog in weather like this. I'll go."

He didn't relent. In her boots and heavy coat, plodding through blinding snow, he followed the rope from shack to barn, where the livestock snuggled against each other in the straw. He fed the hogs and cow and milked the cow. As for the safety of her cattle out on the range—one could only pray.

Rather than a hardship, the days of confinement with Prudence and Evalina were a gift. There was no shortage of ideas to keep them entertained. Bible study in the morning, followed by the singing of hymns. Evalina's strong soprano voice leading, Sister Prudence harmonizing with the alto, Leander bellowing out the bass.

> *From Greenland's icy mountains/From India's coral strand,*
> *Where Afric's sunny fountains/Roll down their golden sand;*
> *From many an ancient river/From many a palmy plain They call us to deliver/*
> *Their land from error's chain.*

Afternoons, the three napped and read; evenings were spent playing Rook. At first, Leander objected, claiming that the playing of cards tempted one to move seamlessly into gambling. But once Prudence and Evalina assured him that Brethren in the East approved of this new game, he took it quite seriously. "Aha!" he would shout triumphantly, pounding the Rook card on top of a round.

On the third morning they awoke to an eerie silence. The gale-force winds had stopped, as had the snow. Prudence mocked his suggestion that he could now return to Englevale—though he didn't really want to leave. Five-foot drifts blocked the lane. Who could predict how long it would take for roads to open?

Aboard the train back to Englevale, Leander took out his pencil and pad of paper. "It is not enough," he wrote, "to say that we cannot keep unwholesome thoughts from rushing into our minds. Repeated efforts will eventually keep them at bay." Evalina's face, while not beautiful, glowed with piety. Her breasts beneath the pleated bodice ... "When an impure thought makes its way into our consciousness, we should at once turn our minds to something beautiful." His hand touching her breast ... "If there be any virtue and if there be any praise, think on these things."

Oh, dear God, forgive my lust.

He saw only one way to free himself from this torture: He must tell Evalina about Mildred. He would say I am married and the father of two daughters. She would—no, he must first apologize for not telling the truth earlier. After the apology he would say I am married and the father of two daughters, and she would blush—she was the kind of woman to blush over her own thoughts. Assuming she reciprocated his feelings. Her eyes said she did. So, she would blush and feel ashamed. He must tell her she had no reason to feel shame. It was his fault for ... no, he had not lied, only offered minimum information. She should not feel shame. But if he told her he was married, she would—because she was a woman of virtue— she would not smile at him and speak of fondness with her green eyes.

All of these thoughts, useless. She was heading to Missouri, and he was bringing his family to North Dakota.

November 20, 1909

Dear Leander,

I arrived home safely on Tuesday. The weather here agrees with me more than that of North Dakota, though during the past two days we have had temperatures below freezing.

Papa continues to experience great pain from lumbago. A neighbor has urged him to seek healing at the Weltmer Institute. Papa is usually a mild-mannered man, but the notion of magnetic healing galls him no end. He says it is all voodoo and un-Christian.

Instead, he asked to be anointed. He was deeply moved by the service and already has more energy than he has had in recent days. I am not claiming he was healed, only that the occasion was laden with spiritual strengthening. Mama has expressed gratitude for my presence, as dealing with Papa has been fraught with trials and tribulations.

My main joy in having returned is that I can again play the piano. In my absence, ours has gone quite out of tune, so I shall take care of the matter right away.

I hope you are doing well and that with God's grace, you are not suffering much from winter. I pray for you daily and thank God for your friendship.

Yours truly,

Evalina

He promised God that his letter in response to hers would mention Mildred. It didn't.

April 27, 1986

Dear Lydia,

What a disappointment that another trip down to North Carolina offered no new information. Your research into Papa's past is a conundrum, to say the least. I'm puzzled that there isn't a Church of the Brethren anywhere in Burke or the surrounding counties. So where are the graves of Clarinda and her mother? It's puzzling that a man named Leander Muller, with a daughter named Clarinda, shows up in Pineville, NC, in the 1910 census with a wife and a second daughter. But that man can't be Papa, as he was in Cuba then, and his wife and daughter were deceased.

I'm sorry I can't be of any help. The thought of spending hours delving into all that genealogical stuff bores me to tears. But I'm grateful for your determination.

Love,
Dorcas

Chapter 26

During the Brothers' first growing season in Englevale, their crops hadn't done as well as anticipated. Swarms of yellow grasshoppers had devoured corn sprouts. A dry spell had stunted the growth of the Sisters' vegetable gardens, a hailstorm had ruined the Aurbachs' wheat. And still, Leander hadn't found a homestead he could afford to buy.

The Fitzwater family planned to spend the winter back in Indiana, where a relative offered hospitality in a house with fireplaces, indoor plumbing, even electricity. Families up in Cando were already leaving for the winter, with plans to return in early spring.

Leander's teeth chattered most of the time, indoors and out. There were days when the wind screeched and swirled so fiercely that he couldn't walk upright. Nights were growing longer and daytime temperatures hovered near freezing. He dreaded mornings, when he had to step from under a pile of quilts out into the frigid room where his breath created wisps of clouds. The single window, its edges stuffed with rags, remained caked with ice. Take Dr. Peter's Blood Vitalizer, Sisters and Brothers advised.

A special meeting was called for a Saturday afternoon. Others knew the two men. From Ohio, Leander was told.

"Sisters and brothers off our southern shores hunger for the Word of the Lord," one said.

"We have the opportunity," the other said, "to again send several families to a single place so that we might win hearts and minds to Christ."

"The climate is warm."

"The government is now stable."

"The climate is warm."

"The sugar cane economy is thriving."

"The climate is warm."

Leander had confidence that his future was with the Brethren. But Mildred, he regretted, instead of being committed to spreading God's word, was applying her energy to building monuments to leaders of the insurrection. And Charity, ill now, looked back with misty eyes to the days when slaves had responded to her every whim. Mother and daughter were devoted to the past. Brethren were focused on the present. Working to further God's kingdom must be done now, and Cuba was the place to be.

The climate is warm.

Evalina. Her expressive eyes, her . . . her . . . her womanly body. Would she go to Cuba? To so much as pose the question would be the same as proposing marriage.

If Mildred would not go . . . If he dared not invite Evalina . . .

The climate is warm.

Another blizzard attacked the area. He spent days and nights in the main room of the Showalters' house, where everyone gathered near the coal-burning stove. Despite the folded braided rug pressed against the front door and rags stuffed around window frames, cold found its way inside.

There was a sameness to snowed-in days. The older Showalter children argued over checker moves, the middle ones moaned about being shut in, the youngest competed for Sister Showalter's lap. Several times she roused an energetic song. "The old gray mare, she ain't what she used to be." Leander yearned for quiet to read the Bible or a book from Brother Showalter's meager library.

Outside, the wind howled incessantly. Every morning, Leander and Brother Showalter, along with the two older boys, checked on the stock, following the rope between house and outbuildings, fighting against the wind to carry hay. Back indoors, they stomped snow from their boots, removed overcoats, caps, and mufflers, then rubbed their hands together in the warmth of the stove. Whirling snow had frozen Leander's eyelashes, and his lips were sorely chapped.

How strange, he thought on the fourth morning. To be awakened by quiet, when all night long the wind's fury had shaken the house. To be greeted by the fragrance of brewing coffee. Bright sunlight made the fresh snow glitter like stars scattered across the night sky.

Word circulated that Brother Shoemaker, up in Cando, had lost his way and frozen to death when returning from town. If this wasn't yet winter, what would January be like?

It was time to decide. Prove his grit by spending the winter cooped up in North Dakota? In the room off the kitchen where his hands were too stiff to write, or in the main part of the house populated by noisy children? Or did God will him to go to Cuba?

Finally, he decided to return to North Carolina, but only for the winter, so that he might convince Mildred to return north with him. Or perhaps she'd be more amenable to moving to Cuba. In either case he could spend the winter writing in the warmth of a fire.

The day before he boarded the southbound train, a letter from Evalina arrived.

November 20, 1909

Dear Leander,

I arrived home safely on Tuesday. The weather here agrees with me more than that of North Dakota, though during the past two days we have had temperatures below freezing.

Papa continues to experience great pain from lumbago. A neighbor has urged him to seek healing at the Weltmer Institute. Papa is usually a mild-mannered man, but the notion of magnetic healing galls him no end. He says it is all voodoo and un-Christian.

Instead, he asked to be anointed. He was deeply moved by the service and already has more energy than he has had in recent days. I am not claiming he was healed, only that the occasion was laden with spiritual strengthening. Mama has expressed gratitude for my presence, as dealing with Papa has been fraught with trials and tribulations.

My main joy in having returned is that I can again play the piano. In my absence, ours has gone quite out of tune, so I shall take care of the matter right away.

I hope you are doing well and that with God's grace, you are not suffering much from winter. I pray for you daily and thank God for your friendship.

Yours truly,

Evalina

Chapter 27

Instead of asking fellow travelers where they'd been, where they were headed, what they thought of the weather/landscape/President Taft, Leander alternated between napping, reading the Bible, and praying for answers.

He'd told Englevale Brethren that he'd return, although going to Cuba remained a possibility. There he could experience the excitement of living in a new culture, the challenge of being part of another mission effort. The downside: Once again he'd have to support himself and his family by farming. He knew nothing about growing sugar cane or coffee or oranges.

Another option: The church in Nevada, Missouri, was small but could offer employment. The word itself implied security and status. Like Reverend Gibson, Leander could incorporate reading and study into his days. But he couldn't take Mildred there. She and Evalina did not belong in the same town, not even in the same state.

When the train crossed into North Carolina, his body recognized the demarcation, the inner conflict between homecoming and a reluctance to return. Later, in South Carolina, when the brakes screeched and the train came to a gradual halt in Yorkville, there was a tightening of the chest, the clenching of teeth.

His first thought upon waking: *I am warm.* Mildred's body lay beside his under a down comforter. The bed springs squeaked as he rolled over to face her. In the dim morning light, he could see locks of hair peeking out from under her nightcap. Faint snores escaped her slightly parted lips.

He rolled onto his back, placed his hands behind his head, and peered up at the cracked ceiling. Evalina was up there, perched on a piano stool, her lithe body leaning to the left, to the right, to the left. Her fingers magically moved from one end of the keyboard to the other.

Father, forgive me.

What was there about Evalina that attracted him? The word *passive* didn't fit. *Receptive*, maybe. He'd originally seen Mildred's spunk as a challenge, but a man could tire of having to corral a woman. Or had Evalina drawn his attention because he was far from home and lonely for a woman's affection?

Far from home. Where was home? Seven years had passed since he and Mildred had lived here with Charity in what was once the overseer's house. There had been little space for him then; there was even less now. His bookcase, which Mildred had moved from their Pineville home, now held Charity's medicines, the girls' toys, and sundry knick-knacks. His books were in crates.

From across the hall came Clarinda's cry, "Mama!" Mildred stirred, stretched, and sprang from the bed. "Comin', darlin.'"

Leander's return seemed to throw the household into upheaval. Accustomed to an abundance of attention, Mother Charity refused to relinquish any on his behalf. She was hungry; she had no appetite; she was exhausted; she wanted to go on a buggy ride. If Mildred wasn't responding to her mother's whims, she was seeing to the girls. At other times she was absorbed in the work of the Yorkville chapter of— *The Daughters*, she called it. Gladys remained ever-present, incessantly talking as she tended to the cooking and cleaning. More like a servant than a member of the family.

The girls had grown in the nine months he'd been away. Clarinda seemed not to remember him. During the day L'il Charity stood back and stared at him as if trying to figure out his relevance in her life.

One afternoon, while Mildred and Gladys were heaven-only-knew where, while Mother Charity and Clarinda napped, L'il Charity stood in the doorway of the parlor, where he was reading.

"Come," Leander said, patting his knee as an invitation. Timidly, she approached and climbed onto his lap.

"How would you like to go to where there's snow?" he asked. "And we can build snowmen, and you can take a sled to school?"

"Will Mama go too?"

"Of course."

"And Clarinda?"

"Of course."

"And Gamma Charity?"

"If she wants to go."

"And Aunty Gladys?"

"If she wants to go."

The long list of potential travelers north took him by surprise. How often had he heard Mother Charity say she would never leave Avalon? She'd even selected a site next to her husband in the family cemetery. If by chance—and chances were slim—if by chance Mildred and Charity agreed to move, Gladys would go too. The image of all three women adopting the Sisters' bibbed dresses and white prayer coverings was almost laughable. Pioneers on the North Dakota prairie? Living in a dwelling bigger and sturdier than Sister Prudence's, but a shack all the same? Gladys would chatter non-stop, and Mother Charity would demand attention, and the girls would be forced to stay indoors on frigid days—all too frequent. Worst of all, he'd have no place to escape to, no place where he might read.

Mildred would never accept the humiliation of mingling with Yankees. In conversations with the Sisters, she would defend slavery, which they would report to their husbands, who would hold a meeting for the sole purpose of dealing with her. She would be dismissed from the fellowship, and he . . . Leander . . .

Cuba? Mother Charity certainly wouldn't cross waters to a foreign country where English was not spoken, and if Mildred had an adventuresome side, she'd kept it hidden.

What if he asserted his headship? We're settling in North Dakota, he would tell Mildred, and you and the girls are coming with me. Only you and the girls. No, she didn't take kindly to being told what to do.

But he didn't want to live in North or South Carolina. The Carolinas meant exclusion. The Baptists had expelled him. The Democratic Party exercised raw power, and a white Republican who spoke out was accused of alliance with colored people and risked being killed by the Klan. Keeping silent was the coward's choice. A man of courage, he was not.

The household had returned to earlier routines as though he weren't present. If his mother-in-law engaged with him at all, it was to reminisce about her girlhood and what a wonderful husband Henry had been and about the day Jefferson Davis came to their house. Gladys and Mildred shared responsibility for meeting Charity's needs—assisting her with bathing, taking her for walks over to the ever-decaying main house, and listening to her repeat memories about her girlhood and what a wonderful husband Henry had been and about the day Jefferson Davis himself came to their house. Seldom did L'il Charity and Clarinda play quietly. Their arguments irritated Leander, trying to read in the warmth of the stove.

"You shooed them outside without their coats on!" Mildred yelled.

"Doesn't anyone discipline those two?" Leander yelled back.

During his absence Mildred had become a woman of incredible energy, darting from one task to the next. She rose early to prepare a breakfast of eggs, grits, and sausage, then spent the rest of her day meeting the whims of Mother Charity and the girls, conversing with Gladys, and working on behalf of The Daughters.

Much of her work for The Daughters was undertaken on a Remington, paid for by her mother. The click-click-click of her typing could be heard at various times of the day. Letters to school officials, urging their support of curricula telling *the true story* of the Confederacy. Letters to women, encouraging them to submit stories of how they had survived Yankee atrocities. Letters to persons of influence, inviting them to attend Confederate Memorial Day.

Leander recognized the Remington's potential in his own writing aspirations. When Mildred wasn't pecking at its keys, he tried to learn the basics of the machine.

He typed a "Letter to the Editor" of The Gospel Messenger: "Pride and fashion are the two great instruments Satan is using today to destroy our church."

He typed a news item:

January 15, NORTH CAROLINA. Elder Leander Muller of Englevale, N. Dak, came to this place and held a week's meeting, preaching fourteen sermons and baptizing seven. He was invited to deliver a temperance lecture in the Methodist Church. There were about 600 people present, and they were not disappointed, for the lecture was excellent. Bro. Muller is a strong temperance worker. Iva Lee Moore, Chestnut, NC, Jan. 3.

February. Still no word in *The Gospel Messenger* about the Missouri church hiring a pastor. The Brethren had abandoned the idea of going to Cuba, Leander had heard.

He ought to tell Mildred what he was thinking. But only in their bedroom could they be alone, and there she would immediately fall asleep, or Clarinda nestled between them, or his body's desires governed the moment.

MINISTER WANTED. The few members of the Nevada, Mo. church are searching for a resident minister. We appeal to those ministers who contemplate a change to correspond with us. Sunday school is held regularly, and there are two preaching appointments a month. Carthage, Mo.

Leander sent a letter of application.

Leander climbed into bed. "I'm thinking we need to get away together," he told Mildred. "Take the train to Charlotte for a day, get a Coca-Cola, maybe shop at Belk Brothers. You could use a new pair of shoes, couldn't you?" He trusted Mother Charity to provide the funds.

Mildred surprised him by moving closer, snuggling against his body. "And we can ride the streetcar and look in store windows. Maybe instead of shoes, I'll get a new hat."

The bed springs squeaked.

It was as if she'd been released from long-term confinement, the way Mildred walked up and down the aisles of Belk Brothers. She wore her mother's hat, a maroon one that sported a constellation of pink feathers and dwarfed her face. Leander followed close behind, lest she turn up an aisle without his noticing. She fingered the Chinese silk of a blouse, the brocade of a purse. She admired the narrower sleeves of blouses and tried on befeathered and beribboned hats equal in size to the one she wore. He turned away as a clerk showed her the latest in corsets. "You'll find them less restrictive," the clerk promised.

"We must take back something for the girls," Mildred said. "Oh, here are some darlin' sailor suits. Wouldn't L'il Charity look cute in this?" In the men's department she playfully plopped a homburg on his head. "And you need a necktie," she said, peering into the display in a glass case. "I hate that suit you wear now. It looks like you belong back in Europe a hundred years ago."

He smiled as if he approved of everything she admired. Finally settling on hair bows for both girls, she opened the silver clasp of her crocheted purse.

At that moment Leander knew. In witnessing the mere act of her handing the clerk a dollar. The purchase was more than a simple financial transaction. It was who Mildred was, the woman beneath the feather-laden monstrosity of a hat. A daughter of privilege, for whom one of life's greatest pleasures was shopping. Not that he'd been blind to her indulgences before. In fact, they had both attracted and frustrated him.

How many times had he transplanted seedlings? A tomato plant, a cabbage plant. Placed in alien soil or set out when it was too cold, their leaves would crinkle, turn black. Mildred would not tolerate transplanting.

Later, when entering the restaurant of Hotel Selwyn, Leander observed anew the sense of entitlement that accompanied her. There was haughtiness in her stride, femininity in the tilt of her head. Once seated, as if she had every right to know who else was present, she looked around without gawking. No matter how nonchalant he tried to appear, he was an interloper.

"Mama says influential men meet here." Finger by finger she removed her gloves. "I'm sorry. I should pay you more mind." Her gaze fell to her lap, where she'd just placed her gloves, then lifted to stare into his eyes. "I take it you have a purpose in bringing me on this outing. Otherwise, you couldn't abide accompanying me up and down store aisles."

He took a deep breath. "I do. We needed to be away from family, in a place where we can talk freely."

She nodded, raised her right eyebrow to suggest a question, but did not speak.

"I've met with success among the Brethren. Their beliefs are in harmony with mine, and they respond to my preaching. In the past I've told you of my longings."

The large hat cast a shadow over her eyes, hiding whatever attitude she held at that moment. But her tone was calm. "You're not asking me to go up to Dakota, are you? You know I can't leave Mama."

"No, I'm not asking you to go there. I've come to accept that you—and I'm not asking you to leave your mother. I'm not sure what I'm asking. Maybe that you consider . . ."

"Consider?"

He took a gulp of the Coca-Cola the waiter had placed before him, a larger swallow than one accustomed to the drink's fizz would have taken. A brief coughing spell overtook him.

"She'll go if you go," he finally said. "I want you and the girls with me. And your mother."

She brought the linen napkin to her mouth, dabbed at her lips. "You said you'd not ask me to go, but you just did."

"Yes, yes," he muttered.

Between them hovered an uncomfortable silence, while in the background could be heard conversational murmurs, forks scraping against plates, plates clanging against each other.

"Mildred, since I was a boy . . ." He abhorred making the comparison but wanted her to understand. "It's a little like your work for The Daughters. You're committed to getting the word out, what you believe is the truth." He took a deep breath. "God has called me to preach his word."

"Then you must follow that call." Spoken without rancor.

He made a sudden decision. "Two other families I know come back East when it turns cold. That way their children can go to school all winter. I'll come back this time next year."

By returning to North Dakota he could be part of the Brethren fellowship most of the year but be a husband and father over winter. Yes, he'd do that.

A letter arrived. The Nevada, Missouri, church wanted him to begin employment in April. God was calling. The church was calling. Evalina was calling.

Dear God, what am I to do?

Clarinda, who had traveled with him by train, sat hesitantly on the lap of this woman she didn't know. Sadly, Dorothy Jane's influence in his daughters' lives would never match that of their maternal aunts, but Leander wished they could recognize her importance to him. He'd have brought L'il Charity along, too, had she not been old enough to understand adult conversation. He dared not risk her going back home and chattering away to Mildred all she'd heard.

They sat in Dorothy Jane's front parlor, brother and sister facing each other on matching wooden chairs with red velvet cushions and ornately carved backs. From the nearby fireplace came pops and sizzles.

"The Good Book says," Leander began, "'Behold, thou desirest truth in the inward parts.' That's why I'm here. I need a dose of truth . . . and some of your wisdom to go with it."

"'Truth in the inward parts,'" Dorothy Jane repeated. "Okay, you've got me all curious. What's going on in those inward parts of yours?"

"I follow the Commandments, I keep the Sabbath holy, I don't steal, I've never killed anyone, and I don't take the Lord's name in vain—well, on rare occasions, I confess. I keep the Sabbath holy and am a serious student of the scriptures. I express gratitude for every meal, kneel and pray every night before I go to bed, pray at other times as well."

His sister tittered. "Am I s'pose to be impressed with your piety?"

Leander chuckled too. "Guess I hold you up there with God Almighty himself. If you say I'm pleasing in your sight, God is sure to agree. See here, an opportunity has come my way, the chance to do what I've dreamed of doing for most of my life."

"Something having to do with politics?"

He grimaced. "You know my own brother-in-law wouldn't vote for me. No, I've been called to a preaching position. A job. A profession. I wouldn't have to work behind a mule in a cotton field. Hopefully, never again."

"Ahn-tee?" Clarinda pulled on Dorothy Jane's collar.

"Mind your manners, child," Leander scolded. "Adults are talking."

"But, Papa, I gotta pooh."

"Josie," Dorothy Jane called, "come help Clarinda." A young Black woman entered the room and took the child by the hand.

"The job offer," Leander said, reminding them both of where the conversation had been interrupted. "It would be wonderful, but a few things stand in my way."

"Oh? Like what?"

"Mildred," he said glumly. "See, in North Dakota I discovered the Brethren and I are as good a fit as a hand in a glove. And now a Brethren fellowship out in Missouri has issued the call."

He leaned forward in the chair, hands on his thighs, elbows jutting out. "Mildred, she's a—you could say she's—I'm afraid she has no room in her heart for a Christian group that values simplicity as they do." He fingered his coat buttons. "What I wear now is the plain suit of the Brothers. No tie, no lapel. The Sisters reject the fashions of the day. Folks recognize them on their treks into town by the white bonnets they have on. You've seen Moravian women wear something similar.

"At issue is—she's under—Mildred thinks I plan to return to North Dakota. It's my fault for leading her to—but it was my intent to insist that she and the girls accompany me. At least on the day I told her. Of course, she'd not leave her mother and sisters, and I'm just as positive that she'll never consent to Brethren . . . the clothing and all."

"You started out talking about truth in the inward parts. Whatever did you mean?"

"I'm like a boy who's outgrown his clothes. I've outgrown the body of my younger self. I'll be forty-four this year. If I don't seize this opportunity, if I don't go, I'll be stuck in the Carolinas for the rest of my life, growing cotton, unwelcome in the pulpit of Baptist churches, and yoked to a woman more committed to the South of old than to Christian values."

He stood and paced, his eyes following the seams in the flooring. "There's more to my dilemma."

"Oh?"

He knelt in front of her, taking her hand. "I'm not meant to be celibate."

"Oh." She pursed her lips. "I see."

"Do you?"

"I reckon these folks know you've got you a family." A question or a statement?

"Uh, no. I haven't exactly lied. I told them I have—I have a daughter down here. I let them assume . . ." He returned to sit in the chair, buried his head in his hands. "No man can hate himself more than I do right now. I already let down one family. I loathe the idea of leaving Mildred and the girls." He ran his fingers through his hair. "But if it's God calling, and if he hasn't touched Mildred's heart, what am I to do? Over and over I've prayed, but he isn't offering clear answers. That's why I'm seeking your advice."

Dorothy Jane stood, took heavy steps over to the fireplace. Her back to Leander, she stirred the sizzling logs and embers with a poker. Kept stirring, deep in thought. "Little brother, I think—since you was a tyke—remember when that story grabbed holt you? Something about a boulder that looked like a face. And the two of us, we talked about you someday being great like the man in the story. I've always known you'd someday be—someday you'd be doing important things."

When she turned to face him, her eyes revealed a sorrow he recognized from when Papa had died. "What I'm about to suggest—God forgive me—what if you was to arrive alone and say your little one died while you were home?"

She rested her hand on the back of the chair as if posing for a photograph. "Many a man's lost his family to disease. Listen, God gave you a good mind. Wouldn't he want you to use it?"

As far back as he could remember, Dorothy Jane had been his closest ally. A speaker on his behalf before he had words. An emboldening voice since his adolescence. Now, *Tell them your little one died.*

Did Dorothy Jane speak for God?

Mildred sat in front of her Remington. In nearly half an hour, she hadn't pressed a single key, just gazed from one corner of the ceiling to the other. Confederate Memorial Day was only a month away, and she hadn't started writing her speech. It was her first time addressing a large crowd, and she wanted her words to make people take notice of both her passion for the subject and the importance of the ideas she presented.

The points she wanted to discuss were all jumbled. The younger generation born after the war, they were the ones who most needed to hear. About the humiliation the South had endured during Reconstruction, and how prominent men of education and wealth had been denied participation in the new government. Carpetbaggers and scallywags, she should mention them, too, how they'd handed power over to ignorant Black men. And the ambitions of Black men to have white women. And how the Ku Klux Klan had stepped forward to protect the honor of the South and Southern womanhood. And the strength of South Carolina women who had been left to manage plantations and survive Yankee humiliation while their men were off to war.

She wanted to ask for Lee's assistance. But he'd mock her ideas, criticize her for wanting to protect the honor of the South. She looked over at him seated in the easy chair, watched as he set aside his book to open the bulky dictionary resting on the arm of the chair.

"I'm interested in how you approach your sermonizing," she finally said. "How do you know what order to put your ideas in?"

He looked up from his book. "I make an outline. Decide what points I want to make. I only choose two or three, because I want people to remember them afterward. Any more than three and they won't be able to tell you even one later on."

"How do you decide what the important ones are?"

"They're the ones I can say more about."

"Can you give me an example?"

He lowered his head and peered at her through the top of his glasses. "Why this sudden interest in how I organize a sermon? You've never cared before."

She took a deep breath, anticipating his reaction. "I've been asked to speak at Confederate Memorial Day."

"Woman, you're fixin' to embarrass yourself."

"I take offense at that. You're not the only one in this family who's able to deliver a stirring message. Once I'm up there talking I'll be fine. I just need help organizing my ideas."

"What I'm saying is that no self-respecting student of history would stand in front of a crowd and spout the malarkey you and The Daughters keep putting out there."

"You're the embarrassment, the way you side with the Yankees. No true man of the South would deny the facts the way you do."

"A true man of the South, one with integrity who's able to acknowledge sins of the past, that man looks at the past and says our side fought for an evil cause. We deserved to lose."

"Deserved to lose! How can you say that? We were defending our way of life. One that was genteel and mannerly and, and . . . Besides, the message I plan to deliver is about how we've stood strong in spite of military defeat. Ours is a priceless heritage. The Daughters honor those who defended our cause and the women who, who . . . Southern women continued to be the guardians of the family. Their valor deserves to be recognized." Her forceful nod of the head signaled triumph.

"Sounds like you've got the beginnings for your outline right there. That's all the help I intend to provide." His attention returned to the book he'd been reading.

Mildred simmered over his arrogance. She, Charity, and her sisters had been correct in their initial assessment of Lee Muller. Through and through, he was a Republican, a betrayer of the Anglo-Saxon race. Nothing was ever going to change that.

It had been easier having him away, not around to judge her and flaunt his self-conferred superiority. She was relieved that he would again be leaving for a spell. Four months was about all of him a woman could tolerate.

He had failed at farming. Failed at being a schoolmaster. What made him think he would succeed out in Missouri? What if he didn't like it out there? What if the small church discovered he'd lied about . . . about everything? What if Evalina's father did not like him? What if Evalina . . .?

It was conceivable that he'd have no choice but to return to the Carolinas. And if he did come back? Mildred must assume that he would. He must keep his options open.

She would expect letters from him. But if she thought he was in North Dakota, he couldn't send letters from Missouri. He would warn her, before he left, that he'd likely be too busy readying a homestead, preparing the soil and planting crops, to have time to write.

A dilemma. If he wanted Mildred to believe he was returning, he'd have to leave some of his clothes and books with her. But parishioners in Missouri would expect him to arrive with a trunkful of belongings. How could he assure Mildred of his eventual return and, at the same time, communicate to Brethren that his stay among them would not be fleeting?

Ah! The only ones who knew what he was leaving behind in the Carolinas were Baptists, and no Baptists were going to be reading a Brethren publication.

"It's already April," Mildred said. "If you're going back up to Dakota, isn't it time to be planting wheat or somethin'?"

Seated in the easy chair, Leander reached for his dictionary. Schismatical. (Siz-mat-ik-al) he wrote in a margin of *The Brethren's Tracts and Pamphlets*. The word appeared in a section opposing secret societies.

"Lee, did you hear me?" Mildred stood over him, her brown hair coming loose from the bun. "I'm wondering why you haven't already taken off for Dakota. Last year you went at about this time."

"It turned out to be too early. There's not much to do until the ground thaws. I plan to go in a week or two."

Truth was he couldn't bring himself to leave. How many times had the narrative of his life been interrupted? A youth destined for greatness had been coerced into marriage. Then in his efforts to support a family he'd been entrapped by debt and forced to escape to Aquone. He'd tried to start anew in South Carolina.

To create this new story required losing his past. Losing yet another family. Losing the man he'd been to become a different—a better—man. But might it turn out to be like the child's game of Drop the Handkerchief? You drop the piece of cloth, but it chases you to the end of the earth.

Chapter 28

Since his return from North Dakota, Lee had regaled the girls with his bedtime stories. Snuggled against him in the easy chair, they listened to Ojibwa tales from "where we'll all live together someday." One night, a story about Kitchi Manitou creating rock, water, fire, and wind. Another night, a story about Spider Woman capturing the sunrise.

Mildred wondered how they would adjust to his leaving again. After his eight-month absence, they'd been cautious at first, more often going to her or Charity or Gladys with their tears or delights. But he'd gradually won them over, mostly with his bedtime stories.

During eight years of marriage he'd displayed two quite different sides of his nature. There was the charming Lee who told stories and kissed his daughters' scratches and bruises, and the scholarly Lee who abhorred disruption. An open book usually offered a clue as to which ruled at any given time.

The day before his departure, Mildred prepared his favorite dinner: thick ham slices, mashed potatoes, fresh peas, and biscuits. Gladys baked a caramel cake. After the meal the girls gave him pictures they had drawn with the wax crayons he had brought back from North Dakota. There were six people in each picture: Clarinda's stick figures with hair and clothes, L'il Charity's attempt to draw human-shaped bodies.

Clarinda pointed at the smallest figure, a dark-haired girl in a bright blue dress. "This is me," she said, looking up at her father.

"And this one is me," L'il Charity said, her finger on a red-headed child wearing a yellow dress and holding a book. Mildred thought she detected his eyes watering. Several times he mentioned, "when I come back from Dakota next winter."

The following morning, Archibald McGregor came in his buggy. Mildred thought Lee would never let go of the girls. One in each arm, he held them both close. "Till we meet again," he said as he clasped the hands of Charity and Gladys. Lastly, he gave Mildred a hasty embrace before climbing into the buggy.

As he rode off, the girls clung to Mildred's skirt. In the nearby field insects made clicking sounds among the dark green leaves of cotton. In rhythm with the flutter inside her belly. She'd considered telling Lee before he left, then decided his knowing would only complicate matters. Soon enough. She'd tell him in a letter.

"Well, that's done," Charity said matter-of-factly and turned toward the overseer's house. Gladys took her hand and accompanied her.

Mildred and the girls remained where they'd said their good-byes, watching the buggy disappear from view.

Chapter 29

He alit from a train in Nevada, Missouri. In the cardboard suitcase he carried all there now was of his worldly possessions: two shirts, an extra collar, a pair of wool trousers, two pairs of socks. His Bible, of course, and *Christian Research in Asia with Notices of the Translation of the Scriptures into the Oriental Languages*. The two drawings his daughters had given him as departure gifts.

Hand over brow, he squinted to avoid the sun's piercing afternoon glare. Watched as the train, with deafening squeaks and groans, lurched forward on its continued trek westward. He removed his wire-framed glasses, cleaned them with his handkerchief. Had anyone noticed and commented, he would not have acknowledged that anything more than a cinder caused his eyes to water.

"Everything lost when the house he was staying at burned to the ground," he'd announced in *The Gospel Messenger*. Yes, there were still Mildred and the girls. With a similar news item, he would—his heart ached at the thought of erasing them from his life, but he'd already gone beyond the bounds of conscience.

Brushing soot and cinders from his suit with flicks of the hand, he lifted his shoulders and inhaled deeply, hoping that at age forty-four a man could begin anew.

Acknowledgements

"We Have Beared Witness," from Chapter 1, was originally published in County Lines: a Literary Journal, Vol. 8, 2021 Issue.

"In Service of One's Mind," from Chapter 10, was originally published in High Country Headwaters IV: an Anthology by High Country Writers, 2022.

I am grateful to many individuals. To Verna Todd, Rebecca Beck, Celia Miles, Jeanne Charters Rustivo, Linda Brown, and James Poling for reading and providing feedback on various versions of the manuscript. To longtime friend Jeannine Steiner, who has always encouraged me to pursue my passion for writing. To online bloggers, memoirists, family historians, and dissertation authors whose names I failed to write down, but whose tidbits of knowledge helped provide historical context.

Nancy Werking Poling writes from her home in the mountains of North Carolina. A lifelong interest in history—more recently in the lives of common women and men of Appalachia—inspires much of her work. Her books include *While Earth Still Speaks, Before It Was Legal: a black-white marriage (1945-1987)*; *Had Eve Come First and Jonah Been a Woman*; and *Paradise Restored*. She maintains a website at www.nancypoling.com and posts on Facebook and Instagram.

Discussion questions for book groups

1. What moral dilemmas did Leander encounter? When did you want to tell him, "Don't do that!"

2. Did you ever feel sympathy for him? Why or why not?

3. What were Emma's choices when Elias left? What were the likely consequences of his decisions on his surviving children?

4. Compare Elias Leander's relationships with his three wives: Emma, Mildred, and Evalina. What attracted him to each one? How were the women similar? How were they different?

5. What was Dorothy Jane's role in his decisions? What was your opinion of her?

6. In what situations did Elias Leander, a white man, encounter African Americans? How do you understand his responses to these situations?

7. What was the significance of the friendship between Elias and Samuel?

8. In what ways did religion influence Elias Leander's decisions?

Similar April Gloaming Titles:

*We Never Took a Bad
Picture*
Ashley N. Roth

Ash Tuesday
Ariadne Blayde

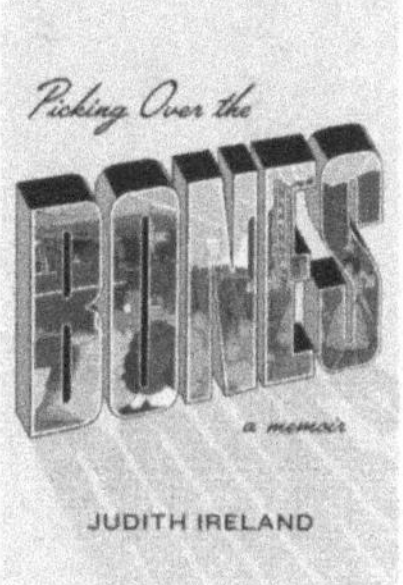

Picking Over the Bones
Judith Ireland

Frank's Bloody Books
Mack Green

Possessing the Seasons
Charles Prowell

*The Peril of Remembering
Nice Things*
Jeffery Wade Gibbs

APRIL GLOAMING

View our full catalog at aprilgloaming.com